USA TODAY BESTSELLING AUTHOR

Dale Mayer

TERK'S GUARDIANS
ALEX 10

ALEX: TERK'S GUARDIANS, BOOK 10
Beverly Dale Mayer
Valley Publishing Ltd.

ISBN-13: 978-1-778865-98-5
Print Edition

Books in This Series:

Radar, Book 1

Legend, Book 2

Bojan, Book 3

Langdon, Book 4

Walker, Book 5

Reid, Book 6

Sanders, Book 7

Nate, Book 8

Royal, Book 9

Alex, Book 10

Royce, Book 11

About This Book

Born with the ability to see psychic abilities in others, Alex finds himself called to help out a mutual friend, someone with similar abilities to Alex's. Plus this mutual friend is on a mission to save innocent children. No way Alex can say no to that.

Taryn is desperate to save two children—both with abilities—from a greedy family member. Taryn needs help, so she contacted Levi, looking to see if he had men to spare. Of course that took her to Terk, with a similar request. In Taryn's world, anyone with similar talents who needs help gets it. Period. Finding out these children were being exploited by their uncle made it doubly hard.

But the uncle looking for an easy way to profit off these gifted children isn't willing to step aside, … not without taking down everyone around him …

Sign up to be notified of all Dale's releases here!
https://geni.us/DaleNews

PROLOGUE

TWO DAYS LATER, early in the morning, Terk sat in the kitchen, his head in his hands, when his phone rang. Sophia came in, putting the call up on the TV. He looked at her in surprise.

"It's Levi."

He nodded, as he looked up at the big screen. "Levi, how're you doing?"

Levi opened his mouth to speak and then frowned. "Are you guys okay?"

"Yeah, it's been a hell of a few days," Terk muttered. "It seems as if Celia's in prelabor, then she's not, then she is. Man, I, for one, find it more than a little frustrating."

Levi laughed. "Yeah, and, for Celia, it's ten times worse. This is definitely a new experience for you, isn't it?"

"Absolutely," he muttered, almost with a groan. "We're all waiting and excited and worried and trepidatious and every emotion in between. But our last job finished successfully, and things are calming down, although it was a little on the rough side." Terk sighed. "We rescued two Americans, and now we're all just trying to recuperate."

"So, I hear you have Bruce over there."

"Yeah, so what do you know about Bruce? He's had a rough go and is still in and out of it. He's unconscious, or still close to it a good share of the time, though he is improving."

"But he'll make it, right?" Ice asked, her face coming into view.

Terk smiled broadly when he saw her. "Hey, Ice. You get kudos from me on having kids. I'm, … I'm still struggling, and the babies aren't even here yet. And it's only our first time."

She burst out laughing. "Yep, there is nothing quite like it," she murmured. "I would love to chat on that, and we will sometime soon, but back to Bruce. What's going on?"

"He's okay. He's just … it'll take some time. We used so much energy to keep him alive as we worked to get him here that we can't really put him into standard medical care. They would never understand what they were looking at, and we need him close by to keep up the energy treatments. I am sure that he'll make it, but it'll take him a while. He was mistreated terribly, and frankly it's a miracle he survived. Without help from Royal during their captivity, Bruce wouldn't have made it. I'm sure of it."

"His prognosis is good to know," Ice told Terk, as she looked over at Levi pointedly. "I guess you didn't get a chance to tell him, did you?"

Levi shook his head, and then another face appeared on the screen.

Terk studied the other woman, feeling a stirring deep inside. "Taryn?" he asked, after a moment.

She gave him a bright smile. "Hey, somehow I found my way to Levi's."

"That's an interesting place for you," Terk noted.

"After leaving England the way I did, not too sure what I wanted to do next, it just seemed right that this is where I landed."

"Anyway, Terk, I gather she's one of yours," Levi stated, with one of those long-suffering sighs. "Seems as if every time I find somebody new and interesting, almost immediately I find out they're one of yours."

"Oh, absolutely. Taryn and I did a couple jobs together way back when, before I started working exclusively with this team," Terk explained to Levi and then looked at her. "I had no idea you were over there."

"After I lost my partner," she began, "I went AWOL for a while. A long while." She gave him a lopsided grin. "But it's all good now."

He nodded in understanding. "That'll do it, won't it?"

"It absolutely will," she stated, then changed her tone to all business. "I understand from Levi that you've had a lot of changes in your world."

He gave her a bright grin. "Yes, and even more in the next day or so, but you guys had a particular reason for calling, I'm sure."

Levi nodded. "Yeah. Taryn brought somebody with her. Another young woman, Amara, who apparently was looking for Bruce."

Terk frowned at that. "If that's the case, she'll be happy to know that Bruce is here."

"She's not sure whether it's him or not, so that just adds to her worry."

Terk laughed. "It should be easy enough to identify him, once we send over some photos."

"That would help," Levi said. "Also, Amara says that Bruce is special."

"I would agree, based on what Royal has shared with me. However, Bruce hasn't exactly been conscious enough to let us know just how special he may be, though."

"She says he definitely has abilities."

"That wouldn't surprise me," Terk stated, with a note of humor. "Yet we have no idea about his skills to date. We're just trying to keep him alive. He's out cold most of the time, occasionally surfacing for a matter of moments, but he's mostly just out."

Levi nodded at that. "Amara's asking your permission to come over and see him."

"Permission granted," Terk replied cautiously, "though it would help to know if she's friend or foe first."

At that, another woman stepped into the visual frame. "Friend, very close friend," Amara added, "at least I hope so. I haven't seen Bruce in many years."

"Right. And why do you want to see him now?" Terk asked cautiously, studying her, trying to get a better handle on her energy.

She whispered, "Because I care. I kept getting all these messages, saying that he was hurt. By way of Taryn, we came to Levi, and, through Levi and Ice, now we're coming to you."

"Bruce is here. He is hurt. I'm hoping he'll make it. It's pretty touch-and-go at times," Terk shared, "but you're welcome to come see him if he's up for visitors." He then looked at Taryn. "Are you coming too?"

She hesitated, then shook her head. "I was hoping that maybe you had somebody over there you could send to help us here, or at least maybe run a ground crew."

"What's the matter?" Terk asked.

"I got wind of a few children being held hostage by a man here in Texas," she began in a tone that made him curious. "And these children, I believe, are gifted."

"He's holding them hostage? Why?"

"Because he wants to sell them to the highest bidder," she stated, her tone harsh.

Terk winced. "*Great,* that's exactly what we need, isn't it?"

"Levi can supply one or two men, and I was hoping that I could get some help from your side."

"For people like us, always, you know that."

Taryn smiled. "Just checking that things are still the same as they were before."

"That will never change," Terk declared. "And you always know that, if you need something from me, you can contact me, without any reservations. So, if this one is happening in Levi's corner of the world, I'm grateful. Things are kind of chaotic here at the moment."

She laughed. "Yet you'll be very happy in another day."

He perked up at that. "I sure hope you're right about that *another day* thing."

"I am. We'll keep in touch, but I do know that we'll need some assistance."

"Okay. Do you have any idea who and what's going on over there?"

"I've heard three kids are involved."

"Does the kidnapper have any biological claim over them?"

"He's the uncle," she said, then hesitated.

"And it has been confirmed that the children are gifted?" he asked Taryn.

She replied with a question. "Do you remember my talents?"

He dredged up the memories in the back of his head. "Yes. Is that how you found these kids?"

She nodded. "Yes."

Terk knew someone else who could sense psychic abilities in people too, just like Taryn. Might be a good person for this job, if Alex is willing. He'd spent so much time in VA clinics, looking for those he could help, that he might not be interested. Then again he'd mentioned getting burnt out. Mentally Terk sent off a message to Alex, as Taryn filled Terk in further.

"They're his sister-in-law's kids. She's dead. The uncle lost track of the family, when the kids' father disappeared after their mother's death—just went crazy and left, abandoning his own children. Because they're biologically related to the uncle, I highly suspect that the uncle is correct in thinking that they do have abilities. And, of course, he's just being the usual asshole, trying to get something out of it transactionally."

"That's something we'll put a stop to."

She hesitated. "If need be, I'm prepared to buy them."

Terk sucked in his breath. "That would not be a precedent we want to set."

"Maybe not, but neither can I take a chance on losing them. Let me know whatever you decide, and I'll keep in touch."

And, with that, she ended the call, and the screen went blank.

CHAPTER 1

ALEX TOGAN STAYED at the back of the convenience store and watched as the three kids—quiet, almost to the point of too quiet—stood beside the tall, pale man, their supposed uncle, as he picked up a few things. The children didn't ask for anything. They didn't look at anything. They just stayed at his side. The man had to be at least six foot tall, maybe six-two, a little slim for his height, and was dressed in a worn T-shirt and jeans that were too big for him. He shot hard looks at the three kids, reminding them to behave. There was no air of happiness between them. On the contrary, an air of absolute terror was present instead. That's what upset Alex.

Of course he'd seen it before, and unfortunately it was all too familiar. Hell, it's why Alex was here in the first place. It broke his heart to see this behavior and the evident abuse—whether verbal, physical, psychological, sexual, or all of the above—but Alex wasn't in a position to do anything about it yet. That would change very quickly at some point, but he didn't have all the pieces in place yet.

Just as the man and the trio of kids stepped up to the cashier's counter, another woman—whom Alex had already observed several times in the store—stepped up behind them as well.

Alex sent her a gentle energy, checking out her aura.

When his energy was rebuffed, his eyebrows shot up. It took a lot for somebody to do that, particularly with his energy skills. He didn't have a whole lot of the crazy talents that Terkel's team had, but Alex certainly had enough to read good versus bad energy in people. As far as he was concerned, an energy scan could tell him everything.

Yet this rebuff was unusual. It was rare for someone to be strong enough to reject his intuitive feelers from their space the way this woman just ahead of him had just done. Of course it was her right. It was her space after all, but most people didn't know when a gentle energy probe checked them out. Not her. This was a very deliberate act, which only meant one thing. She knew about energy.

What made it very interesting was the scenario he was in right now. He noted her smiling at the children, trying to engage with them. Something was going on here. He just didn't know what.

As the woman waited in line, she asked the kids cheerfully, "How are you guys doing today?" The children turned and looked away. Her eyebrows shot up, as if a normal reaction.

However, Alex saw it more as a calculated response, as if she hadn't expected anything else from them. That made him wonder too. He'd heard that somebody named Taryn had set up this op, so was this her? He had earlier studied the photo Terk provided, but it was several years old and hadn't been updated in Terkel's database.

Still, Alex got just a whiff of that same look, that same feel from the woman ahead of him. Chances were this was, indeed, the woman he was supposed to meet up with.

And that would, in many ways, explain her ability to rebuff his energy too. That she did some energy work didn't exactly endear her to Alex though. He'd seen some pretty crazy energy workers in the past, and most were on the edge of not quite normal. *Not quite normal* didn't necessarily mean a hard no in Alex's world, but, if they were unstable, that was a different story. Of course his experience to date had been very different than Terkel's, who had a vast amount of knowledge and years invested. As Terkel kept telling Alex, not every energy worker was the same.

Alex would give her a chance, just because of Terk.

Alex's previous venue had been working with a lot of injured veterans, who'd come back from war, some with crazy PTSD shit that just wouldn't go away. Some had been completely traumatized by what they'd been through. Alex would visit various VA centers, walking through a group of veterans, seeking anybody with gifts, who would need Alex's particular brand of help.

Not that Alex could do a lot, unlike energy healer Terk and his team. However, Alex could certainly find out who was dealing with less of a physical and emotional trauma and more of a psychic trauma. Because, of course, that happened. Just not something that anybody ever freely talked about. Alex tried to help these guys who were otherwise all alone in dealing with the aftereffects of war. Yet Alex had reached a level of burnout.

With a sigh, Alex refocused on the present. Everything about this woman in the store seemed to be calculated, strong, and definitely not showing any weakness that he would have usually expected from a supposed newbie energy worker. However, if this was Taryn, all these observations would make sense.

While the man paid for his purchases, the children with him remained silent, just these silent little ghosts, not a chirp out of them, either good or bad. No request for candy or toys, nothing, making them seem all the stranger. They all trooped outside without one word. Alex grabbed something else before checking out, as he watched the woman approach the cashier now, quickly made her purchase, and slipped out the front door. Alex tossed his own selection and money on the counter, waved off the need for a receipt, and exited too.

The man and the children were getting into a truck. Alex casually walked around the back of it and got a look at the tag number. It was the same as what Alex had followed into this parking lot. He knew it would be, but you can never check these things too often. It seemed as if the more he learned about the criminal world, the more the criminal world had to show him, seemingly one step ahead of the authorities. A pretty sad turn of events really.

Alex didn't give a crap about the man, except that he was an abuser and worse, an abuser of children. Any energy reader would find that to be true. So Alex's only concern was for those children. Taryn had sent out the alarm that these three were in danger. From what Alex just witnessed, he agreed. They were in danger, but he wasn't sure what the hell was going on exactly. How much danger were they in?

Alex had received Terkel's initial case brief, but, as always, it was very incomplete. That was just another part of this energy work that Alex did, at least when he did it. The information was often hard to come by. People were shady, dealing with the underworld, trying hard to do whatever the hell they were trying to get away with. Thus, they weren't too open about sharing information. Alex had to rely on cues, actions, and energy to get a better handle on them.

Regardless of his findings, or Terk's, or Taryn's, any authorities would want more concrete evidence. Alex shook his head.

As the truck drove off with the man and the children inside, Alex walked toward the car the woman was getting into. Just as she went to close the door, he stepped in the way. "Maybe we should travel together."

She froze, her gaze narrowing. "And I would want that, why?"

"I could follow behind you," he suggested, plain and simple, "but, with two of us following the same truck, it'll look mighty suspicious." Her breath sucked in on a gasp, and he nodded. "I'm Alex." She frowned at him, her gaze assessing, sending a strong probe his way. "Hey, if you repelled my probe, don't expect me to allow yours."

Her eyebrows shot up, and she studied him for a moment. "What about your vehicle?" she asked, turning to look at the car beside her.

"We can come back for it later."

"It probably won't be here later," she shared, with a laugh. "Or, if it is, it won't have tires or maybe even an undercarriage at that point in time."

He shrugged. "I'll have the rental company pick it up then." She seemed to consider letting him in her vehicle. He added, "They're getting away from us."

She glared at him. "Get in then."

And, with that, he raced around to the passenger side and quickly took his seat. As he did so, he sent a text to the rental company, asking them to come pick up his rental.

"You won't have wheels after this," she repeated.

"I'll just get another rental."

"If they give you one. They don't usually like it when you abandon their vehicles in the middle of nowhere, especially in a neighborhood like this."

"I don't know about that," he countered, keeping his gaze on the road. "I do it quite often."

She frowned, gave him a quick headshake, then tore down the road after the kids.

TARYN STRUGGLED TO drive and to keep up without being too obvious that she was following the truck in front of her. She blamed it on the distraction caused by the very magnetic man at her side. She was shocked to feel *this* again, since the loss of her partner. Yet it highlighted a void in her life that she thought she had been handling well so far. With a shake of her head, she sighed and shared, "He told me that he was sending a couple people, but he didn't tell me who."

"That sounds like Terk," Alex stated, with a clipped nod. "He tends to keep information close."

She nodded. "Are you expecting some backup?"

"I can get help, if needed. Since Levi is based here in Texas, even if he can't spare a man with boots on the ground for us, Levi can run his satellite for facial recognition, while his team does background checks and online surveillance. Plus, he's got local contacts with the authorities and such, for whatever else we may need. So we may not see his man. As for Terk, he has people all over. He mentioned Riff was somewhere in the US, so maybe he'll show up later."

"Wow," Taryn muttered. "How do you run an op like that? Sounds a little too *fly by the seat of your pants* for me."

Alex laughed. "Maybe because most of us on Terk's team aren't the most obedient types anyway," he admitted.

She gave a startled laugh. "Not exactly sure what that means."

"Oh, I suspect you do," he argued. "We have a tendency to be independent, and we've seen a lot of the world that isn't that great and don't just accept what we're fed. We do this work voluntarily, not for free, but by choice," he explained. "We do it for ourselves because few of us have the abilities and the support to do that, but we certainly don't do it because we have to. It's a calling," he murmured. "Terk knows all that. So, other than providing what we need to get started and to address any immediate safety concerns, he opts not to spend time and resources on things we'll largely disregard and go figure out for ourselves anyway."

She shrugged. "Do you know the family in question?"

"No, I don't." He turned to her. "Do you?"

At that, she gave him a hard look but still answered the question. "Yes, I know Bruce, the maternal uncle to those children. He's recuperating in England at Terk's castle, after being rescued with his cellmate from a shitty Russian prison. I also knew Mary, Bruce's sister, when we were all young. She's the mother of the three children, but she died recently."

Alex went quiet for a moment and then nodded. "That fits too. I'd heard that Terkel's team had some guys the Russians had imprisoned but didn't realize there was a connection to these children."

"After their mother passed away not all that long ago, I heard that Jeff, the paternal uncle, considered the kids more of a commodity than anything else." Alex stiffened. "Exactly," she murmured.

"Terk filled me in," Alex replied, "but it sounds even worse when you put it that way."

"It sounds awful because it is awful," she declared bitterly. "I just can't understand the mindset of somebody who could do such a thing."

Alex sighed. "The issue is not so much the mindset but the fact that no emotions are involved, no humanity. Abusers are totally selfish and don't care one way or another about anybody else. Plus, I understand that the children's father is out of the picture. So, in this stateside uncle's eyes, these children have become a liability for Jeff, so he's trying to get as much as he can for them."

"Who does that?" Taryn cried out softly, even as she kept the truck in view up ahead.

"People who have no soul, people who just don't care," he muttered. "I'm sure all kinds of psychological reasons have helped make Jeff who he is today, but the bottom line is, if he cared at all, he would never consider such a thing."

"Did you see him in that store?" she asked, shaking her head. "Cold, really cold, and the children were these quiet little …" She was bereft of words.

"Ghosts," Alex suggested. "Little ghosts, scared of the future and terrified of the present, with absolutely no idea how to change it."

Taryn bit her bottom lip. "How pathetic is that?" she asked, her voice barely a whisper.

"Do we have any idea if Jeff had anything to do with his sister-in-law's death?"

"I don't know. Of course it crossed my mind, but I have no proof either way. What's worse is that Bruce doesn't even know yet that his sister is dead."

"If Jeff killed his own sister-in-law, it would be a nice way to get those children away from her," Alex murmured.

Taryn agreed. "True. I don't know what this guy's time-line looks like or how he'll even go about it. How do you sell a kid anyway?"

"What I'm also wondering about is," Alex added, "did Jeff have a hand in the disappearance of the children's father too?"

"Wow," Taryn muttered. "I didn't even consider that. However, being blood brothers, maybe Jeff and the biological father to those children are more alike than I want to believe. From what I know, they were both unemployed and not actively looking for a job. Mary, the kids' mother, was working two jobs and was the only breadwinner in that household of three adults and three children." Taryn shook her head.

"Yep, those brothers are not exactly pillars of the community," Alex agreed.

"If you get a hit on the missing father, let me know. We sure don't want either of these brothers granted legal possession of these kids, much less illegal possession. Right now, though, I'm more focused on the sale of those children. I don't have any dark-web experience I can call on to hunt that down, so I'm really hoping that Terkel can handle that part."

"I'm sure he will, but what exactly is Jeff trying to sell the kids *for*? And I don't mean the money angle." Alex hesitated. "Depending on the particular crime involved here, Terk would have multitudes of agencies all over the globe with dark-web resources that can be brought in to help."

She looked at him. "Really?"

He nodded and then added, "You won't like which one is most likely to be brought in though."

She stared at him, feeling her stomach clench. "Child sex crimes?"

"That'll be the big overarching one, yes. Also child slavery, child prostitution, child trafficking, and God-only-knows what else is in that sick bastard's mind," Alex replied. "And that's why we're here, … to confirm that doesn't happen and that those kids end up somewhere safe."

"I want Bruce to get his niece and nephews back."

Alex nodded to that. "Is Bruce the guy who's still sliding in and out of a coma at Terk's castle?"

"Yes, though, according to Terkel's healers, Bruce is doing much better." When Alex didn't reply, she just glared at him. "I have to believe that Bruce will come out of this okay," she murmured.

"He's a good friend of yours?"

"He is. I don't really know too much about his sister in recent history, or even the children really, outside of the fact that they exist," she admitted, with a shrug. "I went off the grid for a while, and now I feel bad about that. I was fostered by Bruce's family. Bruce and I were best friends when we were kids, and I still consider him my best friend today. However, as we got older and went off and had lives of our own, we lost touch. I didn't even know what had happened to Bruce until his girlfriend reached out to me," she murmured. "And that's another story in itself."

"Meaning?"

"Meaning, somebody besides me desperately hopes Bruce survives this and comes back to her."

"Bruce has a partner?"

"Not exactly. At one point he and Amara were partners, but, as it happens so many times in long-distance relationships, they drifted apart." Taryn sighed. "Eventually it got to be too much, and they ended up separating, maybe over his going on that last mission to Russia. I'm not exactly sure of the details. That was a while ago because then he was captured by the Russian government and held as a prisoner under horrible circumstances. Amara didn't know anything about it until recently, and neither did I. Now that Bruce has been rescued, Amara wants to see him, but he's not quite capable of handling a visit just yet."

"No, of course not," Alex replied, "if ever. One of the hardest things to do is go off to war—or, in Bruce's case, a potentially dangerous mission—knowing there's no reason to come back."

Startled, Taryn stared at him, before yanking her gaze back to the road. The truck up ahead just thudded along as if that asshole didn't have a care in the world. Jeff was all about himself and what he could get out of those kids. "I'm not sure what you mean by *no reason to come back*. Bruce had his sister and his niece and nephews and his friends. Besides, Bruce and Amara made a mutual decision to split up."

"Maybe, but I can tell you that the guys who have partners to come back to, the guys who have a reason to come home, … they do much better on military deployments, particularly in war zones, than those who are out there without that anchor, that sense of grounding as to the reason why they are doing this. It's the same for military and post-military private work. A supportive partner makes a huge difference."

That made a lot of common sense to her, and Taryn could understand it, even given the little understanding she had about the human condition. "I'm hoping Bruce will snap out of this. I don't know what shape Amara is in, now finding out more about Bruce and his situation. Still, she's a lovely lady."

"And she didn't want Bruce to go on this Russian op?"

"No, and, … I'm just guessing, I think she probably got a premonition of what would happen to him."

"Ah, that's a different story then," Alex noted, with a nod. "Especially when you have someone who's determined to go anyway, even when the partner has a strong reason for them not to."

"And yet it shouldn't be a deal-breaker," Taryn noted. "There should be a certain amount of trust shared by the couple."

"It depends on whether their relationship had matured to that point or not," Alex pointed out. "You have to understand that most don't ever reach that level of trust. People either don't know how or choose not to go through the difficult work of building their relationship and knowing how their various skills play into it. So, they don't trust their partner—or maybe don't trust the partnership itself—and, if they don't trust it themselves, well, … it's hard to convince somebody with trust issues to have faith outside of themselves."

"And yet Amara is certain that Bruce has skills. Of course, she does too, so wouldn't that make navigating a relationship easier for those two, rather than for two regular people in life? Regardless, if she's got energy-working skills, she's got walls up. Since she's my friend, I don't pry. If she's gifted, she'll tell me when she's ready. … Back when we were young, Bruce and I used to laugh about having superhuman gifts all the time, and I was pretty sure he did have energy-working skills. Of course I didn't know what to call it back then. Yet he laughed about being superhuman and brushed it off as just a strongly developed sense of intuition."

"What did his aura tell you?" Alex asked.

She frowned. "I don't have abilities."

Alex shook his head, smirking.

"No, really. I don't have abilities."

"Yet you can detect gifted children from afar?" Alex asked, raising one eyebrow.

She laughed. "It's my one and only gift. You can imagine how confused I was as a child to have these images pop up in my brain, especially in the orphanage, not knowing what to make of them."

Alex stared at her but nodded. "These gifts are forever changing and evolving. Even Terk gets surprised by someone with particular gifts that he's never seen before."

Taryn shrugged.

"Back to Bruce," Alex began. "If Bruce has a strongly developed intuition, I wouldn't knock it. I know a lot of guys who go by their gut feelings, and that's kept them alive and safe many times over. The problem is when you're forced by bosses or circumstances to go against that gut feeling. That's when you end up in trouble because of it. That happens with energy-working gifts too. Ignoring them is not in anybody's best interests."

Taryn remained silent on the subject, still in denial. Just then the truck up ahead turned down a dirt road. She drove past, studying the driveway. "That's not the address I have on file for the kids."

"But that would have been when they lived with their parents, presumably."

Taryn nodded. "That's exactly when it was. I just assumed that Jeff had stayed in their house after his sister-in-law and his brother were gone."

"Maybe it held memories that Jeff didn't want to deal with. Or maybe it was easier to throw off any shackles of honor he may have had and a sense of what he *shouldn't* be doing by cutting the ties to an absent brother and a dead sister-in-law that Jeff's probably feeling ambivalent about.

Living in a different place just allows Jeff to be more of an asshole now."

Startled, Taryn frowned at Alex. "Do people do that?"

"Sure, it happens both ways, good and bad. Whenever an attachment to a house is holding you back, sometimes it's important to let it go. However, you also must understand that, when you let it go, some people let go of that sense of righteousness, honor, and their ethics because that was also tied to the prior relationships within the home. If they were better with that person around, and acted with love and respect, then they are worse without them. Letting go of those bonds that kept them tied allows them to go back to the part of their personality that they used beforehand to get their own way, and they become those people again."

"*Great*," she muttered. "I can see Jeff doing that for sure. Still, how did unemployed Jeff buy or even rent another house? Surely he couldn't sell the family home? Not legally anyway."

"Terk's looking into all that. However, knowing Jeff, he's probably just squatting in an otherwise empty house." Taryn's mouth gaped open. Alex nodded and continued. "If that's true, we could contact the true owner and have them evict Jeff and the kids, but we don't want to do that to those children, which would only pressure Jeff to sell them faster and to any old Joe Blow off the street."

Taryn had one hand to her heart at this point, stunned by fear into silence.

Alex added, "However, if no furniture is in the place, and they are sleeping on the floor—or the plumbing doesn't work and no running water is in that house—that would not look good to the local social workers. If given notice of that, they would immediately step in and at least get the kids away from Jeff, which is good, but that lands all three youngsters in a children's home, which I know you will veto. However, you can't take them, as you are not related and don't have temporary custody, not legally yet. And the local authorities, once activated, would immediately search for the biological father, which is not a good option either."

"I don't want those kids further traumatized, and I don't like *any* of those choices," Taryn exclaimed. "The missing father has already proven himself to be negligent and irresponsible, and I went that orphanage route myself, and I sure hate to do that to those kids."

"I understand," Alex replied. "Plus, Levi and Ice are working with national authorities, alongside some local ones, all watching movement on that ad."

"And yet we don't know anything yet, right?"

"Nope. We just wait until we hear more." He then asked her, "How did you find the ad to begin with?" She hesitated to answer, and he had a crazy feeling. He raised one eyebrow and stated, "Please tell me that it's more than psychic information."

She flushed. "With Bruce in trouble, I searched for his sister, finding her dead. That sent me down this pathway in the first place," she clarified. "Then I hired somebody to look into this further, confirming the kids and Mary's husband were okay. Of course the PI confirmed the kids' father was long gone, and the kids are with Uncle Jeff. My PI also found the actual posting of the upcoming auction. I have a copy of it on my phone. Then my investigator died from a bad *accident*," she muttered, "and I realized I couldn't get other people involved, not people who weren't pros, who wouldn't understand the danger."

"When we get a chance," Alex suggested, "you need to

show me that posting."

She immediately pulled onto the shoulder of the road and grabbed her phone, brought up the screenshot she'd taken, and handed her cell to him.

He read the ad and whistled. "Wow, Jeff really is an asshole, isn't he?"

"Yeah, my PI somehow knew this was Jeff's ad, but I questioned it. Then someone posted pictures of the kids." She showed Alex three other screenshots of the same three children they had just seen at the convenience store.

"Crap. In the ad, the price point is blurred, but the message is clear. *Open usage*," he repeated in anger.

Taryn asked, "What the hell does that even mean?"

"It means, … Jeff doesn't give a crap," Alex stated, his tone harsh. "Whether they're sold as black-market adoptions or for human trafficking, the sex trade, pornography, *whatever*, Jeff is okay with all that. Terk's people are already tracing that ad back to the person who placed it, which I would bet will be asshole Jeff."

She shook her head, scrunching up her face to hold back the tears. "To think of it happening at all is absolutely brutal," she muttered, "but to know that it's happening to Bruce's niece and nephews while he's not here to do anything about it, or to even be told about it, is crucifying me."

She was startled when Alex gently squeezed her arm. "You and I both know that negative energy will cripple you, if you don't keep it in check."

She took a deep breath and nodded. "Yeah, you're right about that, but you and I both know what can happen when these kids disappear. They get lost out there in the big wide underbelly of the world," she noted, waving her hand around. "It will be almost impossible to find them."

"So, who did you contact, and what have you done about this so far?"

She sighed. "I contacted Terkel."

He frowned at her. "Just Terk? Why not the police?"

She shook her head. "I didn't call the police yet, … and I can't really explain why." He stared at her, and she felt the heat of her face flushing. "Look. I don't have anything against the police, other than their disdain for any woo-woo stuff," she added. "I did go to another couple I know, and I talked to them. Through them, … they contacted Terkel for me."

"Levi and Ice," Alex stated.

Taryn smiled and nodded. "Yes, and I'm hoping they were the right people."

Alex stared out in the distance and nodded slowly. "They are definitely the right people. Not only do they take on cases like this all the time, but they have a lot of connections to law enforcement, the *good* ones. So that's probably the best thing you could have done. Plus, Levi and Ice know which cops are honest and which are dirty." He settled back and smiled. "Okay, so all that should at least ease your mind," he said, trying to make her comfortable. "Did they come up with a plan yet?"

"No, they're still gathering info, working on tracking down Jeff's history and connections, plus bank accounts, looking to see if there's been any recent movement or transactions. They've got watches on airports, but I think their immediate concern is that Jeff might take the kids across the border into Mexico, and they would just disappear."

"Being in Texas, with the border not far away, I suppose that's possible too," Alex agreed thoughtfully. "Although unfortunately enough abuse is certainly going on in the USA—and right here in Texas alone—that Jeff doesn't have to drive to another country."

"I know." She winced, getting back on the road. "I just want to keep an eye on Jeff and these precious children, until I know what the next step is. We must save those kids. So, if we don't get that plan going soon, I'll go in and snatch the kids myself."

CHAPTER 2

TARYN GLANCED AT her watch. "Jeff was only in town for about twenty minutes," she murmured. "He picked up some groceries, whatever the convenience store offered, so nothing out of the ordinary there."

"No," Alex replied, "except that it's quick food, which can be made easily, even while on the run." She turned to face him and frowned. He shrugged. "It's not as if Jeff picked up vegetables and steaks. He picked up macaroni and cheese and canned soups. He would need a hot plate and water, disposable cups and plastic spoons."

She shuddered at that and nodded. "Good point, but that alone doesn't necessarily convict him in this case."

Alex chuckled. "No, it sure doesn't, not as much as we might want it to. I'm a bit of a foodie myself," he shared, "so serving that kind of food to children should be something we can charge him with, you know? Poor sustenance for those kids or whatever."

"I don't think quality meals for the kids is at the top of Jeff's list right now," she grumbled.

"Nope, it sure isn't, but we need to confirm with Levi and Ice that they're searching the dark web for any buyers, even if some governmental agency or two are supposedly on it."

"After my private investigator was killed, I'm hesitant to

have Levi and Ice go in that direction," she shared, "so I've got Terkel on that path."

"You think he would be better at it?"

"Well, he is psychic and has all those gifts to forewarn him, I would hope. Also, with his history of working for the government, plus the international aspect of that job, Terk might have better access to things like that, as well as the means to keep it anonymous, or to at least try to."

Alex pondered that and shrugged. "I agree that Terk may be better positioned, but I don't care who does it—Terk, Levi, some government agency near or far—as long as somebody does. I hope all of them do, confirming each other's findings." He reached for his phone and made a call.

Taryn listened in, and, when Terkel answered, she smiled.

"Terk, it's Alex."

"Yeah, I hear you. Go on. What have you got?"

"So far, absolutely nothing. Taryn and I have connected, and we just followed Uncle Jeff and the three kids back to a rural driveway, after they picked up a few simple groceries, you know, convenience food," he shared and went on to elaborate. "Not exactly ingredients for home-cooked meals, more like mac and cheese."

"And yet," Terkel noted, "if Jeff's sister-in-law was the cook in the family, he might not know how to do more at this stage of his life."

"That's possible. We're just checking in to see if you have any news on the sales ad."

"It's still up, though that doesn't mean some buyer hasn't already closed that transaction. I've contacted a couple other departments," Terk shared, "so we've got more help tracking that website. It's always been a matter of interest to law enforcement the world over, so it's not as if this is the first ad on this website that the authorities are concerned about. However, now you have confirmed a physical location for these children, plus have confirmed the uncle is with the children. We'll see if Jeff is squatting, as Alex suggested, just to cover our bases. Regardless we want to be in a position to pick up those kids before they're put in any further danger."

"Did you tell the authorities anything about what's on that ad?" she asked.

"They got the ad," Terkel stated, his tone solemn, "and weren't happy to find yet another one among millions. They see these all too often."

"One more thing," Alex added. "Are you or Levi's team trying to find the absentee father?"

"You getting something?" Terk asked.

"An inkling. So, if your team or Levi's can locate him, I would like to know."

"Will do. More updates coming, as we get further intel." Terk then abruptly disconnected, as was his custom.

Taryn frowned, looking over at Alex. "Okay, I'm not sure what to do next," she confessed. "I mean, I want to sit here and watch and confirm they don't go anywhere."

"I suggest we set up camp somewhere close by, meaning, hiding the car and mostly waiting inside it," Alex replied, with a chuckle. "We'll need a few supplies, and maybe I can grab my rental car again."

"Sure, if they haven't already picked it up."

"Don't care whether they did or not," Alex stated, with a wry smile. "I'll just get another one. We can get coffee too."

"Yeah, except I don't want to leave the kids to take you back to your rental," she pointed out.

He nodded. "It's not that far, so, even on foot, I should

be back in an hour or less, especially if I hitch a ride there. If you leave here, if you go anywhere at all, let me know, so I don't have to worry about where you've ended up, or your being deep-sixed yourself."

She winced at that. "I can't say I like that idea."

"It's unfortunately a little too common in some of these more rural areas," Alex shared, as he got out of the car and looked back at her. "Don't leave the car." She glared at him, and he shook his head. "I don't know whether you have any experience in this shit or not," he explained, "but I do, and, when things go all to hell, … they have a way of doing it very, very quickly. We don't know how dangerous this man Jeff is. We don't know whether he's completely overwhelmed after the loss of his sister-in-law and the absence of his brother, or he's just a completely unfettered animal now. We have our suspicions, but not really a solid clue. Is he just on some weird sidestep right now, or is he a serial killer, and this is part of his MO? For all we know, it could be anything."

Her eyebrows shot up at the mention of a serial killer. "Maybe we should get somebody to check into that serial killer angle."

"Terk and his people will do a full background check on Jeff, don't worry. It's unusual for a man to go from being a good uncle to somebody prepared to sell his niece and nephews," he declared, trying to keep the bark out of his tone. "There had to be some trigger for the change in behavior."

"And yet we know of one possible trigger," she said. "The one thing that comes to mind is the loss of his brother and his sister-in-law."

"Sure, but it takes a little more than that to push him so far astray. Seems Jeff lived with the married couple, so Jeff got free room and board, or maybe the couple was a sounding board for Jeff, offering him possible solutions to all his problems. Hell, it could simply be all about the children's gifts and the possibility of a con with a huge windfall for Jeff. I don't know," Alex admitted, "but it would help if we figured it out. And soon."

With that, he shut the car door, leaving her all alone.

As Alex walked along the road toward his rental, he passed Jeff's driveway. Alex checked for activity in or around Jeff's house, but there wasn't any. He quickly sent Taryn a text. **Get yourself into a better position. No activity at the moment**. She sent back a thumbs-up, and he kept on walking.

It wasn't long before a vehicle drove by, and the older man driving stopped beside Alex.

"You need a lift, son?"

Alex smiled and replied in a pleasant, grateful tone, "I would love a lift. I'm just heading to the convenience store."

"No problem," the man said. "That's still a good five miles on foot though." Alex quickly got into the vehicle with the old man, who eyed him curiously. "You all right?"

"Yeah, I am. Just had a bit of a row with my girlfriend," Alex replied, with a laugh. "I figured we would both do better if I got out and cooled off for a bit."

The old man cackled. "Isn't that the truth? Sometimes it's better though if you put her on the side of the road instead of yourself," he teased.

"I can see that," Alex conceded, "but I was hoping that she would calm down sooner than later this way."

"Yeah, I hear you there, and, if she's a good one, you've got to do everything you can to keep her."

"Oh, I plan on it," Alex agreed. "You live around here?" He figured it was an opportunity to get the lay of the land. Plus, the old man might know something.

The other man nodded. "Yeah, been here for a long time."

"I don't really know this area at all," Alex noted. "We were just at the store a bit ago and saw a tall guy with three little kids. … Those children looked like timid little ghosts."

"Ah, those are Mary's little ones," he shared, with a sage nod. "That's a sad story."

"Yeah? What happened?" Alex asked.

"She passed away not too long ago, and her old man just abandoned those kids. The uncle was in and out of the home, and, from what I know, he took on those young-uns. … Yet he's just lost. He hasn't a clue what he's doing." The driver sagged a bit. "It's pretty damn sad."

"He's okay though, isn't he? He wouldn't hurt the kids or anything, right?"

The old man grimaced and shook his head. "Jeff's a bit of an odd one. I'll give you that, but I don't think he would hurt the kids. They are his brother's kids after all."

"But, when you get somebody who's overwhelmed in life, like Jeff seems to be," Alex began, "you know, a bit disconnected, passionless, I worry about his committing suicide or something."

"It's hard to know these days. You hear about so many of those bloody murder-suicides going on that it makes you wonder. I certainly don't want to think about that in this particular case, but I won't say it couldn't happen."

"*Great*," Alex muttered, half under his breath.

The old man laughed. "I'm not saying Jeff would do that."

"No, of course not, yet you're not at all sure that he wouldn't."

"No. … I'm not. Jeff's always been a bit of a weird one."

Alex wasn't exactly sure what that meant but was prepared to go with it. "Does he work?"

"Used to, and then he lost his job somewhere along the line, and I know Mary kept working full-time, even though the kids sometimes exhausted her to no end. Yet she wouldn't give up on her husband and her brother-in-law and her kids. Her husband may have been laid off too, if memory serves. So, if both her husband and her brother-in-law couldn't find work, Mary just stepped in and did what needed to be done." The old man snorted. "For that reason alone, I have trouble with both of those lazy-ass guys. That damn husband just ran off to points unknown. The uncle is still here. Surely he could have found some job to do."

"I agree."

"Yeah, I am sure you do. It's one thing for a guy to not have a job for a little while, but it's another thing entirely to not keep looking for a job. I think Jeff just got a little too comfortable, living off his brother and his sister-in-law, with her earning the money so Jeff didn't have to do anything." The old guy shook his head. "In my day, we always looked after our spouses and our kids and our siblings, no matter what. So you're asking a good question. I hope somebody who knows Jeff better has an answer to that because I sure don't. I hate to think of anything happening to Mary's kids. She was a good, hardworking woman, and I was really sad to see what happened to her."

"What happened to her anyway? How did she die?"

"As far as I know, it was a car accident. The way I heard it, when her husband brought her into the hospital, she was already three-quarters dead. It was the saddest thing. When she died, he had her cremated and basically didn't tell anybody it had even happened. He kept it really quiet and just went inside himself and didn't say a whole lot for a long time. Then we slowly started to see Jeff out with the kids. That's when we first heard that Mary had died and that her good-for-nothing husband had hightailed it out of here, leaving his own children behind. The kids, of course, are pretty-well traumatized over losing their mom. She was everything to them. Dad on the other hand, well, he was worthless. … It remains to be seen whether Uncle Jeff will man up and take care of those kids or move on to another woman who will support him."

"I'm sorry to hear that about his sister-in-law. It always seems as if the good ones die young."

The old man laughed and laughed. "Perfect thing to say to an old buzzard like me," he pointed out, still chuckling.

Alex winced. "Oh, yeah, I should say, *present company excepted* and all that."

"No need," the driver said, still laughing. "I'll never argue about having lived a long life because I certainly have. I've lived, and I've lived well, and, when my day comes, I'm okay with it. My kids are all set. My grandkids are doing fine. Everything is hunky-dory. So, I figure I'm living on borrowed time. But the thing is, I know it, so whatever. It's all good."

When they reached the corner store, the old man stopped and let out Alex. "There you go. Have a good day now, son."

As Alex got out, he leaned in and thanked the old man

again. "You too. Thanks for the lift."

And, with that, the old guy drove off, leaving Alex at the store yet again. His rental, luckily, was still here. All of it. A couple phone calls later, it was his again. He smiled as he started to get in, then hesitated and popped into the store. He grabbed two hot coffees, several sandwiches, some bottled water, and a few snacks, not knowing how long they would be sitting outside Jeff's house tonight—and for future nights probably. Then he headed back out to his rental and drove down the road toward where Taryn should be, watching Jeff's house.

As Alex got closer, he looked around for any sign of Taryn and her vehicle. He had told her to find a better hiding spot, which was a good idea on all stakeouts, but he had also told her to let him know if she moved and where to. He hoped she hadn't gone too far. Out here in this rural area, it would be darn hard to track where she was without too much effort. Just then his phone rang, and he checked the Caller ID. He answered it, as Taryn was on the other end.

"You just passed me."

"Okay," he murmured. "Are you in the trees?"

"Yeah. I pulled in between a couple, behind some bushes," she described. "So I have a full view if Jeff leaves, but without his seeing my vehicle."

"Okay, good. I'll drive around a little bit and confirm there is no other exit. I'll also see if I can come up with something that gives me a better way to gauge activity around the back of the house," he shared. "I do have coffee."

"Wow. … You picked up coffee."

Such envy filled her tone that he laughed. "Yeah, don't worry. I got one for you too."

She chuckled. "You're much nicer than me. I probably would have forgotten about you completely."

"I don't know about that," he countered. "I'm hard to forget. Anyway, once I find a spot to park, I'll come by on foot and make you a coffee delivery." And, with that, he ended the call and started hunting. He needed a good place to sit and to lie in wait for an asshole who was into selling kids, even his own niece and nephews.

CHAPTER 3

TARYN WATCHED A shadow approach, but it was hard to see who it was. She stiffened as it got closer and closer to her. Dusk had settled in, and she had seen no movement from Jeff's house. She hoped the kids were settled in for the night. However, she also felt more fear too. She didn't trust anything that happened in the dark anymore. Something was seriously off with Jeff. Considering the ad he had placed, it revealed an awful lot about where he was in life. Other people might give him some plausible excuse, but she wasn't really into ignoring people's shitty behaviors, especially when it came to abusing children.

As the shadow came closer and closer, she recognized Alex's profile and smiled. She waited until he got close enough, and then she opened her car door and stepped out to meet Alex halfway. He handed her a sandwich and a bottle of water. She looked at it in surprise. "Wow, you really did think ahead, didn't you?"

"Yeah, though I wish we had a thermos or something. That coffee won't last long, and it looks to be a long night."

"And that's good. The kids need sleep too." He didn't argue with her, just nodded, and she sighed. "Sorry, I'm pretty uptight about the whole process."

"That's fine. It's also not what you normally do, is it?"

She laughed. "No way." She gave him an eye roll. "I've

spent most of my life in marketing, online marketing at that. So I spend my days and nights on the computer, promoting the more superficial needs of mankind—fancy cars, luxury homes, expensive cosmetic surgery, diamonds and gems and all that sparkles. So, when you start dealing with stuff a little less than prime, you realize how much ugliness is on the web out there."

"Of course," Alex muttered. "I presume nothing is moving here." He motioned to the house down the road.

She nodded. "No. I'm surprised you even came out here again. Aren't you supposed to be watching your area at the back of the house?"

He nodded. "True, but I've got a couple of ... I don't want to say *traps*, but tricks to let me know if anyone is moving out there. I can get back there pretty damn fast, but you're right. I should head back now." Giving her a ghost of a smile, he turned and disappeared into the trees again.

Within seconds he was long gone, reminding Taryn that some of these guys who worked for Terk and Levi had mad survival skills, nighttime hunting, and whatnot, that she couldn't even begin to know about, much less to emulate.

Taryn sighed and remained standing outside her car. All she had was the deep need to confirm these kids were safe. With that in mind, she sent Terkel a text, asking about Bruce's condition.

When the reply came that Bruce was improving, she had to smile. She dreaded telling Bruce that his sister Mary had died while he'd been in that Russian prison, and now Mary's kids were about to be sold by their paternal uncle Jeff. That would send Bruce into a tailspin and probably cancel out any healing he had done to date.

She hoped for enough time to save these kids before

Bruce was fully conscious, before he was finally brought up-to-date. Yet she wanted those kids back right now, without any more waiting. That wouldn't happen. So she needed all those people out there helping in the background to come up with something useful and fast, damn it. With that thought, she settled against her car door and munched on her sand-wich.

Lights came on in the house, and her chewing slowed, as Uncle Jeff stepped outside and appeared to be talking on the phone. She swore under her breath because she wasn't close enough to hear. She sent Alex a text, sharing all that, hoping he was closer to Jeff and could at least hear Jeff's side of the phone call.

Alex texted, **I'll see what I can do**, but then went silent.

She waited, wondering if Alex was close enough to hear something, but not so close for the uncle to hear or see Alex. They sure didn't want that. She waited with bated breath, while the uncle argued with somebody on the phone. He became more and more animated and then started talking louder and louder. After a few minutes of that, he took a deep breath and seemed to calm down a bit.

She frowned because, although she heard one word here and there, she couldn't make any sense from them. Thank-fully none of those words were frightening. She was just too far away to make heads or tails out of whatever this asshole was up to. When Jeff headed into the house again, she groaned because the opportunity to learn anything had just slipped past them.

When her phone vibrated a few minutes later, she checked her Caller ID and answered it without a greeting.

Alex whispered, "Jeff was haggling over the price."

Her breath was sucked away, and, for a moment, she

couldn't catch another.

"Taryn, are you there?"

"Yes," she gasped. "My God. That is so not what I want to hear."

"I know, and he also seems to want the kids to go together, but I think the other party wasn't inclined to do that."

"Of course not, which just worries me more. I also don't understand why they would speak so freely over a phone on this topic anyway," Taryn grumbled. "How is that even possible?"

"Chances are Jeff and the buyer each have a burner phone, which means the call is untraceable, and it'll be the number Jeff's given in the ad."

"Then we *do* need to respond to the ad," she declared in a mad fit.

"You already did, didn't you?" he asked, with a note of humor, just as he appeared by her side.

All she could do was flush. "How did you know?"

"Because you're not the type to leave it to chance. But the main point here is that he wasn't arguing with *you*."

"That's obvious," she snapped, "and I don't like that one bit because it means he's found another buyer, even though he hasn't responded to me."

"He still might touch base with you though," Alex said, trying to keep it light. "He's obviously negotiating, and maybe somebody got in there before you. So, if that buyer causes any trouble, Jeff might very well contact you anyway."

"Or I could raise the price," she suggested. "Should I raise the price?"

Alex hesitated. "You know that you'll have to produce that in cash in order to make this thing go down."

"Why?" she asked. "I can't be alone in this. Won't the government back me somehow?"

"I have no idea," Alex admitted. "I just know, what with government red tape, … if push comes to shove, do you have that kind of money that you can get in a couple hours?"

"I'll get it," she stated brashly.

He sighed at her tone. "That means, no. So, you don't have that kind of dough."

"I can't let these kids get sold off like some sleazy internet merchandise," she grumbled.

"I agree with you fully. Absolutely I do," he replied, "but we need a solid plan, more than a foolhardy dash into the middle of the chaos."

"I had a plan," she stated. "I would buy the kids."

"So, what happened?"

"I put in an offer, and Jeff didn't get back to me," she explained, "and I don't know why."

"That's my point exactly. Even with cash and all that, we seem to be missing something here. Maybe some special exchange of two phrases happens in these things that we aren't aware of," Alex suggested. "Maybe that ad price is a starting point, when it's really a bidding war. I can't really say though, because I've never had any experience with this side of the web."

"Well, if you don't, and I don't, maybe we should ask someone who does."

"Let me check in with Terkel, and I'll get back to you." At that, he disappeared again.

With a sigh, Taryn sat alone in her car once more, her nerves twisting and turning in her gut. To even think that somebody was already negotiating for these kids made Taryn ill. To think that her offer to buy them had been completely ignored made her completely sick to her stomach.

Could Jeff have known that something was wrong with her offer?

Maybe.

How could that be?

Because she didn't act like the other demented buyers?

Too much was going on in her brain that she didn't have answers to, and it was driving her nuts.

When her phone vibrated, she wasn't surprised to see it was Terkel. She bypassed any niceties, like a normal greeting, and asked, "Why can't we go in and do a full-on rescue? They are right here. I don't understand why they can't be picked up for safety reasons."

"Remember that we've got eyes on this sale, along with both domestic and international agencies. They all have skin in the game, so we can't rush in and undo whatever they may have going on in the background. Meanwhile, I've reached out to somebody in Texas who is taking it to a judge to see if it's something they can get a court order for. One problem is, we don't have any viable proof—the kind the courts and the authorities want anyway—tying that auction bid to Jeff and these particular children, although we have an image of the ad, it's a help but it's not enough," Terk explained in a calm tone that was grating on her nerves, and even Terk knew that. "That's what we need right now. Otherwise we won't pull this off."

"So, none of the hackers in your corner have managed to trace that ad back to Jeff yet?" she cried out rather desperately.

"They're working on it," he shared, "but, even so, we can't just go steal children from a blood uncle. What happens if that blows up in our faces? Sure, we can tell the cops, *Hey, sorry about that. We made a mistake.* But the real cost would be that Jeff would be on to us, and Jeff would by all rights be awarded temporary *legal* custody of those kids, and nobody within these various authorities would choose to work with us again. If Jeff chooses to take those kids and to disappear under future circumstances as these? Then we would be far worse off than we are right now."

"What if the kids are hurt?" she asked bitterly.

"Take it easy, Taryn," Terk replied. "As long as they're in that house, and nobody is there to pick them up, we'll leave them in that situation. I don't think Jeff's abusing them, other than verbally. He can't take a chance of doing much, not when he wants prime dollar for them."

Her breath let out in a *whoosh*. "God, I don't even want to think about that."

"Then don't. We're all working as part of a team here, so don't go off half-cocked."

"Yeah, so when do I get to go off half-cocked then?" she snapped.

"If Jeff tries to escape with the children," Terk stated. "Then you stay on his tail, no matter what. Most important is that you let us know every step of the way where you are, even if that means you call me and stay connected to me on the phone during the car chase and to its full completion. And, if you have a chance for Alex to come with you on any car chase, let him drive. He's got the training for it." And, with that, Terkel was gone.

Taryn settled back to wait and to watch, her mind churning with thoughts. Finally she realized she could do one thing. So she sent healing energy to Bruce. She wished she could speak telepathically, but it was a skill she had yet to master. She had no idea whether the children could or not.

Taryn and Bruce had always been close friends, nothing more than that—although they had discussed *more* at one point in time but had ultimately decided they were better off as strictly friends than friends with benefits.

She loved him. She loved him dearly but as a friend. She could only hope that Amara managed to get over to Terk's castle in England to see Bruce and to try to heal their relationship. As a side note, Amara's presence with Bruce, as long as Taryn was stateside, might help Bruce recover faster, should something truly upsetting happen here. Losing those children would break Taryn's heart, along with letting Bruce down, should Taryn *not* save these kids. Taryn had been a kid once herself, taken advantage of in the same way that these kids were about to experience. … That hit a little closer to home than she cared to admit.

She'd always been close to Bruce to a certain extent, partly because they had shared certain gifts, and partly because Bruce's parents had taken her in as a foster kid, which had worked out really well for Taryn. She'd become close to the whole family. It had shown her a life she hadn't seen before, but they hadn't been the first foster home she'd been in. Yet it had been the best, and thankfully for her sake and for her sanity, the last foster home for her.

Taryn had gone in with a chip on her shoulder and an attitude about life that wasn't that easy to deal with. Bruce's mom had quickly surrounded Taryn with love, and it never eased up. Yet Taryn had been so confused about it at the time, not realizing just what a gem Bruce's mom was. Taryn had never been exposed to someone like that. Taryn winced with a pang of sadness now, since Bruce's mother had passed away from a heart attack not all that long ago.

Did she know that Bruce had been in a Russian prison?

Did she know that Bruce was in trouble?

Did she know that Mary and her kids were in trouble?

Did Mary have the same intuition as Bruce did?

Far too many things had been left unsaid among the family members, yet maybe Bruce and Mary's mom didn't need to know this right before she passed. A whole lot of horrible things happened in life, but not many were much worse than knowing that your son was a prisoner and slated for execution in a Russian prison, all during the same time period that your daughter was killed in an auto accident. Wow. That would have been so damn hard to handle.

Pulling back her heavy emotions, knowing it wouldn't help anything, Taryn settled in to watch and to wait, alternately sending energy in the direction of Bruce and now trying to send some to those children in that house with Jeff.

When a voice in her head spoke to her very softly, Taryn frowned, shifted a bit, sitting up, looking forward, still inside her car. She called out equally softly in her mind, *Who are you?*

Nothing but the faintest of whispers was there, then a sigh, and then nothing.

Bruce? Taryn asked. *Is that you?* They had never managed to speak telepathically before, but Taryn's limited abilities had increased somewhat. Maybe Bruce's greater gifts had grown in leaps and bounds, enough so they could talk to each other in this way now. With Bruce's help, maybe she could do more now. She called out once more, *Try to communicate again, if you can.*

Afterward came a weird hum, almost a struggle on the ethers, and then the energy disappeared.

Taryn sat there in the car, dry-eyed for a long moment, and then the tears just gushed. She didn't even know where they came from, but they were so hot and so sudden that she was completely helpless to stop them.

That was the moment she realized they weren't even hers.

ALEX STIFFENED, HEARING the brutal sobs in his head.

"What the hell?" he muttered. He sat up, looked around, but it was most definitely in his head and not outside him. He tried hard to figure out who it was, and yet everything kept coming from the direction of Taryn. He hesitated to ask if it was her because it seemed to be so private, so tormented, so personal. It would be awkward to interrupt. He frowned, hating to be a party to it, and tried to block it out. He'd never heard such painful sounds before.

When his phone vibrated, he answered, only to hear Taryn sobbing away. "What's wrong? What's the matter, damn it? Taryn, talk to me."

"It's not me. Those aren't my sobs," she cried out, and then the call went dead. Alex stared down at it, but, instead of calling her back, he phoned Terkel.

"Yeah, I'm not sure what's going on either," Terkel began, his voice calm but distant. "We're trying to figure it out here."

Alex muttered, "I don't understand. What did she mean that it's *not* her sobs. Did she really mean that?"

"She meant it. I think she's picking up on someone else."

"Why the hell is she picking up on anything?" Alex asked in frustration, "Unless … that's what she does?"

"I don't think she knows what she does. She's always

been a very strong intuitive. My understanding is that she grew up with Bruce, and they used to play all kinds of games based on intuition when they were younger. However, it's not something that she'd ever really used, beyond what she recognized as just her intuition. I think she only shared her fledgling gifts with Bruce. But right now? … She's apparently been attracted to and caught up in some energy that she doesn't recognize, and doesn't know how to get herself out of."

"*Great*," Alex muttered, followed by a hard release of breath. "It's absolutely incredible hearing her in my head." After a moment of silence, he asked Terk curiously, "You're hearing it too?"

"Well, I'm hearing *her*," Terk clarified, "so I don't understand what you mean that it's not her because what I am hearing is definitely her."

"Yes, you're hearing some of Taryn. It's her voice but not her tears." Alex shook his head at that.

"You must think that makes sense," Terk replied, with a note of humor. Then he laughed. "It's not even that it makes sense. It's just what it is."

"God," Alex whispered. "This stuff is so bizarre."

"It can be. Absolutely it can be," Terk confirmed, "but the bottom line is that we don't really have answers for very much in life when it comes to this energy work. Thus, we're as stuck as everybody else trying to figure out what's going on. Everyone struggles to settle into their normal, and this is ours."

"Well, I hope you figure it out because Taryn sounds horrified by it."

"She is, and she's clearly picked up on somebody. Now the question is, … who is it?" And, with that, Terkel disconnected.

Alex was left sitting there all alone, listening to the terrible sobs in his head. He tried everything he could to tune it out but wasn't getting anywhere and finally realized that ignoring it wasn't helping. Damn it, those tears, those sobs, they were so damn strong. He phoned Taryn. "Is that still you?"

"It's not me. It never has been," she wailed, now bawling too in response to these heart-wrenching sobs. "But it's somebody, somebody who's terrified, somebody who somehow latched on to my energy," Taryn guessed. "I don't know how to get free."

"We're supposed to learn these things as we go along, but we never really have a chance to because there's no opportunity to ever really try or practice," he murmured. "We could really use Terk's experience to teach us how."

"I don't know about practice or trying," she choked out between sobs, "but this is beyond the realm of anything I've ever experienced."

"So, what makes you think it's not you then?"

She gave a broken laugh, still mixed in with some sobbing. "Because I'm seeing images. I'm seeing things. It's like …" Then she stopped. "Oh my God," she whispered, "I think I know who it is."

"Who?" he asked.

"The little girl—Cassie, Bruce's niece. I think it's her crying, crying for the loss of her mother," Taryn offered, as the tears started anew yet again. "Oh my God, her pain is just horrific. I need it to stop."

"Well, I'm pretty sure Terkel would tell you to distance yourself from this, but learn what you can, ask why she's doing this, and see if there's anything you can do to help."

Suddenly Taryn gave a strangled yelp.

"Hey, Taryn. Are you okay?"

CHAPTER 4

"**I** 'M NOT SURE I am," Taryn gasped. "Jesus, I don't know what this is, but, God, it's bad."

"Hang on. I'm coming to you."

"No, you have to stay and watch."

"I also have to confirm you're okay."

"That's not part of it," she cried out. "You have to confirm that the children are safe."

"Yeah, it sounds to me as if Cassie's more than safe but is endangering you."

"If she is, it's only because she's scared, but, Jesus, she's strong. … God, I don't know what this is, but I don't like it." All of a sudden she gasped again.

"Now what?" Alex asked.

"I think we got separated."

Suddenly Terkel's voice slammed into Taryn's brain. *No, don't, don't disconnect from the energy, just mute it. Keep it calm. Keep it quiet because, if that is Cassie, we need that connection to that little girl.* And then Terkel left her head too.

Taryn sank back against the car seat, the shudders rippling up and down her spine.

"Are you okay?" Alex asked, now right beside her, outside her car door.

She lowered the window and let out a slow, deep breath.

"I'm not sure," she whispered. "What the hell is going on?"

He winced. "Remember that intuition you spoke of, that intuition you and Bruce shared, that part of you that's always been so strong?"

She nodded slowly and looked up at him, expecting some rational explanation.

Alex continued. "Well, that little girl recognized you for what you are, which is a kindred soul, somebody who comes from a good place in the world. My guess is, Cassie's latched on to you because she can and because she needs that security because she's lost that herself. And I would imagine that, of all the things that she needs right now, it's to know that she's okay and that somebody out there is looking after her," Alex stated. "I'm not sure what Terkel would say, but I have a pretty good idea."

She gave a half-crazed laugh. "He just slammed into my brain and told me to not break the connection." She grimaced and showed her palms. "As if I can control any of this. Terk just told me to *keep the channel open* because it was our only way of keeping track of Cassie." She stared up at Alex with a mix of reverence and awe. "I've never had anybody do that before."

Alex shrugged. "Yeah, Terkel's special."

She stared at him. "You know there's *special*, and then there's *lunacy*."

He softly chuckled at her choice of words. "I don't think any energy worker would appreciate the latter term," he noted cautiously. "And, if you weren't feeling quite so shocked, you wouldn't be using it."

"Are you sure about that?" she asked, staring at him. "Terk was *talking in my head*."

"Yes, it's called telepathy, and it can really make life a lot easier if you can do it."

She frowned at him. "You can do it?"

He shrugged once more, then nodded. "I can do it with Terkel and a few other people I've known for a long time," he shared, "but I'm not sure I can just do it randomly."

She nodded, as if that made all the sense in the world. And, of course, not only did it *not* make any sense, it was just starting to suggest that maybe she really needed some sleep and that this whole thing was getting to her.

Alex gave her a small smile. "You're looking a little bit as if the world just tilted on you." He patted her hand on the steering wheel. "Why don't you try to sleep for a little bit, get a power nap, and I'll keep watch."

She frowned at him. "What if Cassie wakes me up with her emotions again?"

He gave her a sober sigh. "Assuming Cassie connecting to you is happening here, I think you're probably right. You really can't do a whole lot about it. Just try to keep her calm and to keep yourself calm. That is the best option to keep track of here. She's in pain, and she needs somebody right now, and it looks as if she's chosen you."

Taryn took a deep breath and nodded slowly. "I'm up for doing whatever I can to help Cassie, but the rest of this stuff? I'm not sure it's even possible."

He gave her a ghost of a smile and whispered, "You may be surprised about that, but the rest of this is a whole lot easier to handle. Once you open your mind and accept that you have gifts, that it's part of your reality, and that somebody really can talk to you telepathically, chances are you can talk to them in that way too."

Her gaze widened. She shook her head rapidly. "Hell no. No way."

He laughed. "Wait until you talk to that little girl and are able to send her soothing energy to make her realize she's okay."

"But she's not okay," Taryn countered. "How can I tell her that? She's in grave danger."

"Yeah, but we can't tell her that. She's just a child, and she wouldn't even understand what that danger entails. She won't understand the who and the why and where it's coming from," Alex explained. "So it's important that we don't say anything to scare her further."

Taryn let out a breath and slowly nodded. "Okay, I can see that. … I'm so freaked out right now, so it would be way worse for her." She looked at Alex sideways. "I just don't think I'll sleep though."

He smiled. "You may be surprised at just how well you can sleep," he told her. "Partly because you're here to help and that little girl has reached out to you. Cassie needs you, and you need her right now, whether you believe it or not. You two are connected, even if it's only through your love of Bruce. Was he close to her?" Alex asked in a careful tone.

She nodded. "Oh, yes, they were best of friends. Bruce was very close with all three of Mary's kids, before he went back overseas again. But now, it's been so long, and Cassie may not even remember him," Taryn muttered.

"You might be surprised to find out that Cassie may even be searching for Bruce right now on the ethers. Remember that she's young, untrained, yet obviously powerful as an energy worker. Plus, she's looking for somebody or something to help her in this craziness that her world has become. She probably doesn't even know what it is she's looking for, but she's reaching out, and she's latching on. That, in itself, says a lot about who Cassie is as a person, and it's better that she latches on to you than someone else—who could see what she's up to and doesn't have her best interests at heart."

Taryn sucked in her breath at the thought. "God, can you even imagine?" She shut her eyes and whispered, "I think I need to chill for a bit."

"You do that. Move over so I can get in the driver's seat. I'll just stay here and keep watch, … over you and her."

She opened her eyes. "And if something happens?"

"Don't worry." He chuckled. "I'll wake you up, but you'll also wake up anyway because I'll have this vehicle in motion. They will not get past me."

She stared at him for a long moment, and, finding absolutely nothing in his expression that gave her cause for concern, she nodded slowly. "I hope so because I think Cassie is asleep right now, but I don't think she'll stay that way for long."

And, with that, Taryn drifted off to sleep.

ALEX WATCHED CAREFULLY, the house and the woman who slept so peacefully beside him. He was pretty sure Taryn had no idea that he'd helped knock her out. Yet she needed rest because the ordeal to come wouldn't be easy if she was to reconnect to the child without first getting some sleep and recharging.

After a bit of time, Terkel slipped into Alex's mind. *Is Taryn out?*

She is, and she thinks Cassie is asleep too.

Good, Terkel replied, his voice harsher than normal. *Yet I'm not sensing the two boys' presence.*

Alex's heart stopped at that. *Meaning they are dead?*

Not necessarily. I'm just not sensing them. It could be that they have not developed any abilities yet or haven't figured out what's going on in their world. Both boys could be dead-to-the-world sleeping for that matter. Just because I'm not picking up their energy doesn't mean they are not there, he explained, with a note of humor. *I'm not that invincible.*

Are you sure? Alex asked, with a wry smile. *Taryn was pretty shocked to hear your voice in her head.*

After a moment of silence, Terk noted, *She caught that, did she?*

Yeah, were you not expecting her to?

Well, she didn't react as a first-timer, as I would have thought, Terk shared, *so I couldn't judge. Yet, as long as she got the message, I'm good with it.*

Yeah, she got the message, and I think she's just, … how can I say surprised *in its strongest form?*

Terkel laughed. *Yet the fact that she could pick up my message is also massive.*

I know, but she hasn't figured out that part yet, Alex noted, with a chuckle.

What about you? Terk asked.

I'm still here with her in the car. I'm watching the house and the driveway, while keeping an eye on Taryn as well. I'm not entirely sure what's going on with her, but, when she started to bawl like that, well, … it was rough, damn rough.

It wasn't her though, Terkel noted.

No, but I think there was some of her in the midst of it.

That would explain it, Terkel replied, *and, if she's got some trauma in her past, maybe the little girl sensed it and was reaching out.*

I think Cassie was reaching out and didn't need a why,

Alex stated, *but that could be why the little girl could make the connection with Taryn.*

Agreed. Anyway, we may have a thread to pull that leads to the children's missing father. My team is still working on it. Right now though, I need to get some sleep. Things are a bit hectic here.

Yeah? Any movement on the baby front?

Lots of movement, still no babies, Terkel shared, with a sigh.

But nothing to worry about?

No, nothing to worry about yet, as the women keep telling me. Apparently this stuff takes time.

Alex stifled a laugh, so as not to wake up Taryn. *I've heard that a time or two, not personally of course. All the best to you guys, while you work your way through it.*

Yeah, let's just hope this little girl gives us a chance to sleep. It's a little hard to do this work without some recharging time. And, with that, Terkel disappeared.

As Alex sat watching the house, he wondered what the hell this Jeff guy was doing, who he had been arguing with, and how quickly he would make a move. Then Alex got a call from Levi. "Hey," Alex replied in a curious tone. "Are you looking to talk to Taryn?"

"Actually I was looking to talk to you. Terkel told me that you were helping out."

"Yeah, that's what I'm doing," he quipped, with a note of humor. "Although, if I'd had any idea what I would be letting myself in for, I might have given it a second thought."

Levi laughed. "Not likely. We all tend to be in this in-dustry because of our histories and our backgrounds and just because of the people we are. So, once that call went out, and you responded, I'm sure more details wouldn't have changed anything."

"You would seem to think so some days," he conceded, with a sigh. "It's kind of crazy right now though."

"Why? Is Terkel up to his usual?"

"Yeah, that's a full-on yes. … Terkel is definitely up to his unpredictable antics," he agreed. "We've also had the little girl reach out and connect with us."

Stunned silence came on the other end. "Do you want to repeat that?" Levi asked.

"I'm not sure I can." Alex sighed. "The bottom line is that Taryn started bawling her eyes out. She and I were positioned on opposite sides of the house, so I couldn't see her, but I heard her. Taryn was beside herself, and I heard her in my head. I couldn't figure out what was going on. Then she called me, just crying, not speaking. I asked her if she was okay, and she just bawled all the more but stated *she* wasn't the one who was crying."

Levi sucked in his breath. "Good God, this Terkel stuff is enough to derail your brain. That is a new one, even by Terk's standards."

Alex snorted. "Yeah, you're not kidding. Still, it's also pretty weird, yet wonderful."

"I don't know about the wonderful part," Levi noted. "That woo-woo stuff is not for me. I prefer enemies I can see and subdue, not the ones that bounce around on the ethers, causing all kinds of chaos."

"You and me both on that score," Alex murmured. "Anyway, as far as we can figure, the little girl reached out in her grief for anybody on the ethers, likely not even knowing what she's doing. Just reaching out because of her own pain."

"That breaks my heart," Levi said softly. "Can you imagine? I don't think I'll even tell Ice about that part."

"Yeah, that probably won't work out so well for you," Alex noted. "My understanding is that your wife doesn't miss much."

"No, she doesn't, and yet I wish she would sometimes, for her own peace of mind. It just doesn't always work out that way."

"Sorry," Alex replied. "I've got Taryn asleep here in the vehicle beside me, as we keep watch on the house."

"You'll need to pace yourself and get some sleep while you can as well," Levi suggested, "though I guess that's a problem since it's only the two of you. My guys are helping here and there with research and the satellite, but I don't have anybody free at the moment to meet you on the ground."

"Yeah, I heard Riff may be available, as he was in the States. Otherwise I don't know that Terk has anybody to spare to send right now either."

"Let me contact Terk in the morning, his morning, and confirm that angle."

"Things are a little crazy at Terk's end. From what I understand, the babies are on the move but not coming as fast as Terk thinks they ought to."

"Right, Celia is struggling at the end stages of her labor."

"If somebody can come our way—whether from your team or Terk's—I won't say I'm against it." With that, Alex disconnected, then drifted in and out of sleep, as he tried to keep watch on the property.

When a knock came on the driver's side window, Alex bolted awake, then opened the window a bit and stared at a man glaring down at him. "Who the hell are you?" Alex asked.

"Let me in."

"Hell no, I'm not letting you in."

The man gave a long-suffering sigh. "I'm Riff. Terkel sent me. Now, let me in so you can sleep, and I'll keep watch on the house."

CHAPTER 5

Taryn woke up, feeling groggy, as if from a drugged sleep, not the refreshing kind. When she shifted in her seat, she winced and then groaned, slowly opening her eyes wider as she stared at the vehicle she sat in. Noting a stranger in the driver's seat, she almost jumped out the window.

He turned, then smiled at her. "Hey, my name's Riff. Terkel sent me." She swallowed several times. Then he added, "Don't be scared. I'm on your team, so no need to be alarmed."

She stared at him, quickly trying to process things and to catch up. "And I didn't wake up?"

He shrugged. "Nope, you didn't wake up."

"That's not like me at all," she noted faintly.

He cocked one eyebrow. "Better get over it."

Her eyebrows shot up. "Just like that?"

"Yeah, just like that."

She struggled to reorient herself to the chaos her world had become. She brushed her hair off her face and continued to stare at him. "When did you get here?"

"While you were sleeping," he shared cheerfully. She shot him a look, and he laughed. "Obviously that goes without saying, but, hey, we have to start somewhere. Anyway, it's a good thing I came, so now your buddy here can also take a nap and rest up." Riff pointed a thumb to the back seat.

"Any movement on the house?"

"Nope, nothing yet."

"Alex has his car on the other side though," she explained. "He was supposed to stay over there but didn't want to leave me alone here."

"Good call," Riff agreed, glancing at Alex, then turned to watch the house again. "When he wakes up, he can head back over to that side, and we can make a plan, should this Jeff guy decide *not* to leave the house."

"What plan do we make?" she asked, frowning at him. "Isn't it a good thing if they don't leave?"

"As long as we're also tracking whoever may be coming into this picture," Riff added, "because that is a whole different story."

She swallowed hard, then rummaged around and found her water bottle and drank the last bit of it. "I also need a few minutes to walk around a bit, and then some food would be nice." He nodded. She grabbed some napkins, left the car, found some bushes not far away, and relieved herself, wishing for a bathroom and a shower at least, not to mention the rest of the good things that normal people had. Then she reminded herself that a trio of children were at risk of being sold into God-only-knows what kind of a nightmare, so Taryn shouldn't be lamenting the lack of her own creature comforts.

As she walked back to the car, the two men were talking, both now awake and standing outside the vehicle.

Alex faced her, smiled, and asked, "How are you feeling?"

"It was a little weird waking up to find a stranger in the car," she shared, frowning at Riff. "I wish I'd known he was coming, so it wouldn't have been such a shock."

Riff shrugged. "Just because I was coming doesn't mean it wouldn't have been a shock anyway," he pointed out. "Walking in the shadows is something I do regularly."

She still frowned at him, and he frowned right back. She sighed. "Well, you're already here, and we could use the help."

"Thank you, that's most gracious," Riff quipped.

She flushed, realizing she had no say in that or anything else. Besides, any help that they could get would make it easier on all of them. She shrugged. "It's not my deal, and apparently I don't have all the job skills required to pull this off. So I'm sure you guys will do whatever you do."

Riff raised one eyebrow at her. "But you're the one who put out the alarm, right?"

She nodded. "To a certain extent, yes, but I'm not sure how much of an alarm I put out, when you consider how long this may have been going on."

Riff agreed. "Which is another reason why it's important to catch up with it right now. Once the kids are in the trafficking system, it's almost impossible to get them back out."

She winced at that. "I still don't understand why we can't just walk in and grab them."

"Because we have no proof, not per the legal community, regardless of our personal feelings and some hearsay. Until you have proof that Jeff posted the ad, we have no lawful way to intervene. We don't have the right to just go in and remove children from their uncle's care."

"What about under suspicions of neglect and abuse?" she asked. "Surely that would work."

"Maybe, but, if you have nothing concrete to back it up,

the children would just be returned to their uncle Jeff, and the next time you try, you'll have even less support from the authorities," Riff explained. "Plus, it would tip off Jeff, and he could take them and disappear. It's much better to take some time and rally our teams to do it right, while we have a chance to retrieve the kids and also nail Jeff. I'm also not at all against nailing the prospective buyers in this case as well."

She flushed. "Well, if all goes according to plan, I'll be one of them."

He turned and stared, and Alex quickly jumped in. "She was afraid that Jeff would take off with the kids, so she sent in an offer."

"Oh, interesting," Riff murmured. "Yeah, that might work—if you can get him to talk to you."

"Yeah, except Jeff didn't respond." When Riff stared at her, she shrugged. "Alex wondered if there was some code or special catchphrase or something when you buy things on the dark web, so they know you're *legit*."

Riff shook his head. "It's not so much that there's a code, but there is definitely a process. He wouldn't answer you right off the bat anyway, especially if he had other people interested, as in regular buyers Jeff has dealt with before."

"And yet *regular buyers*," she noted, feeling the sickness in her heart, "implies that Jeff's done this before."

"Do we have any evidence of that?" Riff asked them both.

"I don't know," she muttered. "You would have to talk to Terkel about that—or maybe Levi and Ice."

"Are they involved too?" Riff asked her.

Alex nodded, "One or both of the teams are doing a deep dive on Jeff. No word yet on that."

She asked Riff, "Do you know them too?"

"Sure, Levi and Ice are major players in the industry. Plus, they work a lot with Terkel," Riff shared. "So, yeah, I do know them. And, if they're involved, it's great because then they'll have law enforcement working quietly on the sidelines to help us."

"I still don't understand the whole *quietly on the sidelines* thing," she muttered. "I just want to go in there and grab those kids and take them away."

"Yeah, but that's a rookie move. Taking them away is one thing. Taking them away so they never have to deal with this uncle again, that's a whole different story. We cannot fail in this process. We cannot let those children go back to Jeff again, and that's what we're trying to avoid."

She winced. "I get that, and I get why everybody keeps telling me that, but it still feels as if we're not doing enough."

"It always feels as if you're not doing enough," Riff declared, his voice steady as he studied Taryn. "That's just one of the things that comes with this work, because honestly, as soon as we find something's going on, such as this," he stated, carefully gauging his words so as not to pop her bubble, "we just find dozens more cases like it."

She looked around in disgust. "How about I go for a food run?"

The men eyed her, and Riff suggested to Alex, "Go with her." He spoke in a simple tone, no BS, clear-cut.

She stared. "I don't need somebody to look after me."

He turned a hard gaze her way. "You may well believe that, but you're not seeing the bigger picture. The problem with that short-term thinking is that little girl, who is an unknown factor in all this. What if she latches on to you while you're out driving?" he asked. Taryn just stared back, now wide-eyed. "Will you continue to drive while she's overwhelming you? Or even do what you need to do in order to get back here? Am I wrong to worry about that?"

Taryn continued to stare at him, now frowning. "I don't know. I've never had this experience before."

"And considering the work that we're doing right now," Riff clarified, "you yourself know, as well as I do, that it's better off if we stay in pairs."

She flushed. "And yet, if we leave, you're not a pair."

He smiled. "But if anybody here doesn't need to be in a pair, it's me." She glared at him, but he just shook his head. "Don't waste time arguing."

She turned to Alex, already walking toward the road. "Where are you going?" she asked, frustration oozing from her.

"Working my way around to the back to pick up my vehicle."

"Good enough," she conceded. "I'll wait here for you."

He smiled at her. "That's a good idea." Then he quickly disappeared from view.

She pivoted to glare again at Riff. "I don't know that I trust you."

"Good. You shouldn't trust me just because I said who I am. If you haven't checked in with Terkel, how do you know I didn't lie?" She had no answer to that. "I could have lied."

She narrowed her gaze at him. "You're having way-too-much fun in a situation that doesn't call for it."

His eyebrows shot up. "I'm not having any fun. Fun would be surfing in Hawaii. Fun would be doing something with friends, not sitting here trying to stop children from getting served up to some pervert as his playthings," he muttered. "If you don't trust me, contact Terkel."

She frowned, wondering if it was safe to do so, but Riff's gaze was steady.

Riff added, "And you should. You know you should."

She sighed, pulled out her phone, and, when Terkel answered, she said waspishly, "Describe Riff." He gave her a physical description that matched the man in front of her. "Why didn't you tell us that he was on the way?"

"I didn't know he would come," Terk stated. "I put out a word, looking for help, to see if Riff was available. He was in the US at the time, and, as is typical Riff behavior, he just arrives when we least expect it and yet most need it."

"But is it safe to trust him?"

"Yes," Terkel declared, "especially considering he's probably the one who told you to call me anyway."

She felt the heat in her cheeks once more at the accuracy of his deduction. "Yeah, and now he's grinning like a fool."

"He has a habit of doing that, but don't let him piss you off. Just remember that he's there to help and that he's very good at what he does. Anything else is secondary, just noise, so don't let it distract you." And, with that, Terkel disconnected.

She nodded. "Well, he gave you a reference, though I'm not exactly sure it was a good one. Yet he vouched that you are who you are."

Riff snorted. "That's about all he can do anyway." Riff took a skimming glance at the house. "In case you hadn't noticed, most of the people in this industry tend to be free spirits."

"So I've heard."

"We don't take well to orders, and we do what we want because we're here to help. Outside of being part of teams of gifted people who are doing this energy work," Riff explained, "most of us don't enjoy having bosses or being bossed around."

"Ah, that figures."

"Why does it figure?" he asked her curiously.

She shrugged. "Because you look as if you're a bit of a knothead."

He stared at her for a moment and then chuckled. "Well, you're not far wrong," he muttered. "So, when you're out shopping, pick me up coffee and some food, will you?"

She nodded. "I figure we'll probably need to get more than a little bit."

"Well, somebody has to stay here all the time and keep watch," he agreed, "though I would just as soon move into the house."

She stared at him in shock. "How will you manage that?"

"Not sure yet. I'm still working out a viable plan."

"There is no viable plan that'll get you into that house," she stated in exasperation. "You just said that we don't want to do anything that'll put the kids in jeopardy or to give Jeff a heads-up." When Riff turned to stare at her, she raised both hands in mock surrender. "Fine, okay, so you won't do anything to put the kids in danger, but it still doesn't sound like a plausible plan."

"I didn't say I knew how to make it happen," he clarified. "I just mentioned I would prefer to be in there."

"So would I," she muttered, "but Jeff wouldn't let anybody in. He's become very antisocial in this last year, even more so since his sister-in-law's death and the subsequent disappearance of his brother."

"Yeah, the teams are searching for the missing brother,

but I would like a bit more history on Mary's death as well," Riff noted thoughtfully.

She frowned at him. "I've wondered myself if Jeff did something to get rid of Mary, to make his criminal life a little bit easier, but I don't know," she muttered. "It's a bit far-fetched, especially when she was the breadwinner, with her husband and his brother Jeff both unemployed."

"Not necessarily. I've seen serial killers who enjoyed family life, until it just wasn't any good anymore, and they took out the entire family. Then just … moved on to start a new family." When she stared at him in shock, he shrugged. "Remember that it takes all kinds in this world. Just when you think you've seen it all, you haven't. Somebody still has the ability to do things that will shock you."

"Well, all I want to do is get those kids back before Bruce wakes up, when we have to tell him what happened."

Riff faced her. "The Bruce at Terk's? Ah, now that makes more sense. These are Bruce's kids?"

"Bruce's niece and nephews," she clarified. "His sister Mary died while he was in prison, which he doesn't even know about yet, much less about this whole child trafficking fiasco."

"Jesus, that guy's been through the wringer. We definitely need to get these kids back to Bruce. He's been through enough already. The last thing he needs is to wake up and to find out these kids have been sold into sex slavery."

"Let's not even go there," she muttered. "I just want to get them back."

"Last I saw of Bruce, he was beginning to surface a bit. I have high hopes that he'll come back fully."

"What if he doesn't?" she asked.

"We don't need to go there just yet," Riff stated. "The

healers working with Terk are incredible. Amazing, really. They work with people on the cusp of life and death all the time. So Bruce is definitely in the very best place he could be right now."

Taryn didn't know what to say to that. The concept of energy-working healers working with the people on the cusp of death was a little stunning, but Riff certainly seemed serious about his choice of words. "Can you imagine what it would be like to do something like that for a profession?" she asked softly.

"It takes dedication," he replied. "You obviously have abilities yourself, and healing is really not that far off."

She snorted. "I have minor, very minor abilities, and I would call it more intuition than abilities."

"Yeah, most of us are more comfortable calling it intuition," Riff agreed. "That doesn't change what it is." When she glared at him again, he smiled. "Besides, you and Bruce used to experiment a bit telepathically, didn't you?"

"That was a very long time ago, when we were just children, and we used to imagine we could send messages back and forth," she explained. "His family was my foster family, so we lived in the same home. We were together constantly, so it wasn't that difficult to know what the other one might be thinking. His family was really good to me."

Riff frowned at her. "You're a foster child?"

She nodded slowly. "Yeah, and, no, I don't have a clue who my family is. So don't even bother asking because I gave up even thinking about it ages ago."

"Maybe," he conceded, "but you know that also probably explains why that little girl reached out to you."

"I think she just reached out, and I happened to be nearby," she replied.

"I would agree with that to some degree, but I wonder if it wasn't because you're also a foster child and understand loss, grief, and all the other emotions that go along with what Cassie's experiencing right now. Those real and personal experiences you share remain unresolved in your own mind to some degree, and is likely what drew that little girl to you. What you also need to understand is that's why she reached out, but it's also why you reached back."

ALEX PICKED UP the car and headed back around to where he left the two of them. As he drove up, Taryn got right into the vehicle. Riff gave them a salute, and, with that, they headed back to the convenience store. "Did you guys get on okay?" Alex asked her.

She smirked but nodded. "He's different."

"He's very different, but we all are, in our own way," Alex noted. "And having abilities as he does makes him very different. Like Terkel, the energy work makes Riff a very strong, unique character, who can do things you can't even imagine."

"Did he sneak up on you in the car too?"

Alex laughed. "I don't know if you heard him, but that's what he does. He's very shadowy. And I hate admitting this, but I was half dozing, and I didn't see or hear him approach. So believe me that I was quite perturbed at the time, at least until he reassured me that it's just the way he works."

"Still unnerving though."

"Absolutely. *Unnerving* is a good word for it." Alex nodded, with a smile.

As they reached the store, she sighed. "I don't suppose

real food is around here. I've been living on processed food for way too long."

"Well, let's fill up on gas here," Alex suggested, "and we can always ask inside if a restaurant is nearby."

"I'll do that, while you fill up the gas tank."

As soon as he had the tank full and paid for, she came back out, smiling. "Down the road about a mile are a couple fast-food restaurants and a sit-down restaurant."

"We don't really have time for sitting here in town," Alex pointed out, "not when we have Riff out there waiting for us."

"I agree," she said, "but we should at least pick up something more than granola bars and days-old sandwiches."

With a nod, Alex drove into town and pulled up at the first burger joint, one without a drive-through window. She went inside, ordered several burgers, plus fries, milkshakes, and even coffee. She bought more than enough for three people, and, as she got back into the vehicle, she groaned. "This is not much better than corner-store sandwiches, is it?"

"Maybe not, but at least it's something different." Alex focused on the road and headed back to where Riff and her car should be waiting.

As he drove up closer, she leaned forward and asked in alarm, "Where is he?"

Alex shook his head. "Not sure." He drove up and parked at the spot where Riff should have been. Alex got out, looked around, then turned to her, a frown on his face, and got back in the driver's seat. "No sign of him."

She stared at him and started to swear. "Where's my car?" she cried out. "Where's he taken my car?"

He grabbed her hand and said, "Easy now. Riff could have moved your car to a better spot."

"Well, he damn-well better hurry up and tell us where the hell he is," she snapped. "I want to know right now." Instead of a phone call or a text, her vehicle drove toward them, and she stared. "That's him."

Riff pulled off to the side with the window down, so the two driver's side windows faced each other, and smiled at them. "Hey, I thought we better keep changing it up, you know, and move around. That way we're not sitting here at the same spot the whole time. I'll go around to the back where you were parked. I suggest you guys pull a little farther down, so you're a bit more out of view, and see if that works."

"Sure," she replied, a heavy sigh slipping out. "You gave me a heart attack when I saw my vehicle was gone."

He laughed. "Is this your car?"

She nodded. "Yeah, and it's all I really have, so I would appreciate it if you don't just run away with it."

"We can switch if you want, with the rental, so you'll be back in your own wheels."

She looked over at Alex, who nodded. "She'll feel better," he agreed, with a smile. With that settled, they quickly made the switch. That done, she handed over his bag of hamburger meals, along with the coffee, spare water, and snacks that she'd picked up at Riff's request.

"Good enough," Riff said. Then he took the rental and disappeared.

She stared at the dust he created as he left. "You think he's really okay?"

"Yeah, I really do think he's okay." Alex picked up a coffee and smelled it. "What is it about coffee?"

"I don't know, but, while I fully understand that I can exist without it, I really don't want to," she muttered. "It makes me happy, so I picked up enough for all three of us."

He smiled, then nodded. "*Huh*, and here you told me that you would have forgotten me," he teased, referencing an earlier conversation.

She smiled. "Let's just park up here on the roadside, at the little pullout, and eat our burgers. Then we can decide where and what we want to do after this. I still want to go in there and grab those kids. And I remember all the rational excuses why that's a bad idea. I just can't control my emotions. So give me a break." She glared at him. "Beyond that, I have no idea what we can do."

"As we've discussed before, those are the challenges," Alex noted. "It's woo-woo versus the five senses. Balancing what we can do with what we need to do is always the challenge. Plus, we must be patient while we wait."

She muttered, "It still sucks."

He motioned at the burger in front of her. "Eat. You're the one who wanted hot food, so don't waste the opportunity."

She snorted, then picked up the burger and took a big bite. Within a minute, she turned to him and said, "Something's wrong."

He looked at her, tears pouring down her face, and asked, "What's the matter?" He wasn't freaked out like before but still not comfortable with the tears. "Oh, boy, and *this* is exactly why you don't get to stay alone anymore." He moved the food and drinks out of the way, then opened his arms, and she launched herself into them, continuing to sob as if her heart was breaking. While Alex knew it wasn't *her* heart breaking, he also knew, for this kind of a connection to happen, some history in Taryn's world allowed her to be a conduit for this contact from Cassie.

Taryn must have some pain that she hadn't dealt with herself. When the sobs finally slowed again, he whispered, "It really is okay to cry, you know?"

She shook her head. "No, I told you before. These are Cassie's tears," she stated defiantly.

"Yeah, I get that, but they are also yours," he declared, trying to make it seem as if it didn't matter much. "No way it can't be so."

She stared at him, brushing him away.

"Cassie has picked up on somebody else's pain, and it's allowed her to make that connection," he began. "Yet it's also because of the pain you've got bottled up inside that Cassie can connect as strongly and as securely as she does." Taryn stared at him. He knew she needed to hear the truth, so he continued. "So, when this is all over, and when you have a chance to sit back and to reassess everything that's happened, you need to deal with that personal pain of your own, so it can't keep plaguing you."

She blinked at him several times, then slowly nodded and retreated to her side of the car. She pulled napkins out of the to-go bag and wiped at her face with a frantic action that revealed how much she didn't want anything to do with this. When she was finally done, she looked back over at him. "I know I probably don't look normal in any way at this point, but thank you."

"For what?" he asked.

She shrugged. "Not for the lecture. I could do without that," she quipped, "but definitely for the compassion."

He nodded, and, in the same equally formal tone that she'd used, he whispered, "You're welcome." He stared at the house and then turned to her. "Now, if that bout is over, let me ask you something. Are you getting any images or impressions from the little girl?"

Taryn frowned at him.

"With all that crying going on, that little girl is wide open to you, which you could use to our advantage—if you could get a little bit of control, and not be quite so affected personally."

She rolled her eyes.

"You might manage to communicate with her to let her know that it'll be okay."

"But will it?" she whispered. "We haven't got them out of there, and the little girl doesn't know anything at all about what's going on in her world. She just knows that everything is completely changed and that it doesn't feel safe anymore," she whispered. "I can't lie to her and tell her it'll all be okay, … not when she's still stuck in that same nightmare over there."

"But it *will* be okay. No way we'll leave those kids there. We're getting things in place, as we find out more intel. We're doing what we can," he explained, "and believe me when I tell you that Cassie will be rescued one way or another. Get it through your head that she *will* be rescued and *will* have a chance at a new life."

"You promise?" Taryn asked, staring at him intently.

Not surprised that the child version of Taryn inside the adult version of Taryn needed the same reassurance as the little girl Cassie in that house, Alex nodded. "Absolutely. I promise," he whispered. "And there will be a life after all this for you too. But, right now, you need to comfort that little girl, and that means, if you have to lie, you lie."

CHAPTER 6

A ROUGH HAND woke Taryn from a deep sleep. She blinked as she slowly straightened up. Looking around the inside of the car, she groaned. "We're still here," she muttered, her voice thick, her tongue swollen and fuzzy.

"We are," Alex replied, as he turned on the engine, "but not for long."

She blinked, her mind finally kicking into gear, and asked, "Are they leaving?"

"They are," Alex confirmed, giving her a smile. "So, wake up, sunshine."

She groaned. "How the hell does anybody do stakeouts over long periods of time?"

"Well, usually we have people come relieve us," he shared cheerfully. "However, in this case, that's not happening. And, now that we have action, it's really not happening."

"Damn," she muttered, scrubbing her face. "Okay, so presumably somebody's tracking this?"

"Tracking?"

"I guess I'm hoping there's a satellite or something useful done in these situations."

Alex laughed. "*We* are doing the tracking because we definitely have movement, and movement is always good."

She wasn't sure what to say to that because movement in

one way was good, but, in another way, it meant the three kids' lives were in danger again, and Taryn wouldn't go for that.

"You don't have to look quite so despondent," Alex noted. "For all we know, Jeff's heading back out to get groceries."

She tried to contemplate whether that was even feasible or reasonable, but, of course, it was. He hadn't picked up very much last time. "Are the kids with him?" she asked.

"I don't know. So far, Jeff's never been separated from the kids."

"Yeah, wouldn't that be something if this was the one time."

"And then what would you want to do?" he asked her curiously, as he headed out onto the main road, casually driving quite a distance behind Jeff's truck.

"A part of me *still* wants to swoop in there and scoop them up."

"Remember the law and the problems we'll have if you did that."

"The law's a pain in the ass and too slow to react," she stated succinctly. "Particularly when you know that somebody's in trouble, and you can't help them because you're still looking for a way to get around the law."

"We're not looking for a way to get around it. We're looking for way to implement the law in a way that protects those kids for the long haul."

She moaned. "Just feels like an excuse to me." Alex didn't say anything but kept driving. "God, what I wouldn't do for a hot shower, a freshly brewed cup of coffee, and a chance to brush my teeth." She knew she sounded like a brat, and she didn't mean it that way. However, anything to help liven her up and to get her brain kicked in would help.

"Open the window and get some fresh air circulating," Alex suggested. "When we get to the store, if that's where Jeff is going, you can always go use the washroom and grab a coffee."

"Yeah, I would like that," she muttered gratefully. Sure enough, Jeff's truck pulled into the little convenience store attached to a gas station. Alex pulled up and around on the side close to the washroom, where he could still see Jeff's truck, yet it wasn't obvious they were staying too close.

Taryn hopped out immediately, headed inside, and grabbed the key to the washroom. As she stepped out, a little girl stood there, staring at her. Taryn smiled. "Hi," she said. "Who are you?"

"Cassie," the little girl whispered.

Taryn crouched in front of the child.

Meanwhile, Jeff, Cassie's uncle, grabbed Cassie from behind. "Get back in the truck if you can't behave," he yelled, beyond furious and almost bursting at the seams. "You're only allowed in the store if you'll be good."

Taryn's heart jerked at the little girl's treatment. "I'm sorry," Taryn told Jeff. "It's not her fault. I'm the one who spoke to her."

The uncle stared at Taryn in disgust. "You've got no business talking to my niece at all," he said in a thunderous tone. "What are you, some creep?"

Shocked at the violence in his tone and even at his wording, Taryn could only gasp, as the little girl gave her a sad smile and allowed herself to be pulled into the store. It drove Taryn nuts to think that this asshole would get away with this. She almost charged into the store, but just then Alex stepped up and told her to use the washroom, his voice calming and steadfast.

"I'll go in and pick up a few groceries," he told Taryn. "Take care of what you need to in case we have to run."

It took her a moment to shift gears, and then she nodded and went into the bathroom, where she quickly washed her hands and face, used the facilities, and cleaned up as much as she could, rinsing her mouth several times until it didn't feel quite so fuzzy.

As she stepped out, she walked into the store to see the uncle at the cash register. He just glared at her, but she walked past him toward Alex, who even now poured coffee and added several muffins to the shopping basket he carried. Taryn grabbed some beef jerky and a few other items and added them to Alex's pile. He didn't say anything, just waited until she was done, and then he walked up to the cashier.

As Taryn approached the cashier, the uncle and the little girl walked out of the store. Taryn looked over at the cashier, who had a frown on his face.

"Those poor kids," the guy complained in a sad undertone. "Their mom doted on them. Then she passed away, and their lives have turned all to hell. That man is one nasty piece of work."

Taryn frowned at him and asked, "Has he hurt the kids?"

"I don't know," the clerk muttered, with a shake of his head. "None of us knows what he does and doesn't do. It's just that the kids are these pale statues now, cardboard cutouts anytime they come into the store. I don't think he knows how to cook. He keeps buying the cheap processed canned or boxed stuff, not even real fresh food. We're a convenience store," he declared, as he sighed. "We're a temporary stop, until you make your way to a real store and buy actual food—fresh meat and fruits and vegetables. That guy never buys anything fresh here. I don't know what he's up to."

As he turned his attention to ringing up their sale, Taryn pivoted to look outside. She saw Jeff standing outside his truck, making a phone call, while the little girl sat inside the vehicle. Taryn motioned with her head, and Alex just nodded. He handed her money and stepped outside. She paid for the groceries, still keeping up the conversation with the clerk. "That poor little girl, she must be so lonely. Is it just the one child, or did I hear you say *kids* before?"

At that, the clerk frowned, then looked outside. "Twins, two little boys also. Not sure where they are at the moment. Probably sleeping in the truck. … I don't know. It's always sad when you see a scenario go from so happy to what seems like trouble," he declared in disgust. "The guy's a complete asshole and never has anything good to say. He's never got a smile on his face and seems surly all time, if not downright mean."

"I feel sorry for the little girl and her brothers then," Taryn replied. "That can't be easy."

"Hell no," he agreed. "With an uncle like that, nothing is easy about it. That guy's a straight-up dick." He laughed. "And yet he's been around here a long time, and a lot of people know of him, yet nobody really knows him at all—if you get what I mean."

"I do understand what you mean," she agreed, nodding her head. "There always seems to be a few people in each town who are like that."

"Yeah, and I just wonder what we're supposed to do. … If I ever saw any sign of abuse or something like that, I would not hesitate to contact the sheriff. However, when it's her own uncle, and I have nothing to really hang my hat on, what can I do?" the clerk asked, with a shrug. "I keep hoping he gets his shit together in order to look after those kids or hands them over to foster care or something, so at least they would get three meals a day."

"That isn't any way to live, and it seems the little girl is afraid of him too," Taryn shared. "Did you see how she looked at him?"

"No, because she doesn't look at him. I swear, … every time I've seen her, and this only occurred to me recently, but she doesn't look at him. It's like, if she doesn't look at him, she can ignore that he exists, which won't work for her long-term," he noted, with a sigh. "I tell you, it breaks my heart every time I see them, and yet I don't know what I'm supposed to do about it."

Taryn sighed. "I feel just like that too." The clerk was obviously pissed off and frustrated, not really knowing what his options were, and Taryn thought that was probably more common than it ought to be. What are people supposed to do when they feel something is wrong but can't point to anything that would hold water with the authorities because the person in question was a parent or somebody related who had rights to the child, who appeared to be caring for them? Yet instead no caring was involved, and Uncle Jeff was probably more interested in abusing the child than anything. Hopefully Jeff wasn't abusing the children himself, which was a small blessing when he was still heinous enough to sell them outright.

Taryn waved goodbye to the clerk and carried the bag and her coffee out to her car.

As soon as she got there, Alex whispered, "Stay close. I'll

go into the washroom." He nipped into the bathroom, while she stood here with the coffee on the roof of the car, trying to listen in on Jeff's telephone conversation, but once again she couldn't hear because traffic was nearby. She could only pick up bits and pieces. It was more frustrating than anything. When Alex came out and soon joined her, she glared at him. "How the hell are you supposed to hear anything?" she muttered.

He nodded. "I know. It's frustrating," he whispered, putting a finger to his lips. Then he motioned for her to get inside the car.

Once they were both in the semi-privacy of the car, with all its windows tightly closed, Taryn spoke up. "Too bad we didn't have a bug we could put in his truck." When he turned and raised an eyebrow at her, she shrugged. "Next time he goes shopping, we could hide it then. Maybe afterward we could hear something."

He smiled and nodded. "Not a bad idea, though it's illegal, mind you."

She snorted at that. "That's why I'm not a cop," she declared. "I'm all for using whatever it takes to get us some answers."

He smiled at her. "That's because you're on the side of the victims, but you're not necessarily on the side of the law."

"How can there be a difference?" she cried out softly. "The law is supposed to be there to protect the victim."

"The law *is* there," Alex confirmed, "to ensure justice happens. That does not always mean what you think it should. Sometimes these guys just walk because we can't get the case to hold together."

"We?" she asked.

"No, I don't mean *me*," he clarified, with a headshake. "I wouldn't be a cop either. I don't think I could be. … However, I've seen so many injustices where cases were thrown out because someone took a shortcut and compromised the evidence, couldn't collect it properly, or the prosecutors did a sloppy job of putting together the case itself. In those instances, it's just more frustration for the good cops who went through all the work of tracking down things and making an arrest, only to have the perps go free because something about the case didn't hold water. In those instances, there's absolutely no justice at the end of the day, and criminals just get to walk."

She sighed and asked, "Now what?"

"Now, I guess we find a way to stay out of sight and make it look as if we're not involved. Then we'll get back out there and see where Jeff may be headed. While we couldn't hear what he was saying this time either, he sounded pretty upset. Did you check to see if there was any response to your replies to the ad?"

She shook her head. "No, I haven't yet, but that's a good idea." She quickly pulled out her phone, opened up her email, including the one that she had created just for the offer to buy the kids, then gasped. "There's an answer." She quickly opened it up and read it. "He says the price has gone up due to unexpected interest." She stared at her phone, feeling a burning anger deep inside. "What a complete asshole."

"What, for selling the kids or for raising the price?" Alex asked, with a chuckle. "He realized more interest is out there, so he'll milk it for all it's worth. How much have you offered?"

"The going price from the ad," she replied, "which in this case was twenty grand."

ALEX WHISTLED. "BUT you already told me that you don't have twenty grand."

"I can get it if I have to," she muttered. "I was really hoping I wouldn't have to, but I couldn't care less if that's what's required."

"I hear you there, and I'm not arguing that point at all," he stated. "I was expecting Jeff to say that was the price for each child."

She looked at him slowly. "I guess that'll probably be next, won't it?"

"Well, think about it. He's got something other people want. The thing is, if you respond now, he'll know that you're really interested, which to him means you would pay even more. And, if he already has somebody else on the line, they'll pay more as well because this is something they want."

"Jesus, the world is a sick place," she muttered.

"It is, and so are the people who buy these kids."

"But, at this point, we don't know why they're buying them or what they want them for."

"No, but I've never found it to be anything good," Alex replied. "Sure, a lot of people can't get legal adoptions because maybe they have criminal records, health issues, or whatever. If they're desperate enough, they will pay and continue to pay, but that's not necessarily what Jeff's ad is even about," he explained gravely.

Only then did Taryn comprehend the full extent of it. "Right, it doesn't seem to be a black-market adoption. It feels as if we would be lucky if it was only about that."

When he looked over at her, she caught the sadness in his smile as he spoke. "That means you're finally understanding just how bad this is."

"Oh, I've always understood how bad it is," she declared hotly. "I'm the one who offered to buy the kids, remember?"

"You may have to make good on that, you know?"

"That's fine," she snapped. "These kids are Bruce's family, and I could never allow this to happen, not if there's anything I can do to stop it."

"You probably won't have to do anything to stop it at this point. From what Levi and Terk tell me, it seems enough agencies are involved at this point to have all that covered," he shared. "Earlier Terkel told me that he'd found out that this website Jeff used has been on the watch list for quite a while. So all its transmissions are monitored. There is a good chance that whoever Jeff is talking to could be an undercover cop, not his dream buyer."

She stared at Alex in joy. "Seriously?"

He nodded. "They have to make up their own online personas, their own fake IDs on these websites. Then, when something like this happens, they're already in position to set up a sting operation," he told her, watching her expression. "I can't guarantee that's the case this time, and you can bet nobody will tell us either. We're definitely not considered among those in the need-to-know area of the investigation."

She shook her head at that. "And that's just bullshit. You know that, right?"

"I do know that," he agreed cheerfully, "but I've also been on the other side, not wanting people like us privy to the details of an upcoming op about to go active—simply because the more people who are in on it, the more things can go wrong." She slumped back against the passenger seat. He motioned at the coffee in the cupholders and said, "Drink your coffee. Eat some food. We're all over this."

She stared at him and grumbled, "Can't tell it from my end."

He shrugged. "I've given Riff a heads-up that we're here and what's going on. He'll see if Jeff returns home again. Meanwhile, we'll go in a different direction. If Jeff comes home and settles back in again, we'll turn around and find a new hiding spot."

CHAPTER 7

A LEX DROVE, WHILE Taryn sipped her coffee, as they raced down the road in the opposite direction. After Alex had gone about ten miles, his phone vibrated. He pulled off to the side and answered the call to hear Riff's voice on the other end.

"They're back home again."

"Great," Alex murmured. "I wonder if that trip was just to get out to make a phone call. What's the reception like there?"

"It sucks," Riff replied. "So that's very possible, and the internet is even more of a problem. And since his phone and net provider probably aren't as advanced as mine, his service must be even worse."

"That would make sense and would explain why he was so frustrated when he was outside the convenience store on the phone that time." Then he went on to explain to Riff what had happened when they'd encountered him at the store.

"That's too bad," Riff replied. "Now that he has seen the two of you, we'll have to be careful because he's bound to remember you both."

"Well, we can't really blame Taryn for speaking to Cassie," Alex replied, with a smile for her as she glared at him. "The little girl was just staring at her, and I think anybody would have spoken to her."

"*Great*," Riff muttered. "It could also mean that the little girl is reaching out more and more, with that inner instinct that says she's in trouble."

Alex suggested, "It could also just be that the uncle is getting more and more unbearable."

"What gets me is that," Taryn pointed out, as she leaned over and joined in this phone conversation, "I saw no sign of the two little boys."

Riff went silent for a moment. "That's not good," he replied in a bewildered tone. "Would Jeff really leave them in the house alone?"

"They are twins, six years old. Maybe they were sleeping," Taryn replied. "I don't think Jeff'll win any parenting awards, so leaving two young children at home alone probably isn't that big of a deal in his world."

"True enough," Riff agreed. "Anyway they just turned into the driveway."

"Okay, we'll head back and go around to the far side again," Alex murmured. "Did you get any updates from anyone?"

"Just the usual stuff," Riff noted. "Everybody's working on it, but, so far, useful information has been a bit thin. Terk's team has some possible leads on the missing father and will follow through on all of them. There was no local police investigation into his sister-in-law's death and no suspicion on Jeff's part at all. I do understand that an online child pornography group is involved, and another Interpol group is interested in the purchase of these kids as well."

"Jesus, to even hear about that is awful," Taryn whispered.

"I know," Riff agreed, his voice reassuring. "Yet it should

help you to realize that the local and international authorities recognize it exactly for what it is. However, they don't just want Jeff. They want to get the buyers as well."

"Sure, and meanwhile Cassie and her brothers are being tormented day in and day out by this asshole," she cried out.

Silence came from the other end, before Riff finally spoke. "I'm not here to give you the pros and cons on getting these pervs," he began, then took a deep breath. "All I can tell you is that we have to work within the boundaries of the law to best protect these kids, which we're doing." And, with that, he disconnected.

She winced. "I guess I pissed him off, *huh?*"

Alex sighed. He wasn't about to share with Taryn how he and Riff had already spoken to both Levi and Terk, with each reminding them to play nice. It rubbed everybody wrong. Still, it wouldn't calm down Taryn to hear this from Terkel's and Levi's point of view either. So Alex crafted his reply for her consumption.

"It's not so much that you pissed off Riff but that we're all in the same boat. We would all love to go storming in there and get those kids out of there, but we can't do that. We're all just as frustrated as you are, but we know there are limits to what can be done."

"Whereas I don't see those limits because I don't really want to listen to them," she admitted, with a nod, "and that just makes me more of a wild card."

Alex laughed. "You're not so much a wild card, but, because you don't understand the rules we work within, you're kicking back at us, and we don't have any justification that would work for you."

"Sorry," she muttered.

Alex gave her a wily grin. "Doesn't mean that Riff and I

aren't working on doing something rogue. After all, we're not good with rules. Just don't tell Levi and Terk. If we do this, it has to be on our own."

TARYN BEAMED, FINALLY hearing that the guys were really on her side. Heaving out a long breath of relief, she settled into her seat, as Alex pulled a U-turn in the center of the road and headed back the way they had come. "It's just frustrating, all the waiting. I'm finally glad to hear that I am not alone in wanting to go in there and do something drastic." He patted her hand. She looked down at his gesture and sighed. "You know it's a bad day when somebody pats my hand to keep me calm."

He burst out laughing. "Is that not something people do?"

"It's something people tend to do to a child or a very old woman," she stated, with a smirk. "I don't know about anything other than that."

"You are definitely neither of those," he said, "and I certainly don't see you that way."

"Well, that's good," she muttered. She looked over at him and smiled. "We're spending so much time together that it almost feels as if we have a thing going on."

"We do have a thing going on," he declared, as he eyed her.

Enough amusement filled his gaze that she knew he was laughing at her. She shook her head. "Well, laughing at me won't exactly get me on your side," she muttered.

"You are on my side," he countered comfortably. "We're both on the side of those children that Jeff has, and nothing else matters."

Alex was right, and Taryn was just venting. Yet it was hard not to when so much unchecked shit was going on in the world out there. As they pulled into their spot around the back, she pointed up through the trees at a window on the second floor. "Somebody is staring out the window."

"We need a different spot," Alex murmured. "We should be shielded enough by the trees to stay here a short while, as I go scout out the land."

She froze, but he was already outside and gone. She tried to peer through the trees, but it was hard to see. She had just caught that one glimpse of someone in the window, and now all she could do was sit and wonder who the hell it was. So many questions ran through her mind.

Where were the two little boys?

Where the hell was Jeff?

Was he on to them?

That last part worried her more than anything, but she didn't care about her safety. Those little kids, they were everything to her and Bruce, and their safety mattered the most.

She waited, hesitant, when her instincts started to prod her in a really ugly way. Listening to the orders in her mind, she got out of the car, stepped back into the trees, and waited. She saw somebody skulking around in the backyard. Would he come far enough this way to see the car? That would not be good. She wondered if she should hop in and move it, but she figured that might be the worst thing she could do, as the noise alone might only draw more attention to her. Just as whoever it was moved toward her, a loud *bang* came from inside the house.

She watched as the man, now easily recognizable as Uncle Jeff, turned and looked back up at the house and started yelling. Taryn smiled because it was almost as if somebody in the house had done it on purpose. Then she froze for a moment and tried sending out a message. *Was that you, Cassie?*

First came a *click*, a hesitation, and then a soft reply. *Yes.*

Taryn was impressed that Cassie was so strong. *What are you doing?* Taryn asked.

She whispered again, this time very clearly, *We're trying to keep you safe. … I miss my mommy.*

I know you do, honey. I know, but your mommy is in heaven now. And the little girl started to sob again.

Cassie's grief overwhelmed Taryn too. She winced. "Not exactly tactful of you, Taryn," she muttered to herself. "The child is still trying to deal with everything, and here you are, mucking it all back up again." She'd never had much exposure to children and didn't know very much about how to talk to them. She'd been the youngest of the foster kids, and a wary young foster kid at that, not having had a whole lot of good experiences up until she had moved in with Bruce's family.

Still, she knew that Cassie needed one main thing, and it was comfort. Cassie needed reassurance that it would be okay. And that was the part Taryn hated the most, … the comforting and, more so, her lack of tact. The guys were all telling her it would be okay in the end, but still, she was helpless to do anything. What she awkwardly planned to say was something about it being okay soon and that Cassie would be fine, that she and her brothers would be rescued. Taryn decided against it, since she wasn't even sure Cassie knew what being rescued was. So instead Taryn said, *It will soon be okay. You and your brothers will be okay soon.*

My uncle is not the same anymore.

No, I'm sure he isn't, Taryn replied. *I'm sure he's hurting too.* The little girl didn't say anything, and all Taryn heard were sniffles. *We're watching to confirm that you're okay. So you just stay safe, all right? If your uncle tells you to do something, mind him. Don't risk getting hurt.*

He didn't use to hit us at all. Now he hits us all the time.

Taryn winced. *Where are your brothers?*

Another long silence came before Cassie asked, *How do you know about my brothers?*

I saw them with you one day.

My uncle hit them, and it took a long time for them to wake up. They haven't been feeling very good ever since.

Taryn gasped.

He's back. I have to go. Then suddenly Cassie went silent.

Taryn waited, trying to send encouraging thoughts to the little girl. When the car door opened beside her, she watched Alex get into the driver's seat. Starting the engine, he slowly backed it up and headed down the lane. "That was the uncle," she muttered.

He nodded. "Yeah, I'm not exactly sure what happened, but he headed out here, suspicious, so we'll need to find another parking spot. Then he stopped and went back home, when some banging came from the house."

Taryn nodded. "It was Cassie." Alex frowned at Taryn, as she nodded a second time, then grinned, feeling quite proud of herself. "I've been talking to her. She's really scared and worried. She told me that her uncle has changed, and he's not like he used to be. He didn't use to hit them, and now he does," she shared, keeping it simple, when it wasn't simple at all. "He hit her little brothers hard enough that they didn't wake up for a while, and now they are not the same. It sounds as if the little boys are in a lot of pain."

"Damn, that's not good. I would have thought Jeff would be more careful, especially since he plans on selling them. This is bad."

"Maybe he's not selling them or at least not getting the price or the buyers as quickly or as easily as he expected. It definitely sounds as if Jeff's getting angrier and more frustrated," Taryn replied. "That situation will just get worse and worse."

"Yeah, you're right about that," Alex confirmed, then frowned. "Yet a thought in your head isn't something we can take to the police."

She groaned, then sat back, … pissed, yet knowing he was right. Of all the possible leads they could act on, that would be the last they could use as evidence, as least in the eyes of the cops. "It's so not fair that Cassie and her brothers are in that situation," Taryn wailed. "Stuck in there, wishing desperately for somebody to come and help them. Yet I'm glad that she's not saying, *My uncle's hurting me*, or *I'm scared*. She's lonely, and she's afraid because her uncle's changed and her little brothers are hurt," Taryn explained. "Cassie has no idea her uncle has changed in ways she can't begin to imagine. It all makes me very sad. What's worse is how helpless I feel."

"Go ahead and be sad, but don't waste time on feeling helpless. Keep sending healing energy to Cassie and her brothers," Alex suggested. "Also, keep that connection as open as you can. Cassie might be the only source of warning we have."

"She's the one who made the racket that sent Jeff back to the house."

He looked at her. "Are you sure about that? Really?"

"Oh, I'm sure because then she asked me why we were here and what we were doing. I told her we were worried about her, that we knew about her mommy and were worried that Cassie and her brothers weren't okay."

He nodded. "I'm sure that brought about a set of tears."

She looked over at him. "See? I haven't had much experience with children," she pointed out apologetically. "So, I wasn't really thinking that it would bring on the tears, but it did."

"Absolutely it would. Young people don't have the emotional control that we're supposed to have as adults," he noted, with a wry look. "Not that a lot of adults have it either, but generally we have a little more control than somebody at that age."

She pondered that. "She thinks that she's very much in control."

He looked over at her. "So, I've got a question for you. Can you reach the hurting little boys, and what if it isn't the little girl you're actually reaching?"

She stared at him. "What do you mean?"

"A thought occurred to me," Alex began, "mostly because I can't tell who you're talking to, who this person is, what this person is up to. So, is there any chance you are talking telepathically to the uncle?" Taryn had a sinking feeling in her gut, and Alex kept on hitting it home. "What if it's really Jeff, and he's just leading you down the merry path, trying to figure out who and what you're up to?"

She stared at him, her stomach twisting. She went over the conversation as much as she could remember. "I sincerely hope not," she finally said, "but I have no way to know, do I?"

"No, you probably don't," Alex confirmed. "Just keep in

mind that not everything that goes *boo* in the night is a ghost."

She gave a broken laugh. "So far, everything that's gone *boo* in the night has been my worst nightmare," she muttered. "So, I don't know if that would change anything."

He smiled at that. "I get that, and I'm sorry. Adjustments are always required when you come into these matters, and the fact that you have connected to Cassie—or whoever that is—means we have to adapt here." He took a breath to emphasize the point. "It just makes it a little more challenging for the rest of us. If we could jump in there and help, we would. No matter what, it's important that you know we can't do anything to break that connection. And, while she's there and telling us what's going on, there's a good chance she would tell us when she's leaving, when she's in trouble. So, what I am trying to say is, let's keep the connection open, but just remember you can't always trust everything that goes through your head."

"So, you're saying …"

"I get that this is new and exciting, and no way you could possibly understand all the nuances that can happen when you get involved with energy work," he explained. "Short of getting years of experience doing this, hopefully years of experience with Terk as your teacher, the bottom line is, you just need to remember that not everything is always the way it seems."

And, with that, Alex headed down the highway.

ALEX WASN'T SURE if he'd left Taryn shocked, upset, or both. He was thrilled that she'd connected with Cassie, the little girl. Yet he was worried because he had heard stories that were pretty rough, where people thought they were talking telepathically to somebody in particular and found out later they weren't. Alex didn't want to turn it into something scary for Taryn, but he also didn't want it to end up being a murderous event.

He knew it could go both ways, thinking of a case he knew of, where someone lured a woman into thinking that she was talking to her dead brother, but instead it had been the man who had murdered her brother. Alex didn't want any of that happening to Taryn. But to even try to explain something so bizarre was probably well past what Taryn could work with right now, especially as a newbie energy worker.

As they drove past the convenience store again, she looked at him and sighed. "I'm really getting sick of this place."

"We'll head downtown then," Alex offered. "I'll look for some audio equipment, and Levi shipped us some too, so we'll go pick that up as well."

"What for?" she asked, turning to face him.

"Remember your idea of planting something on Jeff's vehicle?"

"Yeah."

"We'll give that a try. It's a good idea."

A big grin crossed her face, and then she laughed. "Oh, I'm glad to see I'm not totally useless."

He smiled at her. "Never that. As a newbie, you're a bit out of your depth, but you've been solid all the way through," he noted. "Don't forget that."

"I think your buddy in the other vehicle would prefer I wasn't around at all."

"Riff just prefers to keep our team tight and small, which I understand. When a team gets too big, with too many people, we end up with added trouble. None of us wants that for you."

"Right," she muttered. "Okay, I can do what I can do. Then I can't do any more." Taryn shrugged. "I'm just trying to stay in control, with all the chaos going on."

"Your role now is very clear. Just keep that channel open for Cassie."

Taryn nodded. "Got it. Yet it'll be awfully nice if we can get her and her brothers out of there. I would love to see them in person."

"Well, you did," he pointed out, with a note of humor. "At the store, the first time." Then he frowned and asked, "Didn't you?"

"Ah, I see what you're saying." Taryn nodded. "Yes."

Alex asked, "Did it feel like the same energy?"

"I think so." Taryn nodded, yet frowned. "I would have thought so anyway."

"Okay, so the next time—if you have a chance and get that opportunity to see her … in person—check out her energy. Check out the feel of her, and see if it is consistent with what you've already connected to on the ethers."

"Back to that possibility that it might not be her I'm talking to?" she asked, with a shiver.

"More like, *let's just confirm*. Maybe she can't send a message unless she's alone. Maybe she's under Jeff's control so much that, when they're out in public together, she can't take a chance to telepathically speak to anyone because she doesn't know how far it travels and whether he'll find out. In my opinion, it seems that Cassie may only be connecting to you when her uncle is not right there." When Taryn nodded,

Alex added, "So we have to consider the possibility that her uncle might have a way to track when she's utilizing energy."

"Oh God. Jeff could be gifted too?" Taryn stared at Alex. "If that's the case, we'll never get her and her brothers out of there."

"Oh, we'll get them out," he stated, "but it would be so much better if we could do it in a peaceful, orderly manner. Otherwise it could be quite ugly."

"But we can't further traumatize her and her brothers either," Taryn stated. "Those kids have already been through too much."

He nodded. "I get that. Believe me that I do. Nobody wants to expose them to more trauma. All I can tell you at the moment is that plans are in the works for the FBI to set up a sting operation."

"Okay, and I liked the idea of that when it was mentioned before. So let's get it going."

"Yeah, it's coming along, but you won't like to hear that we're being kept out of it."

She groaned. "Of course. I should have known." She shook her head. "Even after all we've done?"

"Yes, because, in their minds, we're not qualified professionals," he explained, with a wry note of humor.

"And we can't argue that, since child trafficking isn't a field we've spent a lot of time in, thank God."

"*Thank God* is exactly right," Alex agreed. "Nobody wants to spend too much time in an underbelly world where they buy and sell children." He gave a long sigh. "I imagine the burnout rate on the staff involved in this on a daily basis must be high. It's bound to get to even the toughest of them after a while."

"Of course. Dealing with this daily for any length of

time must be an absolute nightmare," she noted.

"Yeah, I would think so," he muttered. "On the other hand, this little girl and her brothers are getting a rescue, whether they know it or not."

"What about the two little boys, who are badly hurt?" she asked bitterly.

"Yeah, you mentioned that before. Wish we knew more on that."

"I just want to go in there and pull the children out of there."

"But how would you explain their being with you? What do you tell the townsfolk, the cashier at the convenience store, much less any feds?"

"If anybody asks, we just found them walking along the road."

Knowing just how much she wanted this to happen, Alex recognized that this needed to be dealt with delicately. "In a way that might work. The problem would be when the police figure out who the children are and take them back to their uncle Jeff. Then the beatings will get worse than before."

"Won't they recognize the abuse when they check the boys and see the injuries they have?"

"They might," he replied, with a nod. "But the uncle can quite easily say the kids must have fallen. Maybe when the boys got up in the middle of the night, they might not have known where they were and took off walking, until some-body found them and took them to the hospital. Jeff could tell that story or dozens of others," Alex shared. "Believe me, when it comes to excuses, these perverts use a million of them to get out of trouble. And unfortunately, without an extensive record of abuse, quite often the abusers just get to take the kids right back home."

She stared at him, dumbfounded.

He nodded. "Now, if the little boys could say that their uncle had hit them, then that's a different story," he added. "But we're not in a position to do that yet, and, depending on what evidence of injury there is, it would do little more than become a notation on the boys' medical records. Not only will it not stop Jeff from doing it again, it would likely accelerate his time frame and speed up his efforts to get rid of the kids."

"God forbid," she whispered. "Plus, after going through all that, Jeff will be even angrier, just putting all three kids in even more jeopardy."

"Exactly," Alex confirmed. "So, as hard as it is, all we can do is keep up the surveillance and let our people know when something changes."

"Yet something has already changed," she pointed out. "I mean, Jeff's driving around, making phone calls. He hurt both little boys, and he's getting angrier too, at least according to Cassie."

"Did you know her name to be that before all this happened?"

Taryn nodded. "That's her name. Remember that Bruce's family fostered me. Mary, the children's mother, was Bruce's sister. I knew her when she was younger, but I was closer to Bruce, then and now. He and I are friends. We've remained in touch since then, practically family in a way."

"Right, and have you ever met Cassie before?"

She pondered that. "Maybe. I can't remember though. I know we met Mary and her friend at the zoo one time. Some kids were with them, but I don't remember if they were Mary's kids or Mary's friend's kids. The children were very small, and it seems as if there were more than two."

"If there were other kids, some or all may have belonged to the girlfriend then. However, if it was the three we want, that could explain why Cassie reached out to you," Alex guessed. "She would recognize you on an energy level and would already have a connection to you."

Taryn smiled. "That would make sense. I'll have to think about that whole visit. I know Bruce wasn't terribly impressed with the idea of visiting to begin with because, every time he saw his sister, it just made him angry."

"Why is that?"

"Because she wouldn't leave her lazy-ass husband, and, in Bruce's mind, if the husband wasn't *for* her, he must be *against* her."

"Yet how many families argue over the relationships that their siblings and friends get into?" Alex asked, with a smile. "We all know that it happens all the time."

"Sure, it does," she murmured, "and for the sister to be financially responsible for the five of them—hell, actually six, counting Jeff—that's a big burden, one the husband and his brother should have stepped up to contribute to as well. Still," she muttered, "once we get the children out of there, at least we could get the twins some medical attention."

"We would sort that out regardless, whether the twins need it or not. Remember though that we're listening to a little girl."

Taryn groaned. "I know that, and I hear you," she snapped, "but is there anybody in Terkel's group who could check out the twins?"

Alex pondered that for a moment. "There probably is. Terk may already be on it." Alex grabbed his phone. "Let me call him." And he pulled off the road onto the shoulder and called Terkel. As soon as he answered, Alex explained the current issue.

Terkel replied calmly, "We can certainly take a gander and see if we can tell whether the little boys are hurt. The question would be what we could do about it afterward. Remember that we only have two healers here, and they are busy with Bruce and helping out every pregnant woman here too."

"I know. I understand. Taryn remains fired up about us charging in to rescue all the children, now that we know Jeff is beating them."

"I'm sure she is," Terkel noted, "as is every one of the women here. We must be a little bit more circumspect though and confirm that none of the children get returned to Jeff. And the problem with that too is that we don't want the children sent off into foster care either, not while Bruce is still recovering."

"Good point. How is Bruce doing?"

"He was conscious today for about half an hour," Terk shared, a smile evident in his tone. "So, he's getting there."

"Good, we need him to get there a little faster because he's about to become a parent."

Terkel sighed. "It could take a little more time than that to bring him back to that level of care."

"It doesn't matter. He'll have to heal and heal faster, or alternatively we need to set up provisions to ensure these kids are looked after while Bruce heals."

"Yeah, I already have a plan for that," Terk replied. "Seems our castle might just fill up one of these days."

Alex laughed. "I can't imagine that it won't, especially if you keep taking in strays."

"They're not strays if they're part of my group," Terk

declared. "And, by *my group*, I mean anybody with abilities."

"Yes, but, as you're finding out, an awful lot of us are out in the world."

"There are, indeed, more than I ever expected. In fact, a lot more. Anyway, I'll get our admins to see if they can do a scan of the two little boys first, before I interrupt Cara and Clary. I'll get back to you."

Hanging up, Alex turned to look at Taryn to see her beaming.

"Thank you," she said enthusiastically.

He nodded. "We are all about trying to help, you know? However, we also want to confirm that this Jeff asshole doesn't take off and that this website that's selling these children is also taken down. I know the pervs will just pop up on another website, but we must do what we can do right now."

"Got it," she muttered. She sagged back into her seat. "I see Riff's car is there, but it looks abandoned."

"Yeah, I suspect he's gone hunting." At his wording, she turned and frowned at him. Alex winced. "*Hunting* in the sense of trying to figure out what's going on in the house and with the damn uncle," he clarified.

"So, you've picked up the things that Levi sent to us. Now what?"

"That's the thing. I thought Riff would be here, so I could hand them off," he replied in a clipped tone. "Let me drive a little farther down the road, and I'll call him." With that he headed out onto the road and back down another mile or so, then pulled onto the shoulder and phoned Riff.

"I saw you go by," he answered, right off the bat. "Did you get the stuff?"

"Yeah, we did."

"Good, I'll be down at your corner in a minute. Just stay there." And then Riff was gone.

As Alex turned to her and raised one eyebrow, she nodded. "He's a man of few words."

"He is, indeed, but he comes from the heart."

"I'll forgive anything," she said, "as long as he helps those kids."

He smiled at her. "You're becoming quite the mother hen."

"I wonder if it's unique to all women," she muttered. "I've never really had any of these motherly feelings before," she admitted. "Yet right now I am a she-tiger, wanting to go roaring in there, tearing apart Jeff for hurting those little boys and being so mean to Cassie."

Alex grimaced, as he grabbed her hand. "That's why it's a good thing that we are here, calm and steady, to hold you back."

"How is that a good thing?" she snapped, glaring at him.

He smiled. "We need to be united on this. I'm sure not getting into an argument about it."

CHAPTER 8

ARYN WATCHED, AS the handoff of the tracker was completed, plus a radar thing with a cone—another way to amplify sounds, but only under certain conditions, Alex explained. One was with them in the car too, covered by a blanket. Riff once again disappeared into the shadows. She looked over at Alex and asked, "Any reason we can't get out and walk for a bit?"

He eyed her and shrugged. "Did you have a specific place in mind? And please don't say back to Jeff's house, though obviously we'll need to stay close by in order to keep an eye on them."

"I know. I just thought it might do us some good to walk around the place and to get some fresh air. According to the map, a little creek is near here." When he hesitated a moment, she added, "Otherwise I'll go alone, and you can stand watch." He glared at her for even suggesting that, and she threw up her hands.

"I just need a few minutes to reorient myself as to what we're doing and why," she shared. "And that seems to be a hard thing to do when I'm constantly inundated with fears for those children and told to *just wait*. We're waiting for Terkel to get back to us on that FBI sting operation to be set up. I thought agents were already embedded in those sites? So why does any sting op have to be set up? Isn't it already there, just waiting to push the Go button? We're in a constant state of waiting. Meanwhile, these children are suffering. That sting-op bullshit is a total fabrication to placate us, in my opinion."

Alex nodded. "Come on. Let's get out and walk around a little."

She gave him a little smile. "Thanks."

"You're not a prisoner here. You know that, right?"

"I know, but I need to be careful. I have to keep doing the *right thing*. Otherwise I'll mess something up," she acknowledged. "So, I very much just want to get out for a few minutes."

"That's fine. We'll keep a close eye on the driveway and traffic, so we can race back to the vehicle if we need to."

"That would mean Riff wasn't successful in getting his tracker installed," she stated, "and that would be a whole different story."

"Oh, I would put my money on Riff any day," Alex declared.

She frowned at Alex. "I thought you didn't know him."

"I hadn't met him before, but I recognize the type," he explained, with a wry smile. "Guys like that are worth their weight in gold."

She shrugged. "Says you, but I can't get a reading on him at all."

"He's blocked anybody from reading him. And that's what he's used to. It truly is his nature. He does it on purpose. It keeps him a little more distant from everybody, so he can do the work that he does."

"That would be a very lonely way to live," she noted.

He smiled at her and agreed. "It is."

She frowned, looking back at him. "Is that you too?"

"It has been, in many ways at times. I'm not quite as bad as Riff is, but I can see why he does it. I don't want to say I approve, but, in his case, it enables him to be such a good operative." He winced at his choice of wording. "He's private now though, not military, so that's not quite the right word."

"I can't imagine what anybody doing these kinds of rescues goes through," she shared. "I'm a complete wreck already, and I'm only on the first job."

"That's because you're coming from the heart," Alex said in a soft tone. "Most of us doing this work, we have to stop our feelings as much as we can, and yet at times each case seems even worse than the one before. You think you've seen the worst thing possible, and then the next case comes along, and guess what? You hadn't seen the worst thing yet, after all."

"I can't even imagine, and I don't want to."

"No, you can't and wouldn't like it, and that's a good thing, trust me. But the bottom line is, we need to get these guys off the black market and into prison, hopefully for good, as unlikely as that seems."

"It's all just too much to consider," she muttered. As she got out of the vehicle, she slammed the door out of habit, then winced. "Sorry, I shouldn't have done that."

He shook his head. "Don't worry about it. Let's go down to the creek and give you a few minutes to regroup."

Knowing he would keep the house in his rear view, she quickly walked toward the water, then followed a path that ran beside it. She stormed up the trail about one hundred yards and stormed back. Then did it again and again and again. When she finally slowed her steps, she returned to where Alex stood, a smile on his face. Meanwhile she was flushed and sweaty. "I'm sorry."

"Don't ever be sorry for *feeling*," he replied. "It's frustrating, heartbreaking, but it makes us who we are, and that allows us to do this. This is new for you, and, because you have a connection with Bruce and these kids, it's even more personal. We don't want to minimize what's happening to these children in any way," he shared. "However, we must confirm that we not only lock up the players in this network who are profiting from selling children but also get the assholes who are doing the purchasing."

"I feel like an asshole for even putting in a bid."

"It's probably about time for you to respond to that ad. You haven't, have you?"

She shook her head. "No, you told me to wait."

"Good, let me check with Levi on it."

He pulled out his phone and sent some texts, while she sat, her feet in the creek, closing her eyes. For a moment, just a brief moment, it was almost possible to forget about the nightmare going on behind her. When Alex came back and stood behind her, he said, "Levi has a response he wants you to submit."

"Good enough," she replied, as she pulled out her phone, and, following Levi's instructions, she sent out a message, saying she would pay the raised price, but she wanted all three kids and no more craziness. She wanted the deal to be done right and done fast. With the message sent, she sat and waited. "It'll probably take Jeff a long time to respond, won't it?"

"It's hard to say how he's dealing with the other buyers. So far, from what we have seen, Jeff's raised the price so many times that ..."

"That what?"

"That's a part of the deal, and it pisses off people. So it depends on what everybody wants in something like this," he shared. "Think about selling a house, where every person's needs and wishes are different."

"Maybe so, but how godawful is it that we can compare selling a child to selling a house?"

He winced. "Sorry, that was crass, and I didn't mean it that way."

She held up her hand. "It's fine. You got your point across. I'm just … You know exactly how I feel."

"I do," he whispered. He gently squeezed her shoulder. "And none of us thinks any less of you for it. In fact, we all admire that passionate spitfire mindset you've got."

She snorted. "Nothing to admire me for. Admiration would be if I'd gone in there and scooped up those kids and stolen them away from that asshole."

"And gotten yourself shot by the uncle—quite justifiably, I might add. That would put all three kids back into danger and add to the risks of Jeff moving them out even faster. He would get sloppy, not wanting to get caught, maybe dealing with *any* buyer, not waiting for his preferred buyer."

"Right." She shook her head and gave a bitter laugh. "I'll leave all that thinking to you guys. I just want it over with, and I want those kids home. I want them with Bruce, where they belong." She turned, looked up at Alex. "Do you think Terkel will take them in, while Bruce recovers?"

"Oh, Terkel will most certainly take them in—not that he would choose to do otherwise—but all the women in the castle are pushing for that too." Alex laughed. "Terk won't have any other choice in the matter, particularly when they've been working so hard to keep Bruce alive."

Taryn smiled. "I really want to go see him."

"When this is over, we'll go."

She looked up at him and beamed. "You're coming too?"

"Absolutely. I was hired by Terkel, but I haven't seen the man in a very long time."

"Will you do more jobs for him after this?" she asked.

"I don't know," he admitted. "I did this for the same reason that Riff got pulled into it, more or less because of Levi and Terk. But, when you think about it, Levi's team and Terk's team work together and support each other so well that we consider them all part of the same team."

"I think it's wonderful that they can do that," Taryn replied. "It's pretty upsetting to think about how many crazy people are in the world that they keep people like Levi and Terk so busy."

"Plus, Terkel's got his hands full right now with babies coming. He's having twins any minute, if he hasn't already. His brother has twins at Levi and Ice's place, and the other women at Terk's castle are due very soon too." He chuckled. "With all the women pregnant, that just means a steady stream of babies."

"Good God," Taryn noted, "they must need lots of help."

"They're looking for nannies and nurses and cooks and whatever else to give them a hand. I've heard there is one very strange obstetrician who comes and goes. When I say *strange*, the circumstances around her are strange. She pops in when she is needed, stays for as long as necessary, then moves on. She's just getting started at Terkel's place."

Taryn frowned at that. "So how does she know the babies are due?"

He gave her a ghost of a grin. "Remember how that whole group at Terkel's place is a little different."

"So she must have the ability to know when the babies are due?"

"Something like that, and she is also close to Riff—or at least she and Riff have some unfinished business, or so I am told."

Taryn started to laugh. "Anybody dealing with Riff will have unfinished business," she declared. "That man is like a sealed canister."

"What I heard was, definitely some history is between them because he was engaged to her sister."

"Oh, ouch. So why is there unfinished business?"

"Because her sister, Riff's fiancée, was murdered," Alex whispered, "and I know for a fact that part of Riff's deal with Terk is that they help him find who did it, and they haven't been able to get very far yet. So, nothing has broken in the case. It just runs cold until something new develops, and then all hands are on deck again," Alex shared.

"That explains a lot about how closed-off Riff is. He wouldn't want everybody to know his pain and to receive all those pitying looks."

Alex nodded.

"And the OB-GYN? That's bizarre. So she pops in at the castle, whenever a baby is due? Then does her job and leaves again? Where does she go off to?" Taryn frowned at Alex in amazement. "She sounds as secretive as Riff. Plus, can you imagine being so sure of your ability, so sure of what you do, that you time the arrival for each baby's birth? The conventional Western doctors don't know when any of those babies are coming."

He smiled. "I think all of them at Terk's place have an

energy connection, at least among the women while the babies are being born. The men probably don't have much of a say in it."

"So, the men aren't connected?" she asked.

"Oh, sure they are. There are a lot of female healers and energy workers in the castle, so when it's time to give birth, they take over, for a while at least."

She nodded slowly. "I can only imagine," she muttered. "It sounds like a wonderful way to have a family."

He looked at her in surprise. "How's that?"

"Because you're surrounded by people, by family, right from the get-go, something I wouldn't know about," she shared, with a wistful smile. "I've never really thought that energy workers are out there having kids and families of their own? It seems amazing, and I could really get behind it."

He studied her and nodded. "One of their most recent challenges is that everybody who goes to work for Terk and who lives in the castle is forewarned about heightened pregnancy possibilities."

She stared at him in shock. "What?" He laughed and explained further. Taryn was rolling around in a fit of giggles by the time he was done. "Oh my. When you talk about job hazards, that's hardly one that comes to mind."

"No," he agreed, as he grinned down at her. "Apparently that's definitely something they're all very aware of—now, after the fact."

"Yeah, but that doesn't mean they can stop it though."

"They're hoping to get a bit of a handle on it. Several multiple births are happening, including the twin healers at Terkel's place. They're both expecting twins." He shook his head. "I'm not sure who if anyone has delivered yet, but Terkel's wife is expecting twins. Plus, Terk's brother's wife at

Levi's place also gave birth to twins. Several other couples are expecting twins as well. Some don't want to even know yet if they are having a single birth or twins."

"That's pretty amazing, and I'm also incredibly jealous that they've all found something special—a special someone, a wonderful place to call home, a loving family, and a *different* job," she noted. "That is something I never expected to find. Bruce is the closest thing I've ever had to family, and I haven't seen him in ages."

"Bruce seems to be a good guy."

"He's the best," she replied. "He's all heart, and, when he was captured and then held prisoner in Russia, we were all just in shock that it could even happen. But, of course, it was because of the work he did, and that's just wrong too."

"I won't say it's wrong," Alex replied carefully, "because that is the work he did and that work does garner that response at times. When you do get captured, … you also know that you're largely on your own. It's pretty amazing that Terk's people were able to get Bruce out of there."

When a shout came from behind them, Alex turned to see a man racing down the creek bed toward them.

"*Uh-oh*," Taryn muttered, coming to her feet. "That's Jeff." He reached them seconds later, and such fury filled the expression on his face that it was all Taryn could do to stay out of reach of his arms as he tried to grab her. "What is your problem?" she cried out.

He took in several deep breaths, then a step back and pointed. "You! You're my problem. You're following me."

She gazed at him blankly, her mind struggling to process that he was even here or that he was accusing her of following him. The fact that they were down at the creek, some distance away from his house did not matter. She shook her head. "Are you nuts? Look at where we are. I don't even know where you live," she snapped, her voice rising by the second, "and I don't want to." She was practically shaking with fury by then, glaring at him. "What the hell is wrong with you?"

He stepped back again and looked around, almost as if coming out of a fugue state. "Are you sure?" he asked, his tone harsh. "I don't like it when people stare at me."

"What the hell?" she whispered. "We're not staring at you. Look at us. We're sitting at the creek on what appears to be public land."

"Well, my place is across the road," he roared, stepping forward again and reaching for her arm, which she jerked back. "I don't want you even looking in that direction."

At that point, Alex stepped in. "Hey, hey, hey, stop trying to grab her. We're just sitting here at the creek, enjoying a few minutes of spare time," he snapped in a warning tone. "That's got nothing to do with you, so keep your damn hands off my girlfriend and leave us alone."

Jeff frowned, puzzled and confused.

Taking a different tact, Taryn asked, "Are you all right? You look pale and sweaty."

He glared at her. "I'm fine. I'm totally fine. Just leave me alone." And, with that retort, he stumbled his way back up to the road. They followed at a slower pace and watched as he got to the driveway and headed back to his house.

She whispered, "What the hell was that all about?" She looked over at Alex, as if she expected him to have all the answers.

"I'm not sure. Definitely not what I was expecting."

"Yeah, hell no, me neither. He seems to be losing it," she stated. "He's coming apart at the seams at a rate that's …

damn scary. The downside to that is, I don't know why."

"No, I don't know either," Alex agreed. "The troubling part is that you're right. He looks to be falling apart, and now I'm afraid of what he'll do." He looked at her and pointed. "Let's get back to the car."

"Why?" she asked. "It seems even more important to go in there and to get those kids."

"We really don't want Jeff to accuse us of anything, and now that we've been made for the second time, we have to change our spot."

"How did he even know we were here?" she asked.

"Maybe he's been watching us."

She looked at him, startled, and then nodded. "I guess it's possible. Plus, he's obviously paranoid—and with good reason."

"When you're involved in doing something shitty like what Jeff's planning, you start looking around every corner, waiting for the boogeyman to jump out and catch you because you know you're in the wrong," Alex explained. "So, let's get back to the car, and we'll go find another place."

"Yeah, I'm okay with that," she muttered.

They were on high alert as they quietly returned to their car. As Taryn got in the passenger seat, it was hard to tear away her gaze from the house. "God, I hope he doesn't go after those kids now, especially in the mood he's in."

"Let's not go there," Alex suggested. "Let's just stay calm, stay collected. We'll contact Riff and let him know what's going on. We'll also contact both Levi and Terkel and see whether anybody has any suggestions or further intel. Meanwhile, be prepared. Now that we've been made, and Jeff's come out and accused you in particular, they'll want us to back off."

She stared at him and snapped, "I am not leaving those kids behind, and that's that."

ALEX WORRIED ABOUT Taryn.

Since that latest altercation with Jeff, Taryn couldn't stop staring in the direction of the house. "You need to let it go," he said. She looked over at him, and he was so struck by her emotions. "I know. I understand that you don't want to. You would rip off his head, if you could."

She gave him half a smile. "Only if I could do it successfully. Otherwise I suspect he'll rip off mine."

He gave her a shrug. "That could be true."

She sighed. "This waiting is deadly."

"It is," he murmured. "We're still waiting for Riff to get back to us too."

She sighed, visibly starting to relax, which made Alex feel a little easier as well. She must have noticed his reaction because she picked up on it. "I'm not psychotic, you know."

"I know you're not," he replied. "However, you're connected physically and emotionally, which could turn you into a runaway train, if you don't keep it under control."

She stared at him for a long time and nodded. "I guess my connection to Bruce and the kids, especially Cassie, makes it that much worse, that much stronger, doesn't it?"

"Absolutely it does," he confirmed. "Not just the telepathic connection to her, but you also have the Bruce connection. You're desperate to save them all. Yet you don't care how it happens, and you have all these extra emotions, including Cassie's, flooding your system, making you that much harder to control." He faced her as he spoke, watching her shade of embarrassment deepen by the second. "It's truly a dicey time right now."

She winced. "That's the last thing I wanted. While it may not seem that way, I have been trying to maintain some semblance of control."

He gave her a ghost of a grin. "Yeah? How's that working out for you?"

She rolled her eyes. "Apparently not very well."

"No, it sure isn't," he agreed, with a big grin, but he kept his gaze on her. "I just need to know that you will listen and not go off half-cocked over this."

She took several slow, deep breaths, then nodded with the tiniest smile.

"Thank you for that."

"You mean, for the deep breathing to try and get things back in control?"

"Yes," he confirmed, "and for not telling me that I'm crazy for thinking you're running a lot of that little girl's energy in your system, which is making you even harder to deal with."

"Well, I hadn't considered that aspect," she admitted. "And while it's a little unnerving to think that Cassie could be affecting my emotions, it's a relief just to know it might not be all me."

"Whenever you're dealing with an overwrought energy system, you'll have a lot more energy, which can make people very emotional. In this case, you're also dealing with a little girl who's grieving. So her emotions are all over the place. We already know that she affects you, so I must consider everything you do and say that seems a little bit abnormal. It may not be you talking, but it may be Cassie."

She gave a broken laugh at that. "To even hear you say

that sounds wild."

He smiled. "I know. It's crazy. All of it's crazy, but it doesn't change the fact that I must be very aware of it, and you need to be as well."

"Well, I'm glad you're aware of it. At least that makes one of us," she stated.

"Hopefully you can just confirm that whatever is happening is happening because you wanted it to."

She blinked at him. "So. you're saying what I'm feeling isn't necessarily what I'm feeling, and it could be what Cassie is feeling?"

"I don't know what you're feeling," he conceded, with an eyebrow raised, "but I would certainly want to take another look to confirm that you're assessing it properly."

"Ah, so the fact that I want to kiss you, are you saying that's coming from Cassie?"

He sighed and then grinned. "Now, if I thought that was for real"—he was laughing with her now—"I would tell you to fly at it and to lay one on me, so we could check it out more closely. However, I know you're just teasing."

"Maybe. Maybe not."

CHAPTER 9

"HOW DO YOU know that wasn't for real?" Taryn asked, laughing at the cheekiness in her tone. Alex frowned, and she took it as a cue. "I'm fine," she replied, with a wave of her hand. "I'm just relaxing, and I think you're right on point. Some of that energy flowing through me was Cassie's. Some of the frustrations, that sense of being unable to do anything is still there," she added, with a knowing smile, "but I feel less like going over there and pounding Jeff into the ground."

"Well, that's good," Alex said warily.

"Are you sure? Now you're looking at me as if I'm about to jump your bones."

He burst out laughing. "And again, I'm not sure I'm against it. I just want to know it's you talking and not that little girl."

"Jesus, I sure as hell hope not," she muttered, glancing over at him with a smirk. "Still, getting to know somebody while we're cooped up in a vehicle like this is pretty intense."

"Which part? Your former surprise statement or this later one?"

"Well, I wouldn't say jumping somebody's bones was at the top of my list when I got here."

"No, but maybe you haven't had the same experience I have."

She smiled. "I won't embarrass you anymore."

"Is that what I am?" he asked, laughing. "You think I'm embarrassed?"

"I don't know," she conceded. "I think you aren't certain about me. I think you're worried that I'm not who I am and that anything I say and do is not really me."

He studied her and then nodded. "Yeah? Any reason why I shouldn't consider that? I am ready to give it a shot."

She sighed. "Okay, so that little girl is definitely in my headspace. We both know that, but she's not telling me to say that I really like you, or that I want to see you again while we're in England, or that jumping your bones was only half joking," she admitted, along with a nervous laugh. "I get that it's definitely not the topic for here and now, but something just came over me."

"Yeah, that's the part I'm worried about," he stated.

She glanced at him, smiled, and added, "I don't mean Cassie."

"If you say so, but is it somebody else?"

"No way," she replied. "Walking along the creek released all that tension and energy, which was necessary because these other restraints have been holding me back for too long. Seemed to be a good time to release all those thoughts somehow too. So, whatever is going on inside me, letting some of this go also lets go of other aspects of my personality that I've been working on for a long time but didn't think I would ever get there."

She pondered that for a moment. "So, whether it's healing, or whether it's interference from other people," she added, "there are definitely some good benefits to this *release*."

"If you say so," he muttered, but his tone was still hesitant as he studied her.

She smiled and then decided to let him off the hook. "If I'm embarrassing you, that's okay. You can tell me that you're not interested, and I'll stop teasing you."

"It's just that it came out of the blue," he clarified.

"Did it really though?" She gave him a wry look. "You're telling me that you haven't felt some of the energy between us?" she asked. "I'm not saying instant sexual attraction, but I think there was definitely interest. I like you and everything I've seen about you. I'm single. You're single." She frowned and asked, "Wait. Are you single?"

"Yes, I'm single," he replied in exasperation, "but I'm not used to meeting people on jobs."

"Ah. See? That's the whole honor system you've got in place."

He shook his head. "No, but it sounds as if you were letting go of some of these stressors in your life, and it's letting you become a little more unfettered, and you're not exactly sure what you're dealing with."

"Sure, and, because of all that, you're also a safe person to tease," she muttered.

"Safe?" he asked, turning to look at her.

She nodded. "I guess the thing I wasn't expecting is that I trust you."

He gave her a slow smile. "Thank you. That makes me feel good."

She shrugged. "I'm not sure you should thank me for it because that just means I'll push a little bit more."

"I didn't realize you even had a problem that you're trying to work on," he shared, "so go ahead and push away. I don't mind."

"You won't react?"

"Of course I'll react," he stated. "That's why you're pushing, isn't it? To see what kind of reaction you get? You won't know until you try. But you're right. I also like you," he claimed boldly, "and, if this is happening because of all this energy floating around, … and it's helping to heal something inside you, fly at it. Just don't let it interfere with what's going on in that house—or vice versa."

She stared at him, her gaze shooting back to the house, and nodded. "Good point. It's all about them."

"Hey, hey, hey," he said. "Just because it's all about them doesn't mean you don't get the benefit too. There is nothing quite like massive rushes of energy to settle you and to help you release old wounds. The worst thing you could do is hang on to those wounds. They can hurt you each and every time they resurface again, and that's just not healthy. And neither is it something we want."

She gave him a crooked smile. "It's not what *we* want?"

"No, it's not."

His tone was firm enough that she believed him. She sighed. "Sorry, I didn't mean to bring up any of that."

"It just caught me off guard, but energy is like that. You know how, when your friend just comes out of therapy and tells you all about the stuff she's going through, and you're thinking, *It's just the healing process?* … Yet some of it seems so ridiculous. Still, when you go home later that night, and, while you're all alone, all this crap of your own comes boiling up."

"Ah, right."

"Energy is just energy," he stated in a simple tone, "and once you start healing … Did you send healing energy to Cassie and her brothers?"

She nodded slowly. "Yeah, I did. Why?"

"Because then it comes back to you," he declared. "So your body figures it needs healing as well and is working on your own issues."

She winced at that. "*Great*, not what I intended."

"No, it may not be what you intended," he acknowledged, giving her the gentlest of smiles, "but, once you start the process, that energy just keeps on firing." He was deadly serious, and she needed to understand it too. "So, the more you can process, the more you can clear out, all the better. And, yes, I can be a sounding board, if need be."

"I would hope to do some of this without a sounding board."

"In that case," he asked, "do you have a notebook, something you can write down the crazy thoughts that, to you, will seem stupid and made up but are really coming from deep in your psyche?"

She frowned at him. "How do you know any of this?" she asked, frustrated to be so near him and having such a private conversation.

He shrugged. "My sister had trouble for the longest time," he murmured. "I learned a lot from some of the stuff she went through."

"Interesting, but none of this is what I thought I needed to do today."

As if hearing the humor in her tone he smiled. "Sometimes we don't know what we need. However, when the opportunity presents itself, the best thing we can do is listen." And, with that, he pulled his duffel bag from the back seat and dragged out a notebook, handing it to her, along with a pen. "Here. Just write down anything and everything that's coming up. It doesn't matter whether you think it's pertinent or not. Just let it fly."

"Is that ever so easy?"

"Make it so for you. By the end of it, maybe you'll like it, maybe not. Anyway, you can always rip up that piece of paper and throw it in the creek."

"You think that'll do anything?" she asked, staring down at the notebook, feeling like a fool.

"I know it will," he declared. "We used to do that for my sister all the time, and it was just amazing to see what happened. You opened up yourself in order to heal somebody else, but that healing energy came back to you. Now it's sending a message loud and clear that it's time for you to work on you."

"Why the hell does that not sound appealing?"

"It's mostly hard work," he admitted, "but that's your job. To work on you."

She swallowed hard, but she opened the notebook and stared at the blank page. As she did so, words poured through her mind, and she started writing.

ALEX DIDN'T EXPECT the notebook to have quite the immediate impact on Taryn that it did. Yet, considering she had been connected to Cassie and had been sending out healing energy, it did make a loose kind of sense. He sat and kept an eye on their surroundings, with another on his phone, doing research. Meanwhile, the words just poured through her fingers via a pen and onto the page in front of her. He was amazed to see it work, no matter whatever sent him in the direction of making that suggestion to begin with. Regardless, some dam had been released within Taryn.

When she finally lowered the pen, her hands were shaking.

He reached into his bag of goodies they had picked up at the convenience store and handed her a granola bar. "You're getting pretty shaky," he murmured. "This should help."

She accepted it, ripped apart the package, and slowly chewed the snack bar.

Realizing it was a good idea for himself as well, Alex opened another, and they both sat there in companionable silence, chewing away. He waited for her to say something, but she was obviously still caught up in whatever she'd been working on, and that was good. He didn't want to pressure her into feeling or thinking that she was forced to share anything with him.

When she sighed once and yet again and then a third time—the last one being this huge release, almost right from the soles of her feet—he knew that she had accomplished something major. He held out his hand.

She immediately put hers in it and whispered, "Thank you."

He nodded. "When there's healing energy," he murmured, "take advantage of it. It's never there to hurt you. It's always there to help. Sometimes we don't even realize how badly we're hurting, until we do something like this, and then we are shocked to see all the garbage that comes up."

"And yet it does seem to be so much garbage," she noted. "I had no idea all this stuff was sitting in there, just waiting to burst out."

"Because you didn't know you had buried it. You ignored it, and that's fine and dandy, until you can't anymore," he shared. "In a case like this, where Cassie started talking to you telepathically about a subject that you too had experienced, the dam opened up everything for you. So, it's not right or wrong, but I would say that it's a good thing."

She smiled, and he saw the tears in her eyes and knew what was to come. He immediately cleared the space between them and opened his arms. She sobbed once, twice, and then the dam broke, and she threw herself into his arms, and he just held her close.

He hadn't expected anything like this to happen on a job, but, hey, if it helped ease the pain in Taryn's world, Alex was all for it. He tucked his chin on top of her head and just let her grieve. When she finally calmed down, she sobbed several more times and then muttered, "My God, I don't know the last time I did that."

"The last time was when that little girl was bawling her eyes out," he stated, with a note of humor. "Yet this time, I think it was all about you."

She nodded. "It was definitely all about me, but it just seems so foolish to think that I was hanging on to all that."

"It doesn't matter whether it's foolish or not, no judgment here," he declared. "Just lots of peace and acceptance." She smiled. When his phone rang, disturbing the atmosphere, she laughed. He quickly silenced the ringer, checked the Caller ID, but didn't answer the call.

Rubbing her face, she pushed her hair back. "God, I'm such a mess. You have no idea how much I would appreciate a shower right now."

"You and me both," he agreed. "If it was any other day, I would suggest we head to that creek and skinny-dip."

She burst out laughing. "If it was any other day, I would take you up on it."

He flashed her a bright grin. "So there, now we have something we can do when we head back to Terkel's."

"What, run around his place, streaking?" she asked,

laughing even more. "Somehow I don't think they'll appreciate it."

"I have no idea, but I don't think they're stuck on physical bodies back there," he pointed out. "So much soul work happens in that group, so I imagine it's pretty incredible. It must also be a huge adjustment every time somebody joins them," he noted thoughtfully. "The energy of the new person would have to be absorbed into the general collective energy, and people would have to work on their own shit in order to get along with everybody else. I can't imagine, and yet I really want that experience."

"I really want it now," Taryn declared. "And I think it would be perfect for Bruce."

"Maybe, yet I don't know how the kids will react to all that energy housed in one big space."

She smiled up at him. "Kids are kids. They will adapt, especially if all of them are gifted too."

"The way you adapted?" he asked.

She nodded slowly. "It took a long time. It really took quite a long time for Bruce's mother to get inside my heart, but I don't know where I would have been without her … and Bruce too. Then his mother died from a heart attack not long ago. His father died in a car accident soon afterward, leaving only him and his sister. Now his sister is gone too. Mary had a hard time, losing both her parents almost at once. Maybe that's when she started fighting with her husband. I don't know, but it all fell apart for her somewhere around that same time, and I can't imagine what the last of her life must have been."

Alex's phone vibrated now. He looked at the screen. "That was Levi calling before, and again now. I should take this." He quickly answered. "Hey, sorry I missed your call."

He looked over at Taryn and smiled.

She sniffled and settled into the passenger seat of the car, closing her eyes and trying to relax, yet hearing bits and pieces of the conversation.

"They'll move in tonight," Levi told Alex. "The question that I have, and I've been trying to get a hold of Terkel to ask him, is whether this Jeff guy has any ability that'll make him paranoid and potentially jump the gun before anybody has a chance to get there."

"I wouldn't be at all surprised if he did," Alex replied. Then he quickly related what happened down at the creek.

"Good God, how close were you to his house?"

"We weren't close at all, … at least one mile away. The creek is completely deserted and on public land owned by the government. So it's not as if we were trespassing on Jeff's property or anything, squatting rights or not. I'm pretty concerned about his mind set now."

"Did Taryn hear back from her latest email to Jeff's ad to buy the children?"

Alex turned to her. "Levi is asking if you've had any response to your latest email on the ad."

"Oh, right, let me check again." She quickly brought it up and shook her head. "No, there's nothing."

Alex hit Speaker now for the rest of this conversation.

"Okay," Levi said, "one more thing. We think we've pinpointed the missing father. I'll send you his coordinates. You may be the closest man to him, FYI, unless he goes on the move again. In the meantime, keep a closer eye on responses to Jeff's ad, will you? Set a notification so you'll get an alert."

"Will do," Alex noted.

Taryn winced and quickly got busy changing the settings

on her phone, while Alex ended the call with Levi. "I'm sorry, I should have done that to begin with. I'm not very good at this stuff. I'm sure Levi probably thinks I'm an idiot."

"It's fine," Alex stated. "Nothing's gone wrong so far, although now we have Jeff's brother possibly in the mix, and we don't know yet if he's involved in this. We'll figure that out soon enough. I don't know what Jeff's problem is, but he is definitely getting more unstable. But the time frame for an entry to rescue the kids is set for tonight, so, as long as everybody realizes that, we just have to keep them here until then."

"Sure, and I suspect that, as paranoid as Jeff was earlier, he's already trying to get out."

"Maybe, but will he get out and move the kids, or will he just run and abandon the kids and save his own sorry ass?"

"Well, I would prefer the latter," she replied. "At least that would give the kids a fighting chance. However, since Jeff apparently considers them a valuable financial asset, you and I both know he won't leave them behind."

"Unless … Jeff's brother, the father to those kids who just abandoned them, decides to take over the sale of his own children."

CHAPTER 10

T ARYN EXITED THE car and walked around, trying to ease the stress in her stomach, which was knotting up at the thought of which would come first—a move by the FBI being made tonight, or Jeff taking off before anybody got here, or the unemployed and worthless father to those kids reappearing to do no good, once again. She had no physical basis for that panic, other than her gut. She *was* panicked, and that was enough for her. Probably not enough alarm for anybody else but definitely enough for her. She, Alex, and Riff had taken up spots in the woods, crouched in the brush growing below a copse of trees, where they could watch the house without their wheels. That meant, if Jeff did try to make a run for it—or Jeff and his brother switched up positions—somebody would have to run back to one of their cars and give chase.

When she heard a birdcall behind her, she turned to see Alex and Riff talking. She smiled as she made her way toward the men.

Riff nodded at her. "We got the bug into the truck," he shared. "So, if Jeff does try to run, that should help with tracking him and the kids."

"I hope so," she murmured. "Especially since the powers that be are apparently making a move tonight."

He nodded. "I agree with you. I think Jeff's too paranoid, and even now the need to run is probably eating at him."

She winced. "Do you think he'll run before the Feds have a chance to get here?"

"Yeah, I sure do," Riff stated. "On the other hand, that's good for us, so we can capture Jeff."

"If it was all about capturing him, why haven't we just gone up to the damn house and picked him up already?" Taryn wailed.

"Good point, but the Feds want the buyer too. That's the holdup," Riff noted, giving her a cheerful grin.

She groaned. "You do know how irritating you are, don't you?"

"Yep," he agreed, with a nod. "It's something I've really been perfecting."

She stared at him, shaking her head, as he turned away to make a phone call. Taryn then glanced over at Alex to find him grinning broadly. "I'll never really understand Riff, will I?"

"If you want to get along at Terkel's place, I'm pretty sure you'll need to figure it out."

"*Right*. As if I could do that. I'm not doing anything here to help either, and that's driving me crazy too."

"So, we're back to that frustration level and how you just have to deal with it on these jobs," he repeated. "Remember that."

"I know. I know," she muttered, with a groan.

When Riff returned moments later, he shared, "Levi's just getting the sound set up from our tracker, and, from what I have been told, it seems Jeff is already in the truck."

"What?" she gasped.

"He's got somebody who's interested in the two little

boys."

"No," she cried out. "I said I would buy all three children."

He looked at her and nodded. "And yet these black-market guys? … If they get a better offer and have somebody willing to pay way over the asking price, it won't matter what your deal was. Jeff will go for the highest dollar."

"So, I should have just offered more?" she asked numbly. "God, this is a sick world."

"Yep, it is," Riff confirmed, "which is why some of us spend a lot of time in the sewers, trying to clean it up."

"So, what do we do now?" she asked.

"When the vehicle leaves, we'll follow it," Alex stated. "However, if Jeff's only taking the two little boys, I want you to stay behind."

She stared at him. "Can I go get Cassie then?"

"I highly suspect she'll leave on her own," Alex added. "Whether she knows where she's going or not, I would bet that her instincts are telling her to get the hell out of there, and this would be the perfect time. So, my guess is that she'll try to leave, but I don't want her out in these woods all alone."

"Predators are everywhere," Riff noted. "I'm okay with the four-legged ones, but this is about the two-legged variety. They're always on the lookout for little girls, always searching for opportunities. So somebody needs to stay and keep an eye on Cassie."

"I'll stay," Taryn declared. "You guys follow Jeff and the twins, and I'll be here for Cassie."

"You're sure about that?" Riff asked cautiously.

"I am. I absolutely am," she stated, with a smile. "Look at that." She pointed out the truck coming down the driveway. "Here he comes."

Alex nodded, then asked, "Now the question is, does he have the little girl as well, or is it just the two boys?" As the truck drove by, they couldn't see any child at all. Alex turned to Taryn. "Would he have left them all behind?"

"I wouldn't think so. And the two little boys are already injured or maybe asleep or worse," she shared in a confused tone. "Maybe the uncle's got them hiding in the truck." She looked at Jeff's vehicle. "There is an energy trail behind his vehicle."

"When you say, *energy trail,*" Riff asked, turning to her, "what does that mean to you?"

"It means, somebody is in there," Taryn explained, "but I don't know who, and I don't know how many."

"Good enough." At that, Riff took off in the direction of his vehicle.

Taryn walked slowly toward the house, watching as Alex bolted to his rental and headed down the road after Jeff too. Only as they took off did Taryn return her attention to the house.

And there in the distance, moving slowly, almost as if she were injured, came Cassie. She hesitated for a moment. Then her energy seemed to accept that her uncle Jeff was gone and was then committed to whatever she had decided, as Cassie now raced down the road.

"He's gone," Taryn called out, so Cassie would know that Taryn was nearby. Apparently encouraged, the child ran faster as she worked her way to Taryn, who caught her midjump, right as the little girl leaped into her arms and burst into tears. Hanging on tight, Taryn tried to soothe her and to calm her down, even as she carried her into the bushes. Taryn had to keep the little girl safe and out of sight.

Taryn mentally sent out a message, hopefully received by anybody who was listening, knowing that she would need a few minutes with Cassie, before Taryn could grab her phone. She hoped her telepathic SOS got Terk or one of the good guys.

Terkel, his voice strong and clear in her head, stated, *Just keep Cassie quiet, Taryn, and keep her with you.*

What should we do?

Walk down to the creek, and get her away from the house. Somebody will come pick you up soon, Terk murmured.

And, with that, Terkel disappeared from her head. She smiled at Cassie, still in her arms. "Don't worry, little one. You'll be safe now."

The little girl looked up at her and frowned. "I know you."

"We talked while you were out shopping. Are you upset because your uncle left you at home?"

Immediately she shook her head. "No, he just left with Jack and John," she whispered. "I wanted him to take my brothers to the hospital"—then she sobbed—"but I don't think that's where they're going. I think he's getting rid of them because they are hurt so bad."

"We have somebody going after them right now," Taryn replied, as she hugged the little girl close. "We'll stay here in the shadows and wait until somebody comes to pick us up."

"Then what?"

"We'll keep you safe, and we'll find your brothers, then confirm they get the help that they need. I'm afraid your uncle will be in a lot of trouble."

Cassie started to cry again. "He hurt Jack and John so bad," she wailed. "He kept saying he would do the same thing to me if I wasn't good."

"Yeah, angry people can be like that," Taryn whispered, hugging the little girl tightly. "However, that doesn't mean they get to stay that way, and they're not allowed to hurt children."

Cassie brushed away her hair and stared up at her. "You can let me down. I can stand up now."

"Maybe, but it also makes me feel better to know that I have you in my arms, and you're safe," she whispered to the little girl. "It's been a long time coming since I realized what trouble you were in."

In the darkness, the little girl stared up at her. "You're the one I was talking to, aren't you?"

"Yes. When you called out looking for help, looking for somebody"—Taryn nodded—"I'm the one who answered."

Cassie patted Taryn's cheeks gently. "I was afraid it was another bad guy," she whispered.

"Have you met lots of bad guys?"

"My uncle has been taking pictures of me and showing people," she replied, her voice breaking. "Pictures like … naughty pictures."

Hearing that, Taryn's heart hardened against Jeff, and any bit of forgiveness she might have mustered due to the difficult time he'd recently experienced went right out the window. "Well, he won't be taking pictures like that anymore," she snapped. "Don't you worry, sweetie. Your uncle will be punished for not being a nice man."

"He used to be nice, and then Mommy died, and my daddy left," she whispered. "I really don't want to stay with my uncle anymore."

"I understand. Now I really need to make a few phone calls," she said, "so we'll find a place to hide, until somebody can come get us, okay?" Taryn looked around, but she didn't see a whole lot except for the darkness of the night, and that wouldn't be enough, not if Cassie's uncle came back.

Cassie pointed up at a tree. "Can you climb a tree?" she asked. "I can."

"Sure," Taryn replied. "Why not?"

And, with that decision made, yet recognizing a completely different atmosphere took over at nighttime, the two of them scooted up the same tree and settled in for the wait.

BY NOW, ALEX and Riff had been following Jeff's truck for a good forty-five minutes, and Alex was worried about leaving Taryn alone for so long. When his phone vibrated, it was Riff.

"She's got the little girl. Cassie apparently came out of the house and raced right to her."

"Good God, really?"

"Yeah, so why don't you head back and get them," Riff suggested. "I'll stay on this guy's tail. Also, the message that came through is that the little boys are in the truck, but they are injured. The twins need medical care, but Cassie was worried Uncle Jeff might be taking the boys someplace to dispose of them permanently."

"Well, when they left, we knew it wasn't good news," Alex replied. "Yet, if Jeff injured those boys to the point that he can't sell them," even biting at the term himself, he added harshly, "he'll probably just dump them."

"That would be my thought too," Riff agreed. "We can't take that chance."

"No, absolutely we can't. Yet we don't want to leave Taryn and Cassie alone out there in the dark for too long."

"Sounds as if they're in a tree off the creek."

Alex pulled off to the roadside and asked Riff again, "Are you sure you've got this?"

"I'm on it," Riff declared. "You get back there and get them before anything else goes wrong."

With that, Alex quickly turned the car around and headed back. He wondered about Cassie leaving the house and heading straight for Taryn. He picked up his phone and quickly called Taryn while he drove. He put the call on Speaker.

"We're here, and we're fine," she murmured. "We're hiding up in a tree."

"That's a good choice," he replied. "Just remember that predators come in all kinds and sizes."

She snorted. "Yeah, you're not kidding, and just enough assholes are in this world that we don't always recognize who the predators are."

"That's true too," he agreed. "How is Cassie?"

"She's curled up in my arms, asleep right now," Taryn said softly. "She's a whole lot stronger and in better shape than I would have thought."

"That's good. I'm surprised she ran out of the house on her own." He hesitated, then asked Taryn point-blank, "You didn't go in after her, did you?"

"No," she clarified, with a laugh. "I did not. I would have, and I planned to reach out, but the minute her uncle left, Cassie grabbed her little bag that she was always to have ready and bolted out the door, knowing that her uncle wouldn't come back anytime soon. She didn't want to be here when he returned." Then she went quiet. "Jeff's been taking pictures of her, ... then posting them probably."

"Well, we know what he wanted them for," Alex noted

in a wry tone. "Remember that this was all in progress and that Jeff apparently has buyers all lined up."

"Yeah, sure," she replied, "but that sting operation's set for tonight. It may well still be on, but nobody will be here."

He laughed. "That happens sometimes. We do the best we can, and still, they get away from us. However, Riff is on Jeff's tail, and Riff's job at this point in time is to save those little boys," he stated, taking a pause. "So, if Jeff should get away, that's not the priority."

She sucked in her breath. "As long as they don't give Cassie back to him," she declared.

"Yeah, that would be for the best. Can you get her to tell you anything and maybe record it on your phone?"

"I'll work on that," she replied softly. "She's asleep right now, but it's not an easy sleep. She's restless and keeps waking up and crying."

"Crying for?"

"Her brothers. She's devastated about her brothers."

"She's already lost her mother, and her father took off," he murmured. "So losing her brothers at this point would be almost impossible for her to imagine or to even deal with."

"Yeah, you're not kidding," she murmured. "I don't even know what to say to that."

"How about nothing," he suggested. "Just remember that I'm on the way." And, with that, he rang off and hit the gas pedal even harder.

CHAPTER 11

TARYN SETTLED IN the tree, hugging the little girl who still dozed in her arms. There was a chill in the air, even though it was a summer night. Once the sun left, and the winds picked up, it would be hard to keep the body heat in. The fact that she was in a tree waiting for Alex to come get them completely threw her. Meanwhile, here she was, cuddling Bruce's niece, and that was worth everything.

She kissed the top of Cassie's head, causing her to snuggle in closer. Smiling, Taryn gently cradled the child in her arms and whispered, "Alex is coming soon."

The little girl didn't respond, but why would she? The name Alex didn't mean anything to Cassie anyway. As Taryn sat in the tree, she watched as headlights came toward them. She smiled, only to see the headlights turn into the driveway and head up the road to Jeff's house.

Her heart slammed against her chest as frantic thoughts assaulted her mind.

Was that Uncle Jeff? Had he dumped the little boys somewhere and come back home?

But that's not a truck parking in front of the house. Even in the dark, she could tell that much.

If that were the case, somehow both Riff and Alex might have missed Jeff; and it also meant that he would soon be looking for Cassie. Which meant Jeff could be coming after them in a major fury any second now. Not that he knew Taryn was here, but she couldn't help but remember that he'd somehow known she and Alex were at the creek, one mile away. Maybe Jeff knew where Taryn was right now too. She shifted restlessly, sending out as many telepathic messages as she could.

When her phone vibrated, she snatched it, trying to not wake up Cassie. It was Terkel. "Hey," she whispered. "A vehicle just drove to Jeff's house, and I can't tell who it is because it's dark out there. The uncle had driven away, so I don't know if it's him or what."

"Riff's still following the uncle's truck," Terk replied, his voice calm.

"Well, somebody else then has shown up here," she snapped. "And I don't like it."

"Take it easy," Terk said. "Alex is on his way back to you, and you're still in the tree, right?"

"I am, along with Cassie," she confirmed, "and we're just high enough that I can see the house, the driveway, and the vehicle parking there. I can't see much about it, except that the headlights have now stopped at the front of the house. So, I know the vehicle is still there, but I don't know what it's doing."

"It's possible Jeff was expecting somebody to show up there," he muttered.

Then Taryn froze. "Oh, good God."

"What?"

"What if Jeff took off to dump the boys, or whatever he's up to, and just left Cassie there to be picked up by his buyer?" The thought just destroyed her, and she held on to Cassie even tighter. "Would Jeff do something like that?" she asked in a horrified voice.

"For anybody who's prepared to sell their own niece, this makes total sense. Jeff just gets to leave, to go pick up groceries or whatever, then never returns."

"So are the little boys with Jeff?"

"We don't know that for sure. We only have Cassie's account of that, right?"

"Right, and she's sound asleep."

"And she needs to stay that way," Terk noted calmly. "Things could get a little dicey coming up, and we'll want to minimize the trauma she has to go through."

"Too late," Taryn quipped in a broken tone. "Cassie told me how her uncle hit Jack and John pretty hard, and they weren't quite right afterward."

"Well, head injuries can do that, so I'm not surprised if that was the end result of a blow," Terkel added in a solemn tone. "Both boys can be helped, even from afar."

"I understand that you would check on them."

"The healers did, and they have already been working their magic on the boys. Both do have concussions, possibly head fractures too," Terk shared, his voice deep, "which is one of the reasons we're out there trying to pick up Jeff as fast as we can."

"And yet Riff's still tracking the vehicle."

"Yes, and now the question is, if somebody drove up to the house to collect Cassie, what'll be their reaction if she's not there?"

"Well, if it were me, I would be furious. Then I would contact the uncle right away—looking for my *purchase*," she muttered, her tone twisting at the last word.

"Of course," Terkel agreed. "Stay where you are. I'll get back to you in a few minutes." And, with that, he disconnected.

Taryn cuddled Cassie close. Taryn's head bent against the wind that was picking up and whistling through the trees. She watched the vehicle below, but it remained in place, its headlights facing the house. She didn't know if anybody had gotten in or out over the noise of the wind and the phone call, but it was quite possible that they were inside the house now, searching for the little girl.

When Cassie popped her head up a little later, she looked around, sleepy-eyed. "Are we still in the tree?"

"We are," Taryn whispered, "but good people are coming to help us."

"Are they?" she asked, with just enough doubt in her tone.

"Yes, good people are out there helping us," Taryn murmured. "And they're also trying to find your brothers."

At that, tears came into the little girl's eyes. "They didn't even do anything," she whispered. "Jack and John didn't do anything bad."

"I know. Your uncle is probably having a rough time dealing with Mommy's death and Daddy's disappearance."

Cassie looked up at Taryn, with an age-old wisdom that was hard to argue with, and shook her head. "He's changed, ever since Mommy passed away. Uncle Jeff's different."

"Well, death can do that to people," Taryn replied. "Somebody drove up to your house. Do you know anything about that?"

The little girl nodded. "Uncle Jeff told me that somebody was coming tonight, coming to visit."

"Oh. … Did he give you any details?"

She shook her head. "Just that I was supposed to be really nice to him."

Taryn's stomach seized and then wanted to revolt at that

phrasing. "Well, the good news is, you won't have to be nice to him at all. He's at the house, and I imagine he's probably looking for you and your uncle."

Cassie stared back, chewing on her bottom lip.

"Don't worry. You're not going there ever again," Taryn declared.

Cassie twisted to look up at her. "Is he a bad man?"

"I don't know who he is, but he won't be a good man," she replied. "Honey, did your uncle ever touch you?" she asked.

Cassie shook her head. "No, he didn't, but other men wanted to."

"And that's not right," Taryn stated. "Nobody gets to touch you. Not that way, not in a bad way."

Cassie's chest rose and fell. Then she sighed and took a big, deep breath. "I don't want to go back into that house," she announced.

"You won't have to, honey," Taryn stated firmly. "We'll stay here until my friends get here, and then we'll leave."

At that, Cassie looked up at her. "I don't know your name," she whispered.

"I'm Taryn, a friend of your uncle Bruce. You may not remember me from years ago, but you remember Uncle Bruce, don't you?"

At that, the little girl perked up. "Yes. I do. Can I go to Uncle Bruce?"

"That's the plan," Taryn stated. "We'll have to take a plane to get there though. Plus, I want to talk to Bruce first, before we head in that direction."

"So you know him?" Cassie asked, looking for that same reassurance.

Taryn realized just how much this little girl must have

gone through already. "I do know him, Cassie. We were really close friends when we were growing up. And I knew your mom back then too," she added. "She was older than me. When I left home, where Bruce and I had been raised with your mom, I didn't call Mary like I did Bruce. He and I stayed in touch."

The little girl stared up at her. "You knew Mommy?"

"I did, back when we were all kids."

Cassie relaxed against Taryn. "My mommy was the most beautiful lady in the whole world," she whispered.

"She was. I agree." Taryn nodded. "And, Cassie, we will keep all these ugly people away from you. You don't need to be worried about that."

She nodded. "She wasn't happy."

"Who wasn't happy?"

"Mommy," she said. "Mommy was not happy at all. She told me that we needed to leave before something bad happened."

"Oh dear." Taryn winced. "I hope nothing bad did happen."

"Uncle Jeff hit her once," Cassie shared. "I know it really hurt her. She cried lots, and then he got angry because she cried."

Not a whole lot Taryn could say to that, but it reinforced what kind of a man they were dealing with. "I'm so sorry. That couldn't have been very pleasant to see or hear or go through."

"I just wanted Mommy safe," Cassie stated. "I told her that we had to leave, and she agreed that we should, but she didn't know how."

"She could have contacted her family."

"They didn't like Uncle Jeff, so she couldn't call them.

She wanted to contact Uncle Bruce, but she didn't know how."

"Yeah, honey, that's because Bruce was having a hard time too," Taryn replied. "He was overseas, working in Russia, but he got captured and was a prisoner for a long time." Cassie stared up at her in shock. Taryn nodded. "Which is one of the reasons why he hasn't been able to come for you, but he's getting better now. So he will see you soon, after we take you over there," she clarified. "I don't think he'll travel for a while."

Cassie seemed to accept that at face value, and she settled back again. Then she froze and asked, "What about Jack and John?"

"Jack and John are coming with us," Taryn declared.

"Even if they are not …" Cassie hesitated and then asked in a whisper, "Even if they aren't normal?"

"Do you really think they won't be normal?"

"Uncle Jeff hurt them really bad," Cassie whispered. "There was lots of blood."

"So why would you think they are not normal?"

"John wouldn't speak or couldn't. When Jack talked, … his words sounded funny, and Uncle Jeff laughed at him and said that nobody would want him now, not like this."

Taryn struggled to keep her temper reined in. The more she heard about Jeff, the more she wanted him in front of her, where she could kick the crap out of him—or worse. "Well, your uncle is not a very nice man," she declared, "and Jack and John will be just fine. We'll do everything we can to help them heal from their head wounds, and we'll get all three of you over to see Uncle Bruce."

Cassie went silent for a moment, and Taryn saw the little girl's face in the shadows of the moon. Cassie seemed to be thinking about something, something that was bothering her. "What's the matter, honey?"

"What if Uncle Bruce doesn't like us?" she whispered.

Taryn's heart broke. "Uncle Bruce absolutely adores you, always has and always will," she stated. "He loves you all dearly, and you're his sister's kids. So believe me that he will do everything he can to protect you. He would be here right now if he knew about all this, but he's been badly hurt himself. He's only just now starting to recover. However, he will heal, and he will be fine."

"Are you sure?"

"Yes, I'm positive, and he'll be so happy to see you," she added. "Sadly he doesn't yet know about your mommy, so I need to tell him about that as well."

And, with that, Cassie settled back into Taryn's arms and didn't say any more.

WHEN HIS PHONE vibrated, Alex swore, then quickly answered it, his heart sinking at the thought of more bad news reaching him.

"Somebody has driven onto the property," Levi stated, his voice calm.

"Where are you getting that from?"

"From Terkel, who got it from Taryn. We have no idea who it is or what he's doing there, but, according to what Cassie told Taryn, somebody was coming to visit her."

"Jesus Christ," Alex muttered. "That little girl has good instincts. I thought it was unwise of her to leave the house, not knowing Taryn was there. Yet, if Cassie got out of the house in the dark and ran on her own, that little girl is all kinds of brave."

"She is, but she may have been heading toward Taryn without even realizing it."

"Exactly, and again that's back to good instincts," he murmured. "It makes me feel pretty shitty that this animal is out there to hurt a little girl like Cassie. She was this quiet little ghost beside her uncle. Well trained—or more likely well beaten into submission," he shared.

"But we won't let it stay that way."

"Is she doing okay?"

"She is. How far out are you?"

"About four minutes." Alex pushed the gas pedal even flatter on the floorboard. "I'm getting there as fast as I can."

"She's doing fine, and they are still hidden. It would be great if we could catch the asshole who headed up to the house."

"Yeah, that is my first priority," Alex declared, "assuming the two of them are still safe in that tree. If Cassie and Taryn are okay, I'll head up to the house and see if I can pick up the buyer."

"Well, the sting that was supposed to happen tonight has been called off, since Jeff bailed early. However, the police are still on the way, even set up a roadblock or two, and remember that they will have control of the operation, once they get there."

Alex swore at that.

"I know," Levi replied. "It's frustrating, but we must work with local law enforcement, and, in this case, they had the chops to go in and to make a seizure."

"Right, I get it." Alex groaned. "So, do I go in the house or not?"

"You can go in, but you'll have to identify yourself when

the locals show up, just to confirm they don't include you as part of the sting."

Alex thought about that, wincing. "*Great*, that could really delay my getting to Taryn and Cassie."

"It could, but let's not go there. Yet I've warned the authorities that you're on the way. Of course they've stated flat-out that you're to stay away."

"Yeah, I know the drill," he muttered, "and I get it. I really do, yet … it makes me crazy."

"Keep driving," Levi said. "You should be coming up on the gals, if you weren't that far away."

"I'm really close now," he muttered, as he slowed down, based on his GPS directions. "Jesus, it's dark out here. No streetlights, no nothing," he complained.

"Yeah, I'll bet, but, according to Terk, Cassie could see by the moonlight."

"Yeah, I'm sure she can. There's just enough to make it a beautiful evening—under any other circumstances," Alex noted. "Only this situation makes it suck."

"People have a way of making everything suck or making everything great. We can't get hung up on one or the other. We just do the best we can," Levi shared, and, with that, Levi rang off.

Alex phoned Taryn as soon as he was off the call from Levi.

"Where are you?" she asked anxiously.

"I'm just approaching the driveway right now. The sting group has been called off, since Jeff left the property. However, the local authorities are coming, hopefully to pick up this new guy, but I want to confirm he doesn't leave before the cops get here. So my thought was to head up to the house first." There was silence on the other end. "Unless you need me," he asked in an undertone. "If you need me, … I'm there. Matter of fact, I'm coming right up to you now."

"No, we're fine," Taryn replied. "Go get that asshole."

"And yet we don't know exactly what he's doing there."

"No, we don't—yet at the same time we really do."

He agreed with her. "Fine," he muttered. "Give me ten with him." He saw the driveway coming up. He slowed and shut off his headlights, then turned onto the driveway. He knew that Taryn was watching. He drove most of the way up the driveway, and then, finding a good spot, he turned his rental vehicle sideways on the drive, in between several trees to try and prevent the guy from making a run for it. It also meant that anybody coming behind him wouldn't get any closer either—like the cops—which Alex knew he would probably take flack for.

But, if they were close enough that they could run out and lend a hand, then Alex was okay with it. He stepped up to the front of the house and rather than calling out and announcing his presence, he checked the door. Finding it unlocked, he slipped inside.

The place was dark and silent. At that, he tilted his head, assessing the space. It was too silent.

It had an emptiness to it, and he frowned at that, then did a quick search of the inside of the house, but no one was here. No real furniture was here either. Frowning at that, he turned and headed back outside, checking over the vehicle out front, to see if it offered any information. It had a rental sticker on the windshield, which seemed as old as the car itself, which the guy probably picked up locally. So Alex figured there would also be a fake name used on the application to rent it, … paying for it with somebody else's credit card.

He quickly texted Levi the information that he'd found so far to run a title check, then headed back inside for another search. What would have made the new guy book it, and why now? Would he have left the vehicle on purpose? That didn't make a whole lot of sense, unless the rental was somehow linked to him. Maybe the guy got very suspicious and was spooked. Guys that worked in this illegal field, especially if a pro, or anybody who had done this before, he would be very knowledgeable about keeping himself hidden from the authorities. Alex slipped out the back of the house, looking to see if anything would lead him to finding this new guy.

But he had absolutely nothing. Not a thing. He quickly sent a text to Levi. **Nothing is here. The vehicle is parked, but it's empty.**

Levi replied with a text. **Could be a trap.**

Alex nodded and texted back. **I know it.** And, with that, he slowly retraced his steps to the vehicle and moved away from the front of the house. If the new guy had been watching him, Alex had no feeling of it. His senses hadn't picked up anything, just a sense of emptiness, as if nobody were here. Frowning at that and not liking anything about the situation, Alex got back in his vehicle and headed to the gals. He drove down the road a bit, parked off on the shoulder far enough away that nobody would know that he was going to the creek, then raced to where the two females were in a tree.

As he got closer, he sent Taryn a text. **I'm here.**

When no answer came, his heart froze. He sent another text and still got nothing in reply. Frantic, he looked around, hoping against hope that nothing had gone wrong. When yet another text got no answer still, he quickly phoned Levi. "Taryn and Cassie, they're gone," he cried out. "They're not here."

"Whoa, whoa, whoa. Tell me what happened."

He was frantically looking up and down, as he wandered under the trees. "I've called her phone, texted her. She's not answering, and I've called out several times too," he shared, feeling the panic crushing his chest.

"Jesus Christ. When I mentioned how it could be a trap, this decoy effort was the farthest thing from my mind. I wasn't thinking about a trap like that. Seen any other vehicle at all?"

"No, I drove past the creek and parked farther down the road. So there's a chance that the kidnapping could have happened while I searched the house, then drove here. After all we're talking about a fifteen-minute window here."

"And yet you and I both know that fifteen minutes is time enough for all kinds of hell."

"Jesus Christ," he whispered, staring up around the trees. "Taryn didn't contact me. She didn't say anything."

"No, me neither. What are the chances that she couldn't have?"

"I would say pretty damn high, if that's the case," Alex muttered.

"Do the best you can. I need to contact Terkel." With that, Levi disconnected.

Alex stared around, his gaze catching something pink. He raced over. It was a strand of yarn from a sweater. He sent out as many telepathic alerts as he could, hoping that Taryn was out there and could hear him or that the little girl was paying attention. When a voice crept into his mind, faint and teary-eyed, he whispered, "Cassie?"

Yes.

"Where are you?"

I don't know, she cried out.

"Is Taryn with you?"

Yes, she whispered, *but she's sleeping.*

Alex winced at that because *sleeping* could mean so many different things. "Are you in a vehicle?"

Yes, she whispered again.

"Did you see who it was?"

No, something hit her, and she cried out, told me to hang on to a branch. Then she collapsed.

"*Great,*" he muttered. "Is she bleeding?"

I don't think so, but I can't really see anything, Cassie said, sobbing now. *I'm really scared.*

"I know you are, honey, and we'll find you. Did you see where the man came from?"

No. I don't know, she replied, starting to get hysterical.

"It's all right. You're okay. Now, if you're in a vehicle, do you know anything about it, like what color it is?"

It was dark outside. I couldn't see.

"Okay." Alex thought as fast as he could on his feet. "Did you see anything about the man?"

No.

"Did you see anything about which direction he went? Are you in the trunk?"

It's a van. A dark one, and we're going down the road.

"Okay, I'm heading to my vehicle. I'll be at my car in seconds."

Hurry. I don't like this man.

"Did he say anything to you?"

Just that I shouldn't have left the house. Then she started to sob.

"Great," Alex muttered. At that, he turned on the ignition and raced down the highway, sending out a telepathic message to Terkel. *We're looking for a dark van up ahead, probably fifteen minutes out. Our guy shot Taryn with something, and it sounds as if she fell from the tree. Whether this new guy caught her or not, I don't know. He might have just let her drop. He scolded Cassie for leaving the house. I'll let you update Levi, since I'm on the road in pursuit. Since I didn't cross paths with a vehicle getting here, I'm heading out in the same direction. It's a risk that I'm going the wrong way, but I'm taking it.*

Terk muttered, ever calm, *What the hell is the kidnapper up to?*

Not only that but how did he find them so quickly?

The only thing that comes to mind is that Cassie's got a tracker on her.

And that tracker would be courtesy of her asshole uncle.

Yep, that would be my take on it, Terk agreed, his voice grim.

And given the complexity and the security behind these kinds of sales, Alex began, *I wouldn't be at all surprised if a tracker isn't something that's standard practice. Jeff had to leave Cassie home alone, and maybe this is the reason he felt comfortable doing that because she has a tracker on her.*

CHAPTER 12

TARYN GROANED AS the pain slammed into her head and all down her body. She noted the musty cloth in her mouth, gagging her in two ways. Then a tiny insistent squeezing of her hand made absolutely no sense. When a soft whisper came, she heard a child's voice, telling her to wake up. Taryn wasn't sure why she wouldn't have been awake in the first place.

She opened her eyes, now being jostled back and forth. And there in front of her, barely visible in the darkness, was Cassie, tied up, with dried tears on her face as she stared at her. The details of the situation all came flooding back when Taryn saw Cassie, which made her heart ache when she realized something had gone horribly wrong. *What happened?* she whispered, belatedly realizing that they were speaking telepathically, not out loud.

Cassie looked at her. *You fell out of the tree, and he grabbed you. I don't know who he is. He has a mask on. He was pretty upset that you were there, but he picked you up and threw you in the back of the van.*

Great, that just means he'll be looking to dump me off as soon as possible.

At that, Cassie shook her head, tears welling up yet again. *Don't leave me. Please don't leave me.*

I'm not planning on it. She looked around the back of the

van, trying to minimize the movement because her head just burned with whatever he'd done to her. She could only think it must have been a tranquilizer. Her whole body ached. She asked, *Did you say I fell out of the tree?*

Cassie nodded. *Yes, I heard something, and you looked weird for a minute, shoved me against the tree limb and told me to hold on tight, and then you just fell. I didn't even see him, until he was suddenly right there.*

How the hell did he know where we were? Taryn wondered.

I don't know. Cassie started to cry again.

From the front of the vehicle, a man yelled back, "Stop your damn sniveling. You've been more damn trouble than you're worth already."

Taryn tried to silently soothe the little girl, but it was pretty hard when Taryn was fighting off the headache and her body aches, plus the effects of whatever drug he'd given her.

"That friend of yours won't be out for long," he snapped back. "I need to find a place to get rid of her."

Taryn stiffened at that because the last thing she wanted was to be separated from the already terrified little girl. Taryn could tell from Cassie's panicked gasp that it was the last thing she wanted too.

Taryn tested the bonds on her hands, but they were pretty taut, as were the bonds on her feet. She didn't want him to know she was awake, but even her perceived element of surprise wouldn't be enough if she was still tied up. It wasn't hard to see that Cassie's hands were tied too, but her feet were free. Taryn wasn't sure that made a damn bit of difference.

She willed her brain to kick in and to make sense of all

this, when she heard a voice in her head and recognized it was Terkel. *God, I didn't see this coming.*

I understand. Apparently you were shot with a tranquilizer and knocked out or something.

I'm more or less awake now. He just told Cassie that he has to get rid of me somewhere. He's pissed and really angry that I was even there.

You were a completely unexpected element that he didn't plan on having to deal with.

How did he even find us? she whispered into the ethers. *I don't understand that at all.*

We're wondering if Cassie has a tracker on her.

Taryn froze at that, then looked over at Cassie and asked her, *Did your uncle give you something special?*

Cassie looked at her blankly and shook her head.

Did he poke you with anything or clip something to your hair or something like that?

Cassie just stared at her blankly.

If there is a tracker, she doesn't know anything about it, she told Terkel.

I can't say I would really expect a young girl to understand it either, Terk noted. *Now, Alex is behind you, although maybe ten, fifteen minutes out.*

Great, Taryn muttered. *That's a little too far for me to be comfortable.*

Sure, but it's better than nothing. He was supposed to be right there by you, but he went up to the house first.

Right, and I urged him to do it to confirm we didn't have this guy coming after Cassie, she clarified, with a slight moan out loud. She grimaced and waited to see if the driver heard her. *The only element of surprise I have,* she whispered, *is the fact that I'm waking up.*

That's an element you need to keep to yourself, Terk reminded her. *We're sending reinforcements and doing everything there is to be done. We just don't know how big the gap is between you and Alex and where your kidnapper is going. That stretch of road is pretty deserted, but it's not deserted enough.*

She knew what that meant. *Great. … Hey, any chance our kidnapper is Jeff's brother, the father of these kids?*

We've got him tracked by Levi's satellite. I would have to check his current coordinates. Meanwhile, I want you to just stay positive, stay strong. Keep Cassie with you as much as you can, and keep the line of communications open, he ordered her.

Sure, great. You don't ask for much, do you?

Taryn heard the smile in his tone as he replied, *I'm asking for the world, but, considering the potential consequences if this goes wrong, I don't think I'm asking for all that much.*

She didn't say anything to that. Her aching head now made her entire body shudder. She closed her eyes and relaxed, telling Cassie that she was okay and that she needed to rest a bit because of the shot the guy had given her. Taryn told her that they needed to make sure the guy didn't find out that Taryn was awake. *You also need to be ready to move, should we get a chance to escape,* Taryn added.

Cassie didn't say anything but squeezed Taryn's hand in acknowledgment.

Taryn suddenly realized she didn't even know if Cassie was hurt. At that, she immediately asked her, *Are you hurt at all?*

No. Just you.

I'm all right, honey. It's just fine, she reassured her. *Besides, I don't mind if it keeps you from getting hurt.*

I don't want you hurt either, Cassie whispered, her tears threatening once again.

You're very sweet, Taryn replied. *All we need now is to find a way to get away from this guy.*

What does he want with me? Cassie whispered tremulously.

Nothing good, Taryn replied. *I won't lie to you, honey. He's a bad man.* Cassie didn't say anything to that, but Taryn could feel the tremor as she pressed her tiny body up close. Taryn knew that being tied up, drugged, bruised, she wouldn't be much help, but she had to be. She had to get them out of this. No way she would allow Bruce's niece to get caught up in something so horrible.

The fact that any child had to deal with this was just so wrong, but, when Cassie looked to Taryn for help, it just broke her heart. When the van slowed, and she heard the driver swearing, she realized it was probably some unwanted company or maybe even a cop car up ahead. She quickly sent a message to Terkel. *He's slowing down and swearing, so possibly a cop or something.*

Good to know, he replied. *We're tracking him, just not very closely.*

Yeah, not close enough no matter what, she muttered. *We need help.*

I'm trying to get somebody on the other end who could locate any roadblocks in the area, so Alex could be watching for it.

Our guy's making a turn now, turning left, she told Terk, feeling the waves of pain slowly starting to knock her out. *And I'm starting to lose consciousness.*

Hold on if you can. Just hold on a little bit longer, so we can track you better.

She shuddered in place, trying desperately to keep her mind engaged, as the van made a sudden turn. *We're turning left again,* she shared, *but that depends on where you're coming from.*

That's fine. It's okay. Don't worry about it, Terk told her. *I've got a fix on a roadblock, and we have messages going out to the local cops, as well as to our guys.*

She didn't say anything because messages could be sent out all they wanted, but, if they didn't move fast enough, it would be too damn late anyway. She wanted to laugh, yet she wanted to cry. Neither were options with Cassie sobbing gently at her side. Taryn whispered telepathically to her, *These turns are a good thing, honey. They help us pinpoint where we are.*

But Cassie was beyond being consoled. She'd been through too much already, and right now, knowing that this much of her world was twisting into such a nightmare, it was almost impossible for that little girl to see anything positive in any of this.

Taryn didn't blame Cassie, and, if they didn't have somebody coming to their rescue soon, Taryn would be pretty despondent herself.

At that thought, she snapped back and told herself to knock it off. A lot of people were in bad situations, like Cassie, who didn't have *anyone* out there looking for them, and those people needed far more help than Taryn did. When this was over, she needed to do something to help others in these situations. Even though it would hurt her to get involved in child trafficking, she had no excuse for turning a blind eye to all this nastiness in the world around her.

At that, Terkel's voice stepped into her mind again. *Why do you think we do what we do?* he asked. *It's not because we want to, and it's certainly not because this is the life we ever wanted to live. It's because we can't turn a blind eye to what others are going through, not when people like us are in a position to stop it.*

I want to help, Taryn declared. *If I get out of this, and, when it's all over, I want to help.*

We'll talk about it when this is over, and, of course, you're getting out of it, Terk stated calmly. *I already figured you would be coming over to spend some time with Bruce. It's seems you two were pretty close at some point.*

We always have been, she whispered. *We drifted apart for a long time once we grew up. … My head is so fuzzy, I can't remember if I told you that I lived with him, his family. You know, me through foster care.*

That's right, Terk said. *And you and Alex sure seem to be hitting it off. Is something more developing there?*

Yes, I believe there is, she admitted. *Although I don't know how you know everything*, she said, with a suspicious note to her tone. *Like how he feels. Unless he mentioned something to you.*

Nope, but remember that I'm an energy guy, so I can see the way it flows, and his definitely flows toward you, he explained, *so hold on to that thought too.*

ALEX DROVE AS fast as he could, skidding off the shoulders of the highway on each corner as he raced to catch up to the van. When his phone vibrated, he hit the button impatiently. "What?"

It was Levi. "Your kidnapper has gone off the main road. We've been tracking the roadblock up ahead of you, and your kidnapper hasn't shown up, but, according to Terkel and Taryn, he took a hard left, then another one pretty soon afterward."

"I'm on it," Alex replied, "although I don't see very many lefts up here."

"Probably not. Chances are, it's some dirt road that he knew about, or his GPS picked up on it."

"Well, shit," Alex muttered, as he tried to check his GPS map. "I don't suppose you have satellite on this asshole, do you?"

"We're working on trying to pick him up, trying to narrow it down," he replied, "but I'm not sure we'll get it fast enough though."

"Of course not," Alex said, his frustration boiling over. "Jesus, I should never have gone up to the house," he cried out.

"You can't second-guess yourself now," Levi stated. "It's all about staying the course and finding them before this asshole manages to do anything else."

"Yeah, sure," Alex replied bitterly. "I had them. They were right there, but no, I had to go for this asshole at the house."

"What else would you have done?"

"I should have got them out safely first," he snapped.

Levi went silent for a moment and then added, "Sure, that would have been one avenue, but we all thought checking on the house and making sure this guy didn't get loose was the way to go, considering that Taryn and Cassie were safe for the moment."

"Right, it made sense at the time. It never even occurred to me that somebody would find them up a tree, of all things."

"The only way they could have done that was if they had a way to track the little girl, which is something that we're all considering."

"That would make sense. Plus, if she was a prized possession, or worth a lot of money, I don't think too many people would leave her behind, not without some way to track her."

"Which means that these guys had some method to track Cassie."

"Most likely, … and the uncle probably let our new guy know right where the little girl was, which is just another betrayal for Cassie," Alex whispered.

"That's not what we're focusing on right now," Levi stated, his tone sharp. "Come on. This isn't the time to lose it."

Alex gave a bark of laughter. "There's never any time to lose it, but knowing I was right there and could have put them somewhere safe is too much."

"They were stashed, and you couldn't have stashed them any safer, not if Cassie had a tracking device on her. You can bet that this asshole would have found them anyway."

Alex took a deep breath. "Right, so, in other words, forget all that bullshit and carry on. Any word from Riff?"

"I haven't heard, but I'll check with Terk and give you an update soon, even if just to confirm the car chase is still on. Meanwhile, you stay with me and give me the blow-by-blow of what's going on there. Then I'll call Terk."

Alex sighed, then returned his whole attention to the road ahead. "Oh, hang on." Up ahead, he saw a dirt road with fresh tracks. "I'm taking a hard left. Fresh tracks are here, heading down into some godforsaken who-knows-where."

"Good, afterward take the very next left. Stay on the phone and tell me what you see."

"Nothing," he snapped. "It's dark out here and getting

darker by the minute."

"Yeah, I hear you there, and we're hearing that from everyone involved. Storms are moving in too."

Alex groaned. "Of course."

"That's all right," Levi noted. "It also means that this asshole is likely to go to ground somewhere too."

"No way," Alex argued. "He'll drive through the night to get as many miles between him and this nightmare as he can. He doesn't dare get caught with Cassie either," he noted, his tone harsh. "He knows what the penalty will be."

"I hope so," Levi muttered. "At least then he won't go into this lightly. So, when we put him in prison for the rest of his life, he'll know that's exactly what he deserves."

"And yet he won't care. We both know that. These guys just destroy everything around them, and they could care less, not as long as they have their nasty little pleasures," he grumbled.

"And again we won't focus on that right now," Levi reminded him. "Terkel is in contact with Taryn, and we'll leave it to him to keep that up. So, when you get to wherever you're going, be sure and keep yourself under control."

"Oh, I'm in control," Alex declared, "and don't you worry about that. Do you have backup coming?"

"Yes, though now that you've taken two offroad turns, we still don't know for sure that was correct or that was where our kidnapper went," Levi pointed out. "However, we've got two cruisers coming your way."

"Good, but don't let that roadblock come down yet, just in case."

"No, we're not. The cops are all over it. They've heard that there's been a slight shift in the kidnapper's direction, but they'll still check everybody coming through the checkpoint. They're looking for the dark van of course, but, just in case he ditches it, we're checking everything."

"Yeah, we pretty well have to," Alex agreed, as he drove up ahead slowly. "This road is getting really rough and ugly. So I'm forced to slow down."

"The kidnapper will have to as well."

"Hey, what are the chances our kidnapper is Jeff's long-lost brother?"

"We've got people monitoring the children's father via satellite. I'll check on that. So watch your back. Terkel's calling me. I better go."

Alex drove carefully, but the road was getting rougher and rougher. He could only imagine what Taryn and Cassie were going through, as they bounced along in the back of a van or whatever vehicle they were in now. Alex hadn't seen any sign of the dark van anywhere, at any time, which meant that this guy may have had an accomplice, or he had another vehicle stashed ahead of time, which made sense too.

Sure. Park the rental, leave it there at the house, leave a trail to the uncle, particularly if the uncle was being a bit of an asshole over the whole purchase thing, and then … what? A trail to the uncle would still show that the kids were missing. If the uncle was pissed off at this kidnapper guy, the uncle might very well turn him in. But, if Uncle Jeff had been well paid, that wasn't likely.

Alex pondered the vagaries of the criminal mind set as he drove, picking his way as fast as he could, being as careful as he could to avoid the potholes in a very rough backroad in the dark. He didn't dare risk getting stuck. He had no idea where the hell this road was taking him. His GPS was completely lost and kept telling him to turn around. He finally shut it off, instead of listening to any more instruc-tions about rerouting and making road changes, especially when there was barely even a road to drive on here.

That was the problem with these country roads.

The GPS maps weren't complete when it came to these dirt roadways, and, as soon as you went offroad, the GPS kept trying to plot you a new pathway to get to your initial destination, but, in this case, it wouldn't work. What Alex needed was the destination of the getaway vehicle. He didn't give a crap where he ended up, not as long as it was someplace he could reach Taryn and Cassie.

Up ahead, he had to slow up a bit to take another sharp corner. As he came around, he caught sight of red taillights. He immediately shut off his headlights, in case his were noted as well, and continued a little more carefully, as he had absolutely nothing but the moonlight to navigate with. Moonlight was usually right up his alley, but right now? It was not working in his favor. Even as he drove now at a snail's pace, he was comforted by the fact that whoever was up ahead couldn't be moving much faster.

There wasn't any way to move faster in this darkness. It was sloppy and soupy black out here and getting thicker by the second. At the same time, if this guy knew the area, knew where he was going, he had an advantage that Alex didn't, and that just pissed him off.

Nobody should have an advantage when it came to this bullshit, and, if it happened, it should go to the good guys. But too damn often these criminals were set up in a way that nobody else knew about, until things started to happen. If they were skilled and a little lucky, the good guys could change plans on the fly, but all too often these kids just disappeared into the nasty underbelly of Earth. Plus, in this case, Taryn was likely to get dumped by this guy as well.

Alex wasn't about to let that happen.

He could not let it happen.

CHAPTER 13

TARYN MOANED AGAIN, as her body was slammed from one side of the van to the other. She heard the driver muttering something up ahead, sounding pissed off and angry as hell. She didn't know what was going on in his world, but he had taken a turn off the road they were on, which might be good. However, the angrier he became, the more dangerous it would be for Taryn and Cassie. So maybe that turn was just to a more desolate part of the countryside. That was the last thing Taryn wanted. There had to be some relief coming up, but not soon enough. She didn't trust this new guy, and she didn't want him anywhere close to Cassie.

Taryn tried hard to pull on her inner strength. She focused on whatever she could utilize in order to get the hell out of here—as soon as the vehicle stopped, but it just wasn't stopping.

The driver hit another rough pothole, and she bounced again, another moan coming out. She clenched her jaw tight, trying to stop the sounds that might suggest she was awake.

"God damn it to hell," the driver muttered again. "Where the fuck are we anyway?"

That caught her attention like nothing else would and was music to her ears. If he was lost, he didn't have this game planned out in his mind, and that meant Taryn and Cassie had a chance. Taryn didn't quite know how to make it work, but, if their kidnapper was lost, she could potentially get them out of here, even if she had to pick up Cassie and carry her. Taryn didn't know how far she would get though. That would depend on whether or not she could first disable this asshole somehow and get her hands and feet free of the ropes that bound her. Her weary mind spun with ways to try and get the hell out of this predicament, and she kept sending telepathic messages about rough roads and potholes. Finally Terkel's voice slipped into her mind again.

Alex is right behind you, he said. *We're not sure how far away he is, but he saw taillights, which means hopefully he's near your vehicle, so stay strong.* And, with that, he slipped out again.

She groaned as the vehicle took yet another bounce, and her body was slammed against the side of the van again. Finally the vehicle came to a stop, and she heard the driver swearing even more from the front seat. What she didn't know was what had stopped him. Was it the fact that they were someplace he didn't know, or could he have seen a vehicle coming up behind him?

She didn't want this guy to get out and run, leaving them behind. Yet that might be the best for them. What she preferred would be to have him run off on his own but where they could find him. She didn't want him to come back and do this to some other young girl. She felt Cassie's hand squeezing hers in terror, as the vehicle's engine shut off.

Taryn didn't know what to say to Cassie or how to comfort her at this point. All Taryn could do was stay quiet and wait, wait for that chance, wait for something to break, an opportunity to jump free, to knock this guy off his feet, and to make a run for it. The problem was, Taryn's hands were still tied up, as were her feet. So, if their kidnapper came around with a bullet intended for her, Taryn couldn't do anything. All her plans would be in the wind very quickly.

Cassie slunk deeper into the shadows around her. Finally the big door behind the driver's seat opened up, and Taryn saw the shadow of their kidnapper.

"God damn it," he swore. "What the hell are you doing all the way back over there?" He hopped inside the rear portion of the van to drag Cassie forward.

Taryn waited until he was off balance, then kicked out as hard as she could. Even as he stumbled back, she was trying to get to her feet and land on him, hoping to find a way to knock him out and to keep him down, so he couldn't come up after them again.

She couldn't run hard or far because of the ties on her, but, if help was coming, she just needed to keep this asshole down and out for a bit.

He roared as he tried to jump up, but little Cassie was there beside him, hitting him, but her efforts were frail and futile. Taryn caught sight of a rock and grabbed it with both hands and slammed him in the nose with her elbow first. Then, with both hands tied together, thankfully in front of her, Taryn smashed the rock into their kidnapper's face. He roared and reared up, trying to get away from her. As she rolled over, she hit him as hard as she could, again and again, out of her mind with fury.

Though the blows might have jarred him, they sure as hell weren't stopping him, and that was the bad news. He slammed Taryn to the bare floor of the van, and she felt the breath knocked out of her. Suddenly he was on top of her, slamming his fist into her, again and again and again. Just when she thought she would lose consciousness, she heard a hard *thud* and looked up to see Cassie, holding the rock over her head, as the kidnapper slumped to the floor beside them.

Cassie immediately dropped down beside Taryn, bawling her eyes out. Taryn wrapped her arms around the little girl, desperate to try and figure out if it was over or not.

Hushing the crying girl as much as she could, she reached up and pulled off her own gag, even while she cried out telepathically to Terkel. *I need Alex. I need him fast.* She struggled toward their kidnapper. *We're free for the moment, but I don't know if this asshole's out cold or not.*

Confirm that he is, Terk stated, his voice strong. *And that's an order. This isn't the time to be a shrinking violet.*

She snorted. *Didn't think I would ever be accused of being one of those. We had a hell of a fight, and I'm still pretty groggy. Plus I'm still tied—*

Grab that rock and hit him again, Terk interrupted.

She rolled over until she was on top of the kidnapper. Then she ripped off the mask that he wore. Taryn frowned and looked over at Cassie.

Cassie stared down at him in shock and muttered, "It's Uncle Jeff."

ALEX DROVE CAREFULLY in the darkness, barely noting a dark vehicle stopped on the dirt road, with the van doors open. "Shit." Terkel's voice slipped into his mind.

The gals are free, and they're okay. They're both in shock, so I don't know how badly injured they are or the kidnapper either. You need to check on all of them. They should be in the van still. They overpowered him and slammed a rock into his head to try and get free.

Alex was stunned to hear that, yet at the same time incredibly grateful. "I'm here now," he muttered, as he shut off the engine, threw open the door, and raced over. He saw Taryn, collapsed on the floor of the van but heaving, trying to catch her breath.

She lifted her hands, still tied, and waved at him. "It's been a hell of a journey," she muttered, coughing and trying to get a full breath. "That was the longest five minutes ever."

Swearing at that, he dropped down beside Taryn and Cassie. "Are you both okay?" Neither answered, just pointed to the battered man beside them. Alex frowned, then asked Cassie, "Your uncle Jeff did this?"

Cassie nodded, staring down at the man with loathing. "Yes, that's Uncle Jeff."

Taryn asked, "Who left the house in your uncle's vehicle earlier then? You told me it was your uncle Jeff with your brothers."

Cassie looked up at Taryn and nodded. "It was, but I don't know if he took the truck."

Not worrying about it right now, Alex quickly untied Taryn and Cassie. Then using their rope restraints, Alex tied up their kidnapper. He pulled out his phone and filled in Levi. "We need EMTs here now," he declared. "Our kidnapper is suffering from injuries. They probably won't kill him, and that's unfortunate, but I guess we need him alive," he muttered in a harsh tone. "Besides, Cassie is in rough shape emotionally. Taryn has taken a beating or two."

At that moment, Cassie curled up tightly in Taryn's arms, and Alex knew there would be no way to separate them, and he shared as much to Levi.

"There shouldn't be any need to separate them, but both need to be checked over, especially Taryn," Levi noted. "Plus, why the hell was Jeff driving this other vehicle? If he had the little boys in his truck, and now he is here in a dark van," Levi began, "what the hell is going on?"

"Yeah, all good questions," Alex agreed, "and I definitely want answers too, but we won't get any from him at the moment. He's out cold."

"The gals did a good job, *huh*?"

"They did a *really* good job," Alex declared, pride in his tone. "Sucks that they had to do this at all though."

"Absolutely it does, but that's not what we'll focus on right now," Levi stated, his tone firm. "They did what they had to do to survive. Their lives were in imminent danger, and, even if they had killed him, that would be justified."

"Well, I won't share that with them," Alex noted. "Cassie is pretty upset as it is. Any word on finding the twins?"

"No word yet on the twin boys, and my guys gave the most recent coordinates on Jeff's brother to the nearest police station," Levi replied. "I'll pass along any updates. Terk will update me when he has something to share. And, of course, Cassie is now more upset, especially after finding out that her kidnapper is her uncle Jeff. Still, that's not the most urgent issue right now. You should hear the deputies coming your way soon. I'll hang up and send out some messages to our people. I'll tell them we need two ambulances as well." And, with that, Levi disconnected.

Alex looked over at Taryn to see her holding on, fighting back tears herself. "The cavalry is on its way," he whispered.

She looked up at him, and her tears were ready to spill over. He sat down and pulled both of the gals into his arms and just held on as they cried. Once the tears began, no way they could put that genie back in a bottle, and they just flowed. The crying didn't stop until they heard vehicles coming toward them.

Cassie stiffened, ready to bolt. He held on to her a little tighter. "It's all right, Cassie. It's the sheriff."

She stared up at him. "Will they hurt me?"

"No, not at all," he replied. "Why?"

She just stared at him.

"It's okay. You did what you needed to do. Don't be afraid. You won't be in trouble."

"Yes, I am," she whispered. "I would be in trouble if I ever did anything like that. I was not allowed to fight or to say anything. Uncle Jeff told me that the police would come and would pick me up and that I would never get free again. I would never see my brothers again."

"Your uncle Jeff lied," Alex snapped, his tone harsher than he intended. When he saw Cassie wince, he sighed and gently stroked her back. "I'm sorry your uncle Jeff was so mean, but he only said things like that to control you, and it's not right. He didn't have your best interests at heart when he told you that."

Cassie didn't say anything else but stared with trepidation as two vehicles finally came to a stop. As soon as the first people jumped out, a man and a woman, Alex called out to them.

"I have the two female victims over here," he yelled, "and the kidnapper is here too, unconscious." They quickly approached, the man dropping beside the kidnapper, and the female deputy coming over to check on the gals.

Cassie reared back in terror, but Alex held her close. "It's all right, Cassie. Remember what I told you? It's okay now."

She shook her head and buried her face against him. Alex looked up at the female deputy in front of him and shared, "She's pretty traumatized."

"Of course she is," the other woman replied. "Do we

have an ID on this guy?" she asked, pointing at the unconscious man.

Alex nodded. "According to Cassie here, it's her uncle Jeff."

The deputy stared at him in shock for a moment and then turned to look at Cassie.

Cassie nodded. "That's my uncle Jeff."

Confused, the woman looked back at Alex.

"I don't know who is driving the other getaway vehicle, with Cassie's twin brothers inside," Alex explained. "I'm afraid at this point, it was a decoy or ..." He hesitated, knowing that Cassie was hearing everything. "It's somebody who is *helping* Jeff here," he said, with emphasis on the word *helping*.

Cassie perked up. "Maybe he took Jack and John to the hospital."

"Who are Jack and John, honey? Why do they need to go to the hospital?" the female deputy asked Cassie.

Cassie nodded. "They are my brothers. Uncle Jeff got mad and hit them, and Jack didn't talk right afterward, and John was sleeping for so long."

"When was this?"

She shrugged. "A couple days ago, I think. I don't remember."

"And that's okay," the deputy noted. "Don't you worry about it. We're looking for that truck right now, with your brothers in it."

Cassie bit her lip, and she stared up at the woman in uniform. "Am I in trouble?"

The deputy crouched in front of her. "Absolutely not."

"But I hurt him."

"You hurt your uncle?"

"Yes. I smashed him in the head with a rock. But Uncle Jeff told me all kinds of bad things would happen to me if I didn't listen to him," she shared, staring over at the unconscious man, who was being attended to by two deputies at this point.

"Well, apparently he thought that would work to control you," the female deputy said, with a note of humor, "but, honey, you have every right to defend yourself, especially if somebody is hurting you. And definitely if you're kidnapped." She looked around and asked, "Were you restrained?"

Cassie nodded. "Yeah, and Uncle Jeff hurt Taryn too. He shot her with something and made her fall out of the tree. She was knocked out, and he tied us both up, even though I begged him not to, but I didn't know it was him. He had a mask on. He told me that it was my punishment for being bad and for leaving the house."

"Well, he was wrong, and he isn't allowed to hurt this lady here either." The uniformed female pointed at Taryn. "None of this is your fault, sweetie." She spoke to Cassie in such a firm but kind voice.

It was definitely the right thing to say in that moment, as Cassie slowly relaxed against Alex. He sent a thumbs-up to the deputy, who just nodded, but the anger in her expression was very clear, and he well understood it. Little girls tormented by the very family members who were supposed to look after them was difficult to deal with.

All that Cassie had been exposed to, even just tonight, was trauma she would spend the rest of her life trying to resolve. This was a cluster fuck of mass proportions, and they still didn't know about Jack and John. All of it would leave a marked impression on this little girl's mind and heart. Alex just cuddled the two gals closer.

The female deputy stood up and added, "We have an ambulance coming. Two of them actually. We need to take them in to get checked over."

Cassie shook her head and wrapped her arms tightly around Alex. At the same time Taryn shook her head too.

The female deputy was firm. "You will both get checked out. Alex can come with you, but you'll go to the hospital to be checked over." Taryn sagged against Alex, as if realizing she wouldn't have any choice in the matter. Once Cassie saw Taryn giving in, Cassie relaxed as well.

When the first ambulance pulled in, Alex shifted himself to his feet, bringing Taryn up on hers as well. "Can you walk?" he asked.

She nodded and took several steps. Suddenly she stopped and looked at him with an odd expression. Then her eyes rolled up in the back of her head, and she collapsed into his arms.

CHAPTER 14

W HEN TARYN WOKE, she was being bounced around on a rough road again. She moaned and heard a soft voice telling her it was okay and to go back to sleep. She slept again. When she woke the next time, she was assaulted by bright lights, with white curtains surrounding her, and she was up against a heavy weight. She rolled over gently to find Cassie curled up at her side. She wrapped her arms around the little girl and pulled her into a gentle embrace. She just held the child, who looked exhausted and seemed to have crashed.

The curtain was pulled back to the side, and Alex walked in. He took one look and smiled. "Sorry about that. I saw her curl up beside you, but I didn't have the heart to tell her that you might need some space."

"I'm fine," she whispered, "and I'm so damn grateful that she's okay and that she can stay right here."

"She is okay, but we're still trying to find her brothers."

Tears came to Taryn's eyes, but she brushed them away impatiently. "That just reminds me what an asshole Jeff is."

"Well, he is here in the hospital as well, but under guard, so there is that. Apparently you guys did a good number on him with the rock."

"We were trying to get free of him, which wasn't that easy, considering we were tied up," Taryn shared. "I struggled to get my own bonds off to secure him but couldn't. So, if he had woken up again, before you got to us, I don't know what we would have done," she muttered. She groaned as she rotated her body ever-so-slightly. "I don't know what the hell he did to me, but, man, I hurt."

"Well, to start with," Alex replied, with half a smile, "he probably tranq'd you, letting you drop out of a tree. Rolling around the back of that van on that dirt road while tied up and unconscious couldn't have helped either. Plus, according to Cassie, Jeff also tried to beat the living hell out of you, after you hit him with the rock."

"Yeah, there is that too," Taryn muttered, glaring off in the distance. Then she looked down at Cassie and smiled. "She's a strong little girl. You should have seen her tag him with that rock to get him off me."

"She is a strong one, no doubt," Alex agreed, with a nod. "I'm sure her uncle Bruce would be very grateful for all you're doing."

"Cassie's an innocent little girl, and she had a mother who loved her, and I know her mother is looking down from heaven and is so grateful that Cassie is safe now." Taryn stared at Cassie, struggling to control her tears. "Just as I would be if she were mine."

"I know."

"Yet having a child of my own has never really been on my radar," she shared. "And, after all this, a part of me says absolutely no way I would even want to try to raise a child in this totally psychotic world, with dangers around every corner. But then I think about having somebody as special as Cassie close to me, and it's something that I desperately want."

Alex smiled. "There's both good and bad when it comes

to raising kids, the love and the fear," he noted. "You do the best you can and hope they have the tools to become decent human beings. Although, somewhere along the line comes these assholes, like her uncle Jeff, and I still struggle to understand why. I can't believe that he was the one who did this. I do realize that sometimes things go horribly wrong, and society ends up with a piece of crap like him to deal with, but still …" Alex shook his head.

"How could her uncle Jeff have kidnapped us?" Taryn whispered, looking up at Alex. "He drove off with Jack and John in his truck from the house, so where the hell are her brothers?"

"We're assuming Jeff had a second vehicle hidden on the property. We didn't know about that, and then we didn't know about the one guy who left in Jeff's truck, that was clearly a decoy. I was looking for the kids, not confirming Jeff was the driver. The truck may have been Jeff's, but he was not the driver. Whether that driver knew we were on to him doesn't really matter. However, when Cassie slipped out of the house, maybe not even knowing that Uncle Jeff had a second vehicle, he either followed her on foot or had a way to track her. We checked her over for some tracking device in the ambulance, and so did the hospital staff here. Short of taking X-rays for an under-the-skin tracker, nobody found a tracker."

"But if her uncle Jeff was at the house as his truck left the property, Jeff could have easily followed Cassie right to me, while I tried to figure out what our plan was. He could have taken her at that point in time and wouldn't even need a tracker. It's almost more sophisticated than I can see that asshole being."

"That is a consideration as well," Alex agreed, with a

nod. "We'll get to the bottom of it eventually."

"But will we find Jack and John?" she whispered. "I can't just take one of these kids back. What will I say to Bruce? And how will I face Cassie?"

"I know." Alex's heart ached for her. "Maybe you can just focus on you for a change."

She shook her head and then groaned. "Oh God," she whispered one hand reaching up to her head. She took several deep breaths, while she tried to control the pain. As she looked up at him, she saw the wry look on his face and nodded. "I get it. I'm not exactly in good shape right now."

"Nope, you're not. Yet you won't stay in the hospital tonight."

"Good, I want to get Cassie someplace safe."

"We'll stay in a hotel close by because the doctor wants to see you tomorrow. You're only being released because I knew you would fight him hard to get out."

She looked up at him. "You mean, I can leave?"

He smiled and nodded. "Yes, but we can't go very far away."

"That's fine," she replied, trying to sit up without waking up Cassie, and then she froze. "Is Cassie not allowed to leave?"

"Cassie is not allowed to leave in your care. So, we'll all go to a hotel, but we'll have some FBI agents with us."

She stared at him in shock. "What? Why not?"

He hesitated and then shrugged. "First, we don't have any proof that you are related because you're not. It might be possible if you had Bruce's permission to take on Cassie, but again he's not able to do that at the moment. So, from a purely legal perspective, even Bruce has no legal claim as of yet. Of course the authorities want to make things as legal as they can and confirm that they're doing everything right by Cassie. Second, there is your response to the ad to buy the children."

Taryn grimaced.

"Yeah," Alex noted. "That's problematic. Therefore, the Feds don't want to give you permission to take Cassie out of the country. Not on your own and not without doing their due diligence."

"Of course they don't," she muttered, staring at him. "But they have to believe that she is Bruce's niece, right?"

"No, they don't. Not just on your say-so. This is law enforcement we're dealing with, and, no matter what we know, the laws are designed to confirm that the child is safe and secure *and* in the custody of someone with the legal authority to have her."

Taryn let out her breath in a harsh *whoosh*. "Now that will just piss me right off."

He nodded. "I know that, and I'm just telling you, for the moment, that you don't have custody of her. You can't take her to Bruce, and you can't do anything in any way, shape, or form without getting the law on your side first. In this case, the law is saying that they need proof that you have permission to look after Cassie. They aren't trying to take her away from you," he added, keeping a hand on her shoulder to console her, "so keep that in mind. Cassie has made it very clear that she doesn't want to go with anybody else but you, so this FBI custody-guardianship is a temporary arrangement, until we can figure out a permanent solution."

"What about Bruce? Can anybody contact him?"

"That requires that he's awake and cognizant enough to talk and able to talk at a level that can convince the FBI he's capable of looking after the kids and making decisions on their behalf. But you and I both know where he's at right now."

"Then what? Can we get them out of here or not?" she asked.

"First off, we only have one child in hand at the moment, and we do need to find the two boys and see to their immediate medical needs," he explained. "Then I imagine it'll require tons of paperwork and reports, but considering Uncle Jeff tied up both of you, and, yes, I vouched that you were completely tethered when I found you and that Cassie said Uncle Jeff had already seriously hurt the little boys," he clarified, trying to calm Taryn. "That's all adding weight to our argument."

Then suddenly it hit her, and she realized that, if they couldn't prove that Jeff had done something to deserve what he got, she herself could be in trouble for harboring Cassie and assaulting him. "You do know the law is messed up, right?"

With perfect timing, one of the FBI agents stepped in just then, looking at Taryn, all stern and businesslike. "How are you feeling?" she asked.

"Pretty shitty, hearing there is a question about letting Cassie stay with me. Do you understand what she has been through?"

"We've worked out an arrangement for a little while," the woman stated coolly. "But you do understand that we have to do our own due diligence too, right?"

Taryn took a deep breath and nodded. "I guess that sounds about right. Bruce has already been to hell and back, without having this headache on his shoulders as well. It'll be hard for him to accept what has happened already, so the sooner he can wake up and talk to you, the better. Their uncle Jeff, on the other hand, is a real piece of work."

"Oh, I can assure you that we agree on that. Assuming the story checks out, if this Bruce guy is their uncle, and, given the situation here, I'm pretty sure he'll have a very good case for custody."

"A good case?" Taryn asked, staring at her. "Surely there is no possibility that the children could be forced to return to their abusive uncle Jeff?"

At that, the other woman shook her head. "No, we've identified quite enough from the crime scene to realize that the little girl's life has not been comfortable for some time. If nothing else, she was being verbally abused and criminally neglected. We have also established that you were attacked and kidnapped, and that too will weigh against Jeff."

"That is all fine, but … eventually he'll wake up and say all kinds of things," Taryn replied bitterly, "like I stole Cassie out of the house, and he was just trying to get her back again."

"I'm sure he will," the agent agreed, eyeing Taryn carefully. "For that matter, are you up to giving us your side of the story?"

"*My* side of the story? As if there is *another*?" She stared up at the agent, Taryn's heart sinking, realizing that she really could get into trouble over all this. She looked over at Alex. "Did you talk to them too?"

"I told them exactly what I knew, and they've also already talked to Levi and Terkel."

"*Great*, and yet they still want to talk to me."

"Of course they do," he replied. "You're the one who was there when Cassie came out of the house. You're the one who was there when you were attacked, and you're the one who woke up in the vehicle, tied up with ropes."

"I don't suppose you caught any images of that, did you?" she asked. "I already feel as if they won't believe me otherwise."

"Are you kidding? You have rope burns and bruises, which they can easily match to your skin on the rope that we secured Jeff with," Alex told her. "Remember that the FBI agents aren't the bad guys."

Taryn groaned. "It feels as if everybody out there is a bad guy right now."

"And you're not wrong in the sense that a lot of bad guys exist," the agent acknowledged, "but we are not among them, and we will not let anybody else abuse this little girl."

Considering that was exactly what she wanted for Cassie, Taryn nodded, then slowly and as distinctly as she could, she explained what had happened from the beginning and how she had contacted Levi and then plans had been set in motion.

"Okay," the female agent said, "and now I just have a few other questions."

And, with that, the questions and answers continued for another twenty minutes, until Taryn felt her brain throbbing, things getting fuzzy. "I can't answer any more questions right now," Taryn gasped, as the pounding in her head started to build. "God, my head is killing me." She moaned softly as she shifted in the bed.

A little voice beside her whispered, "Are you okay?"

"I will be," Taryn lied, looking over at Cassie to see her waking up. "How are you doing?"

She stared at the people in the room, then wrapped her arms around Taryn and whispered, "Who are they?"

"Well, you know Alex," Taryn replied, pointing to where he was half hidden. Immediately Alex stepped forward into sight, and Taryn reached out a hand to him.

He grabbed her hand and looked over at the agents. "Maybe you should identify yourselves to Cassie as well." They quickly did that.

Immediately Cassie's eyes grew wider. "Will my uncle Jeff hurt us anymore?"

"No, he won't," the agents replied simultaneously. So many voices spoke at once that Cassie frowned and turned to Taryn. "If you tell me so, I'll believe you."

"Your uncle Jeff will not hurt you and your brothers anymore," Taryn stated firmly. "Right now, he is already in serious trouble for a lot of different things."

"He needs to be in trouble for hurting Jack and John," Cassie wailed, and then her eyes widened. "Did they find my brothers?" she asked, struggling to get up off the bed. "Did you find my brothers?"

Delores, the female agent, shook her head. "No, I'm sorry, sweetie. We're all still looking for them."

Cassie's face scrunched up, and her tears flowed freely. Taryn grabbed Cassie and held her close. "They're looking, and friends of ours are looking too. We'll find your brothers. I promise."

She sobbed. "But will you find them before they are dead?" Cassie asked.

At that question, everyone looked at each other, and Delores added hurriedly, "If you are ready and able to leave, we do have a place for you for the night."

"Good." Taryn slowly pulled back the blankets and slipped out of the hospital bed. She looked over at the others, then said in a waspish tone, "Clothes of some sort would be nice."

"I've got some for you," Alex replied, stepping forward

and handing her a small bag. "I also have your purse and your carry-on."

She smiled up at him gratefully, then looked over at Cassie. "I'll just go to the bathroom."

"I have to go too," Cassie whispered.

"In that case, we'll both go." She held the little girl's hand gently. Trying to put aside her own pain, Taryn led them into the bathroom, past all the agents. There, the gals washed up, used the facilities, and, with a somewhat tenuous smile on Taryn's face, she opened the door and announced, "We're ready."

ALEX FROWNED AS he watched Taryn. She really wanted to leave the hospital, but Alex wasn't so sure now that she should have. Alex helped her and Cassie out of the vehicle at the hotel, but Taryn was clearly woozy and not walking well. The three FBI agents were right behind them. Alex glared at Taryn, as she stiffened and glared back. He smiled. "I didn't think you wanted to go back to the hospital."

Her glare increased in voltage. "No way," she muttered. "Besides, if Cassie is out, I'm out."

He snorted at that. "In that case, you better not collapse on the way to the hotel room."

"I've got some high-powered painkillers in my system, so cut me some slack here." He gave her a wicked smile. "And here I thought you were concerned about me and not just your back."

He laughed. "Believe me that I'm concerned about both. Yet I want confirmation that nobody has any reason to order you back to the hospital."

"Ouch. That would not be fun."

"No, but it would be well within their rights if you collapse."

"I'm not collapsing," she declared.

"Good, because the FBI agents have you in their sights." Alex nodded but kept a close eye on her as she made her way to the hotel room. As soon as they were inside, Taryn walked to the couch and collapsed on it. "What would really help is some food."

"That can certainly be arranged," replied the FBI agent, Delores. "I can get something for you." She looked over at Cassie. "What about you, little one? Are you hungry?"

Cassie nodded. "Yes, please." She had slipped into being this formal, polite little ghost that reminded Alex very much of the little girl at the convenience store.

Delores immediately left, but one male FBI agent remained in the hotel suite with them, while the other excused himself to stand guard outside the hotel room door.

"It's all right, Cassie," Alex said, standing at her side. "You're safe now." She just stared up at him, and he could see her fatigue. She hadn't even had a chance to process any of this, on top of worrying about her brothers. It was all taking a toll.

She just nodded and didn't say anything.

Taryn reached out a hand to Cassie, who gripped it like a lifeline, and the two just clung to each other.

Considering what they'd been through, it made sense. Alex did worry that Taryn would have some problems dealing with Cassie when she got to Terkel's place. Bruce had been away for a long time, so neither Taryn nor Cassie had a close or even recent contact with him. Alex asked Taryn about this telepathically, since an FBI agent remained in the room. *Will this be a problem for Cassie to live with Bruce, after not seeing him in so long?*

She almost shook her head, then winced but regained her control again. *No, not at all. Cassie remembers me and Bruce and understands how I know her uncle Bruce and that I knew her mother a long time ago too. We just need to get things wrapped up over here, so we can get to Bruce in England.*

And that will happen, but it'll take some time.

Taryn frowned. *What about passports and all that?*

That'll be a hiccup because we need passports for all three of the children, possibly visas too, and we'll do both to be overly cautious. Plus, we'll need to file all kinds of related paperwork, Alex shared. *We also need Bruce to be awake and aware.*

Taryn winced. *Great. As much as I want to expedite that process, I want to be sure it's foolproof and prevents Cassie's uncle Jeff from ever coming back after us. I don't want any of this in the children's heads as a memory.*

Alex watched as Cassie clenched her fingers around Taryn's. This wasn't a conversation to have with a little girl right here, even telepathically, if she could pick up on their own exchange here, but it was obvious that Cassie had already been privy to far too many adult conversations. Alex smiled at her. "You'll be fine, Cassie," he said out loud. "I know that we keep saying that and that it's hard for you to believe, but it will be okay."

She looked up at him. "Did you find my brothers?"

And that completely brought the conversation back around to what was most important to her. He smiled. "Not yet, but we will." She didn't say anything and just stared steadily at him. He realized how hard it was to convince a child who'd already been treated badly by the adults who were supposed to protect her, not to mention the fact that she'd been lied to, time and time again. From her perspective, just because Alex said they would find Jack and John didn't mean they actually would. It didn't mean that at all.

He sighed, then looked over at Taryn. "Do you want a nap?"

"I need some food first," she replied.

"It's coming. Then afterward you can have a nap."

"After that I'll have a shower." When he frowned at her, she glared back. "I haven't had one in a very long time," she muttered.

"A bath maybe, but I'm not sure that standing in a shower with that heat will be good for your head," he noted. "It might feel great, but it could also make you pass out."

She stared at him, then shrugged. "I don't care. A bath will do. I just want to be clean again."

"Got it." Alex tilted his head at the little girl. "How about you, Cassie? After some food, do you want a nap?"

She shrugged. "I don't care," she replied, almost listlessly, as if the adult conversation was now too much for her to handle. She literally didn't care, and he could relate to that.

Another ten minutes passed before Delores returned with food, and a lot of it. All different kinds. Delores shrugged. "I had no idea what anybody wanted," she began, "so I just brought lots."

She hadn't exaggerated a bit, as she had everything from fried chicken to sandwiches to burgers. Cassie picked up a burger and ate it slowly. Taryn had fried chicken, and Alex went first for a burger and then fried chicken.

The other FBI agents shared in the feast as well. By the time they were all done, there wasn't a whole lot of food left.

Alex watched as Taryn yawned several times.

She caught him looking at her and glared again. "I'm

not ready to go to bed yet."

"I was wondering if you wanted to try that bath."

She did appear to assess her energy level, and then her shoulders sagged. "I really want one, but I think you're right. I just might be a little too tired."

"Maybe a nap and then a shower?"

She nodded, then looked over at Cassie, who even now started to fade again.

"Cassie and I will go lie down," Taryn announced, as she slowly got up. Cassie immediately went along, joined at the hip from the looks of it. With no argument from anybody else, the two headed into a bedroom, but, when they got closer, Cassie turned and looked back at Alex. "Are you coming?" she asked.

He frowned at her for a moment and asked, "Do you want me to come?" She immediately nodded. Smiling, he got up. "A nap sounds good. I'm tired too." He walked into the bedroom, and the three laid down, with Cassie between them. He pulled a blanket up over them, then whispered, "Now both of you get some sleep."

Cassie immediately closed her eyes, and—almost like magic, as if somebody had flipped a switch—she went to sleep.

Alex whispered, "Now that is the innocence of a child."

"It's damn sad, whatever it is," Taryn murmured. "Thank you for coming in here with us. It'll likely be a while before Cassie sleeps well."

"It'll be a while before anybody puts this nightmare behind them," Alex stated. "She will need some help down the road to sort it all out."

"And that's fine," Taryn agreed, with a yawn. "At least she'll have that opportunity. However, she won't truly rest until we find her brothers."

"I understand that," he replied. "If you're okay for now, I'll slip out and see if I can get some updates."

"Good," she whispered, as she yawned again. "You do that, and maybe you'll have something for us when we wake up." And, with that, she drifted off.

Alex slipped out of the bed, then stood for a moment, watching them. Shaking his head, he walked out into the living room. One of the FBI agents looked up at him, one eyebrow arched. Alex shared, "They're both asleep already. I don't suppose we have coffee, do we?"

"One of ours just left to make a run," he replied. "Meanwhile, we're writing up our notes and asking for an update on what's happening on the chase of the little boys. We have several other agents helping out your … *agent*," he explained, with a wry tone.

"You can call Riff a war agent, a government agent, a private agent, or whatever you like," Alex noted. "What I call him is a skilled brother-in-arms. I would trust him with my life any day. Since these issues typically come down to good versus evil, I never can understand why it always seems as if the FBI considers us to be on different sides."

"Not *different*," Delores clarified. "We're on the same side. There's just not a whole lot of communication."

"And that is sad too," Alex agreed, as he settled in a chair. "I have my laptop here and need to get some work done as well."

"What are you working on?" Delores asked suspiciously.

"Catching up on reports, just like you," he said. "I have a boss too."

The agents just nodded and didn't say anything in response to that.

"Have you worked with Terkel very much?" Delores finally asked.

Alex smiled. "Terkel is kind of a law onto himself."

"In many ways, yes," she agreed, "but he's not lawless by any means."

"Of course not. He works within the law, but he does a broad range of work all around the world."

"Right. Is it true about his being psychic?"

"Absolutely it is, but I'm not exactly sure what that term means to you," Alex acknowledged, with a smile. "You have to realize that his abilities really do defy the definition of what is considered normal, even for a psychic, even for an uncommon man."

Delores considered that, but her gaze was wary. "Can he read minds or anything?"

Alex burst out laughing at that. "I don't really know about that, although I wouldn't put it past him, considering he's been known to talk telepathically. However, I do know he can assess a situation pretty damn quickly and can make decisions that I won't say are always exactly right, but, in my experience, they are mostly spot-on."

She nodded. "We've all heard rumors about the secret agency programs he was involved in, and his name is kind of legendary, even in our circles," she admitted. "Yet none of us really knows what he does."

"Well, in this case, he simply supplied manpower to help make this happen," Alex shared in a friendly tone. "You guys were working in the background on a sting, but we needed to be on the ground."

"Well, it would have been a hell of a lot better if we had been on the ground, too, with you." Delores glared at him. "Yet certain people didn't tell us fast enough."

"Oh, certain people told you all right, but it has to filter down through so many layers of red tape that, by the time you get wind of something that's happening, it's already happened."

At that, one of the male FBI agents turned to Delores and nodded. "Don't even bother arguing. You know how it works."

"I do know," Delores admitted, "but it's damn frustrating. We could have been on this a lot earlier."

"Yet *a lot earlier* doesn't mean that *we* even knew about it," one of the male agents pointed out. "And Alex is right. They are the ones who found out about this problem and brought it to us. They had a better system to jump start this op, but we'll bring it to an end."

Delores added, "It's not as if we have eyes and ears all over the country. Therefore, we can't keep track of every child who goes missing. It seems as if we never get close enough to keep track of any of them," she complained, "and that just sucks. I guess I'm tired of always being too late."

"Well, I'm still hoping we're not too late in this instance," Alex replied. "I need to confirm those little boys will make it through this." The agents frowned at him in confusion. "According to what Cassie told us, the twins weren't doing very well. What she described were symptoms of a concussion," Alex explained, "but we can't really base our actions simply on her information alone. She's just a child herself, and she's clearly been traumatized. It could have been any number of things, but her uncle Jeff is culpable in all of it, and I want to ensure that all three of these children are protected from Jeff regardless."

"We all want that," one of the agents replied. "We also need to know who Jeff was selling them to."

Alex sighed. "I understand you have agents trying to meet up with Riff's pursuit." When Delores nodded, Alex continued. "I presume you sent a team to search Jeff's house?"

"Yeah, with a fine-tooth comb," Delores replied cheerfully. "We haven't got anything back yet."

"And again we're back to that slow process of working with you guys." Alex smirked, but Delores again glared at him. He smiled and replied, "No offense intended, but it's the truth. I'm just saying, when you have private money involved, we seem to get results a lot faster than the red-tape-involved government agencies."

"But you haven't got any results either," Delores pointed out, "so it's not as if you're doing any better than we are."

"It's not a competition," Alex noted, staring at her. "All I'm saying is that private money offers opportunities to get out of the gate much faster."

She sat back and frowned at him. "But is your money going into processing the scene? Otherwise you're not bringing anything to the conversation."

"I did get Taryn and Cassie back. Plus, Riff is working on rescuing her brothers." Alex could have gone on, but considering Delores was obviously quite pissed off about something, Alex just shut up and settled back to work on his laptop. He needed to find Jack and John.

TERKEL SENT OUT a message. *Riff, you there?*

Yep, still driving. What the hell is going on here? I feel as if I'm in a search circle, only going wider, not narrower.

It appears you have a decoy driver, or, at any rate, somebody else we don't know about. Oh, and a heads-up for you. Jeff's brother, the children's long-lost father, has been located via satellite and facial recognition. He seems to be in your neck of the woods too.

So our unknown driver may be circling to finally cross paths with the children's derelict father? So a handoff, maybe, or a brief meetup, or just joining our mystery driver and the twins? Regardless, that can't be good news.

We notified the nearest PD, and I understand a BOLO is out for Jeff's brother. Plus, two Fed cars are trying to catch up with you. So if you hear sirens or see two standard black government SUVs, remember we have a relative on the loose out there and the FBI on your tail.

Great, and I heard you've got Cassie. Is that true?

We do have Cassie, and you have the trail on the little boys.

Do we know what the hell is going on here yet?

I'm not sure, but we need you to keep on it.

Oh, I'm on it, Riff muttered. *No thanks to this asshole up ahead. I don't know how his truck has even gone as far as it has without needing more fuel, but he was obviously fully tanked up and committed to driving. I did stop and get gas and that slowed me by ten minutes, but I caught up to him. Maybe he gassed up too at some point. I had my feelers out for the little boys, as I got back on their tail, in case our driver dumped them somewhere along the line, when I didn't have eyes on him. I got no notice of that, and I'm still getting multiple energy readings off the truck ahead of me.*

No visual sighting of the little boys?

No. I've seen no signs of the twins, Riff replied in frustration. *I still don't have a clue where this guy's heading. Wait. … Hang on a minute. The driver took a turn up ahead.* With that, Riff changed highways. *Well, that's interesting. Looks as if we're leaving the Greater Houston area.*

Okay, keep an eye out and share with me when you can. Meanwhile, we are tuned in on that tracker on Jeff's truck, Terk noted. *Since you are in Levi's neck of the woods, do you need some help? A backup? A relief driver?*

What about Alex?

He's standing guard over the two gals.

Lucky him, Riff muttered, followed by a yawn.

Yes and no. He's also dealing with the Feds, and they're in the same hotel room with them.

At that, Riff gave a harsh laugh. *Oh, Jesus. Alex can keep that job then. Trapped with the Feds? You know I don't handle bureaucracy well.*

Yeah, I don't think Alex is that comfortable with it either, but somebody has to stay with Taryn and Cassie.

I hear you. I don't trust anybody right now, particularly not when I don't know who's behind all of this in front of me.

What about Merk? He can spare you some time, so you can hopefully sleep at least once every forty-eight hours.

Ha. I will take you or your twin brother anytime. You did run down that license plate off this truck, didn't you?

Absolutely, and you are following Uncle Jeff's truck. The van he himself was in to kidnap the gals is being worked up by the Feds, checking for fingerprints, etcetera. We thought it might be stolen, but it seems to be Jeff's too. He just hasn't registered it or insured it for a long time.

Which just makes him suspicious as hell.

It all makes him suspicious, but, if he's been planning this for a while, he would have taken a lot of care to confirm he didn't get caught.

Right. Riff opened up the car window a bit to get fresh air in to stop him from getting tired. *I'll let you know how this end works out, but you keep an eye on that little girl. I hate to say that they're worth more than little boys on the black market, but this is apparently not a case of dumping the twins. It's looking more to be somebody buying damaged goods at a somewhat reduced price, who fully intends to make good use of the purchase,* Riff suggested, his tone harsh.

Terkel sucked in his breath. *I sure as hell hope not. Watch for Merk. Lucky for us, as part of Levi's crew, he is currently in town.*

Great. How far out is he?

Give him about thirty minutes, and he should be on your ass. And, Riff, I know you don't like handing off the wheel, not being in total control, but do a pit stop, will ya? Leave your car on the roadside and jump in Merk's vehicle. Let him drive to give you time to close your eyes and to recharge.

As long as Merk's moving it, I'll consider it. Our mysterious driver can't keep his vehicle going without fueling up soon, and believe me that he won't get another chance to get into that vehicle. I would have already run him off the road if we didn't think those little boys were in there.

Yeah, don't do that, Terkel warned.

No, I won't, but no way in hell I'm letting him take those little boys any farther once he stops, so our pervert can just piss off. Riff closed the connection, but he grinned because Terkel knew him, and Riff knew Terkel. They had maintained a relationship over the years as both of them dealt with their various abilities, bouncing back and forth off each other. Riff just hadn't been government material way back when, and, now that Terkel was private, maybe it changed things enough, … but maybe it didn't.

Terkel slammed him with his response. *Of course it does. You're just too damn stubborn to admit it.*

Damn right I am, he agreed, with a ghost of a smile. *It's kept me alive too.*

That's not living, Riff, Terk stated. *What I have now is living, and I already know for sure that what you have, which is what I used to have, ... is only half of the life you could enjoy. You live for the job, so you're not out there working on yourself.*

Don't need to. Been there. Done that. The pain is too much.

And yet it's not over.

I understand, and I sure as hell still want to know what the hell happened to her.

We'll get there ... soon.

When is this soon *you keep talking about?* Riff snorted. *We haven't had the tiniest break in my case to date. No matter who did this job, whoever killed her seems to have done it in a way that none of the rest of us can trace it back to him.* Riff's tone was filled with fury. *That pisses me off more than anything.*

I know it does. You hate being beat even temporarily, but this case is much more than just being beat. It's not getting the answers that you need in order to move on after losing your fiancée. Those answers are out there, and one day soon we will find them. And, with that, Terkel finally stepped out of Riff's mind and disappeared.

Meanwhile, Riff focused intently on the getaway truck driving down the highway about a mile in front of him, shook his head, and called out in frustration, "Keep driving, asshole. You'll run out of fuel eventually, and it'll happen long before I ever give up. No way in hell you're taking those little boys anywhere out of my reach."

What Riff didn't want to admit was—and in his heart of hearts was the one thing that terrified him right now—what if those hurt and bleeding little boys weren't inside that truck? Or worse, were slowly dying in that vehicle? That would be a worst-case scenario. Riff couldn't help thinking about it now that he was drained and tired, yet no way he dared put any further thought into such a possibility. Still, he knew that, somewhere along the line, they might have missed something. For all they knew those little boys were already buried in the backyard of Jeff's house.

Riff didn't want to stop Jeff's vehicle, only to do a full search and find it empty. He punched his foot down on the gas pedal and moved up closer behind the driver of Jeff's truck, hoping the asshole would finally slow down, but no such luck. And, with no other choice, Riff kept on driving into the night.

And just seconds later, Merk flew past him and immediately pulled to the shoulder.

CHAPTER 15

TARYN WOKE EARLY in the morning and cuddled up tight against her was Cassie. But, of Alex, Taryn had no sign. She heard voices out in the other room. Slowly extricating herself from Cassie's arms, Taryn got up and headed to the bathroom. When she came out, she walked into the living room to find the FBI agents with furiously busy expressions on their faces, making phone calls and talking in clipped tones.

Immediately sensing the tension in the room, Taryn walked over to Alex, who smiled, opened his arms, and gave her a gentle hug. "What's going on?" she asked.

He sighed. "So, the FBI has Uncle Jeff, still in the hospital, and he's talking to some degree. The problem is, he isn't in great shape mentally. We're not exactly sure what's going on, but it looks as if he ended up with a significant drug use habit after his living situation changed drastically, what with his wage-earning sister-in-law passing away and then his brother disappearing on his own kids and Jeff as well—which more or less allowed Jeff to fully develop into the asshole he'd always been on the inside."

She rolled her eyes at that. "And?"

"He sold the little boys."

She stared at him in horror. "Even though they were injured?"

Alex nodded. "Even though injured. Jeff says he told Cassie that somebody was taking the boys to look after them, but, of course, the *looking after* part was definitely dubious wording."

Taryn shook her head. "I can't believe it," she whispered.

"Anyway, the guy who bought the little boys has been informed that we're after him, and he says he's happy to give up the twins, but he wants something in return."

She stared at him, at a complete loss for words. "Giving back both boys is good, but doesn't that mean he still goes to jail?"

"From what I've gathered, he wants a free pass. We get the two little boys, and he gets to walk."

"I presume the little boys are too hot to handle in terms of a commodity for him to move on," Taryn stated harshly.

One of the FBIs agents nodded at her. "Exactly."

"But we want those little boys," she declared, her hard gaze narrowing.

He nodded. "We do, indeed, though the buyer says the boys are okay but have headaches."

She snorted at that. "I highly doubt that they are all that *okay*. And their asshole of an uncle? What will happen to Jeff now?"

The FBI agents were slower to answer her question than Alex.

"He's injured, but not critically so," Alex shared. "He's talking, but not enough. I see a jail cell in his immediate future."

Taryn snorted. "So Jeff's in trouble too, and now will try to figure out how to minimize that impact."

Alex nodded. "I hate to say it, but you're starting to get good at this."

"I don't want to get good at this," she cried out passionately. "I just want to take these kids back to Bruce and let them have a decent life, without living in fear all the time." She frowned at that. "So, what'll happen to Uncle Jeff? Will he try to prevent that?"

"No, he won't get near those kids again. He'll get jail time for sure, just from selling the kids," one of the FBI agents confirmed, turning to her.

She nodded, then realized that Delores wasn't here. Whether she had been moved to another case or was getting a chance to rest or was on a food-and-drink run, Taryn didn't know. However, Delores's absence definitely changed the atmosphere around the hotel room. Taryn turned to Alex. "So, how do we do a trade-off with this unknown buyer?"

"The trouble is, the FBI wants the little boys, but they also want Jeff and this buyer."

"Of course they do," she snapped, glaring at the FBI agents in the room. "That's not fair."

At that, one of the FBI agents faced her. "What makes these children any more important than the next to be sold, and the ones after that?"

She swallowed hard. "And yet those are all nebulous *other children*," she replied hotly. "You don't have any others that you can rescue right at this moment. You also don't know of any future children to rescue that today's process would allow for. I want this piece-of-crap pervert caught as much as anyone, but we can't risk Jack and John in the process."

"We aren't," he stated shortly. "However, if we capture the buyer somehow—or take down the driver who can lead us to the buyer—we offer him a deal. And you can bet he'll be willing to offer up all kinds of other things, once we can get our hands on him—*if* we let him go free."

Taryn groaned. No way to argue with that because this unknown buyer had clearly already proven himself to be a piece of slime who she wanted nothing to do with. Yet the thought of losing John and Jack to the child trafficking system or making them spend one moment with such a horrible person was enough to make Taryn physically ill.

She felt Alex tugging on her gently. She looked over at him and glared. "You're always so reasonable and trying to make me see reason," she muttered, "but I just can't. Not with this."

Alex grimaced. "I'm just trying to do what's best for all of us. And by that I mean, saving those two little boys, who are hurting right now, plus all the future little Jacks and Johns and Cassies out there, by taking another asshole or two off the planet."

"But will the twins' buyer be off the planet?" she asked. "If this goes down, there's still a good chance that he'll work himself free somehow, so he can do it all over again."

"Which is what we're trying to stop," said one of the FBI agents. "So, we set up a deal, only—"

She interrupted him. "Only you lie."

He winced. "Yeah. An unethical part comes into this."

"No," she countered quickly, "there isn't any ethics. Not with guys like this."

The agent nodded. "I'm glad you understand that much at least."

The last part got her hackles up immediately, but Alex hugged Taryn to calm her down.

She sighed and collapsed in his arms. "I need coffee," she announced.

The FBI agent snorted. "You and the rest of us."

"Is that not something we can get delivered?" she asked.

"Somebody's gone on a coffee run already. They should be back soon."

"Well, I hope they bring lots," she muttered. The agent looked over at her, shook his head, then returned to his work. She realized that she wasn't making herself popular, but then again she really didn't give a crap. She was all about getting Jack and John back. She turned to Alex. "Have you heard anything at all about Bruce today?"

"I did talk to Terkel, and Bruce has surfaced a little bit. Every day that he surfaces and talks is a good day," he added. "So remember that."

"And is he …" She hesitated, not sure how to put it.

"Is he all there?" Alex smiled at her. "Yes, he's all there. He understands his name. He knows that he and Royal escaped from a Russian prison. Bruce understands that he is alive and free and why."

She sighed happily. "Good, so all is not lost."

"No, and it's never lost in this instance," Alex stated. "And I know you don't believe it yet, but we are working to help him too."

"Of course I do," she said. "I know that. I do. Everybody's been helping Bruce."

At that, the FBI agents looked over at Alex. "Seriously? He was rescued from a Russian prison?"

Alex nodded. "Yeah, Bruce was being held prisoner. We sent in a small team to rescue his cellmate, who was one of ours. The rescue team ended up getting Bruce out as well. He was in terrible condition, and the rescue itself was pretty arduous but came just in time, as their execution day was set for the following week."

"Jesus," the agent muttered. "Helluva rescue."

Taryn didn't say anything to that, but her sentiment was the same. "The world sucks when you're on the wrong side of whatever asshole is trying to overpower you." She hated to see the world as one where it was all about survival, but it sure seemed to be that way sometimes. She settled back and waited, hoping the coffee would come soon. She realized her fingers were wrapped around Alex's, and he was gently stroking them. She squeezed his hand and sighed. "I'm okay, you know?"

"I was just thinking that," he declared, giving her that same addicting smile again. "Because honestly, you look pretty good for somebody who was knocked out of a tree, drugged, pinballed in the back of a getaway van, then beaten senseless."

"Yeah, thanks for that. You're such a funny man," she muttered. "*Not.*"

He burst out laughing. "Hey, if you can get your sense of humor back, that's worth a lot."

"I don't know if it's worth anything at all when the world is still so sucky," she muttered.

"It absolutely is sucky, but that doesn't mean it has to stay that way."

"That's why I'm fighting so hard to get these kids back to where they belong. It's so not fair that they've had to go through so much already."

"And yet they have people fighting for them. A lot of kids out there don't," he reminded her.

She winced. "That's not fair either." She frowned at him. "I can only help those I know about."

The FBI agent added, "We're trying to help those we know about *and* those we don't know about—the ones lost deep in the underbelly, some of them there for years and years. Believe me that the more you find out about those long-lost ones, you don't even know about yet, but you realize just how many cases are out there, you only wish you'd found out in time to do something."

She sighed. "I get it. I do, but I can't even emotionally begin to think about all those other children. I just know about Jack and John and Cassie, and my head's about to explode as it is. So pardon me, but I'll focus on them because that's something I can do. Everything else … is just too much. Too horrific and too damaging to anybody's sense of well-being," she muttered. "How is it that these assholes even get a chance to live without disintegrating from their own evil before they get a chance to hurt these children?"

"They get the same chance at life as everybody else," began one of the FBI agents. "They just don't want to live as we define it though. They want to do what they want to do, no matter how many people they hurt," he shared, his tone firm. "And we'll continue to do our best to thwart them at every turn."

Just then the door opened, and Delores walked in, carrying trays of coffee and bags of fast food. She smiled at Taryn and said, "Good thing I brought more coffee. I was thinking you might be awake by now."

"Absolutely I am." Taryn walked over to help her. "That's quite a load you brought."

"Well, there's a bunch of us, in case you haven't noticed," she teased.

Taryn noted that same sense of humor from Delores that had seemed so *off* before, but now Taryn understood it was likely a coping mechanism. She smiled and nodded. Then, accepting two coffees, she carried one to Alex.

Delores turned to the male FBI agents. "Okay, you told me to get my ass back here because we had a development. So tell me. What's going on?"

One of the other agents explained about uncovering the potential buyer who had bought the two little boys. He was well-known all over the world and on everybody's watch list to apprehend. Unfortunately nobody knew what he looked like, and he used hundreds of aliases.

"Well, shit," Delores muttered.

"My thoughts exactly," Taryn piped up.

Delores looked over at her and frowned again. "We can't have that."

Taryn listened to the FBI agents as they worked on a plan, but the voltage of her glare increased.

"So, set up a sting, posing as the buyer to pick up the twins from the driver or the middleman or whatever," Delores muttered. "Grab the driver, figure out who the hell he is, then await the buyer's appearance, and nab him next."

"It won't be that easy," said one of the male agents. "This particular buyer is pretty wily, and everybody suspects he's been doing this for quite a while. He's too well versed on how this black-market child trafficking works, so how do we even know he himself will pick up the kids from the driver? What if he calls the driver to circle all around Houston again? We can't make any *get out of jail free* deals with this one. I don't think lying to this one will work."

Just the thought that somebody was so well versed on how to buy children to abuse made Taryn's stomach want to heave. She waited while the FBI agents battled out their next moves. If it didn't go the way Taryn wanted, she would raise all kinds of hell.

Alex understood exactly where she was coming from because he whispered for her to wait. "Just give them a chance."

She glared at him but remained silent.

Delores turned to Taryn. "And, of course, you want us to do everything we can to get the little boys out."

"Of course. And if you had any personal connection to those two little boys, you would want that too."

Delores nodded. "The trouble is, both of us, all of us"—she motioned around the room—"have had way too many scenarios with way too many kids, and we know that, for every one we save, literally hundreds more are kidnapped and sold, who we can't save." Delores sighed in an exhausted way. "So one *normal* predator is worth capturing and releasing to rescue hundreds of kids instead. However, *this* buyer? He goes by many names, but one of his aliases is James Gordon, so that's what we'll call him here. Capturing and releasing Gordon is the equivalent to finding *hundreds of thousands* of kids lost in the black-market underbelly—*only if* we let him go free."

ALEX COMMUNICATED TELEPATHICALLY with Terkel and Riff, asking them when all of them could share their intel, trying to get their own plan ready, while the Feds still worked up one of their own.

Riff called back Alex, conserving his energy by avoiding that telepathic conversation at the moment. "I don't have much to add. I've got Merk with me, driving for now. We are tailing Jeff's truck still, but this driver is really pissing me off. I'm not sure why he's not stopping, just driving around, but I don't like it, and I'll stay on his ass because of it."

Alex replied, "And I don't like that we have no clue who this guy is. Terk has his people ready to run facial recognition, but this driver's shielding his face with a ball cap or a cowboy hat or whatever." Alex frowned and then asked, "Do you think he's got strong instincts?"

"If you really mean *energy abilities*, no way to know. However, if you mean instincts, as in self-preservation, absolutely. All these pervs do. I figure he's another pervert if he's involved in transporting kids. These guys know what happens if they get caught, but they can't resist the urge to keep up their nasty little habits. Unfortunately, most of the time, they risk it and get away with it," he muttered. "But I can't let this guy go, not until I find those little boys."

"And that's the problem we're dealing with right now too. Everybody wants to find Jack and John. Yet they want to take down this driver and promise him no jail time, hoping to find the bigger buyer in the background."

"And that can come at the risk of losing Jack and John," Riff added, "which is the problem we're up against. You know that the Feds will do whatever the hell they want to do, and it won't matter what we say, one way or another."

"That is also what Taryn's finding out the hard way. We've got three agents on the three of us, so you can bet things are pretty dicey over here right now."

Riff snorted. "What a waste of manpower. I'm surprised Taryn hasn't taken them down already."

"She's not quite feeling herself yet. She took some hits physically, between the fall from the tree, the drugs, the rough getaway ride, and the kidnapper beating her. She's a tough nut though. Yet she feels a little touchy now that the Feds are involved, who have made it clear that Taryn has absolutely no legal status where these kids are concerned."

"Oh, crap," Riff muttered sympathetically. "Not my idea of a fun time."

Alex nodded at that. "I get the idea you don't do law enforcement … or any authority at all for that matter."

Riff's tone was way too cheerful as he replied, "Oh, hell no. That's the reason I do the work that I do, so I don't have to deal with those guys."

"We're stuck with three here, but, other than that, I keep my distance." Alex knew all too well that it took someone like Terkel to finesse his fairly-rogue energy workers into something usable.

"I'm staying on this guy for however long it takes," Riff declared. "Oh, and finally now we've pulled into a motel, and, if I find an opportunity to grab those little boys, you can bet I'm taking it."

Alex sucked in his breath. "Just so you know, the Feds will not take kindly to that."

"They want their man though," Riff countered. "So, as long as they get the driver, who can ID the buyer, it'll be cool. I care about those little boys. So, whether the FBI gets their man or not, that should be secondary. I get the basic premise as to why it's important we get this asshole, the driver, and I want him pretty badly myself right now, even if he's some hired courier, some middleman, some lowly lackey—"

"I know," Alex interrupted, "but some money trail should lead us to the buyer. So you're on the same page as we are."

"Because we're all about the people, the ones we can see and can help right now," he muttered. "It's very different to be dealing with them rather than the others we know are out there, and they exist and need help too. Yet it's so much harder to find them, just like any other missing person, whether an adult or a child."

"And ultimately to help them," Alex added, "but, when we do find the ones we can help, we need to step up." And, with that, he rang off, then looked over at Taryn, studying everybody around her, probably trying to figure out what made them tick.

EVERYBODY HERE SEEMED to already be heavily involved in this kind of work, which brought up something Taryn didn't really understand. It was one thing to not have a detailed plan ready if you *weren't* involved in this particular work. That made sense, but, if you, as an FBI agent, *were* involved in this work all the time, why wouldn't you already have procedures and plans in place to make all this happen in short order?

Taryn wasn't sure they had any workable plan at all, and, more than anything else, that worried her.

CHAPTER 16

"**I**'M REALLY SCARED that something'll go wrong." Taryn's heart slammed against her chest, as her nerves took over.

"Well, it could go wrong in all kinds of ways," Alex replied. "Riff's out there keeping a watch on the motel room, so they don't disappear again."

"What if the driver's abusing Jack and John right this minute?" she whispered, her heart breaking.

"Riff said our driver's been glued to the window, staring out, probably fully aware that he's being tracked."

"Whoever the hell he is, what if he gets nervous, sees us coming, then just dumps John and Jack somewhere or sells them fast and someone else takes them away? Maybe the buyer has a fail-safe plan in effect to save his rotten self, should any cops or whatever get too close."

"If the buyer—or his representatives—do anything that renders him empty-handed, he will have given up his most tangible means to negotiate with the FBI." When she just stared at him, not moved at all by that logic, Alex smiled. "I get it. I really do. I am all too aware of our situation, and, as far as you're concerned, no one involved can be trusted. I don't know that you're right or wrong in this instance. I just know that we don't have a whole lot of choices, and this is the FBI's area of expertise, so we've got to at least trust them for that.”

One of the Feds looked over at him and snorted. “*Gee, thanks.*”

Alex shrugged. “Taryn doesn’t have experience with any of this stuff,” he explained, “so what do you expect her to feel? At the moment you guys and the perps hold all the cards, and she’s all about these kids.”

The agent just nodded and didn’t say anything more.

As they kept watching and waiting, a phone rang. All the FBI agents jumped, galvanized into action. Taryn’s eyebrows went up, and Alex placed a finger against her lips and whispered, “It’s probably *him*.” She nodded, wide-eyed, as she listened to the buyer, in a frail wispy computer-generated voice, spelling out his demands. He finished with, “I’ll call back.” Then he quickly disconnected.

“That wasn’t enough time to track him, was it?” Taryn asked.

The Feds looked over at her, and one of them shook his head. “No, it wasn’t.”

“Of course.” Taryn added, “If there’s anything we can do, just let us know.” When they looked at her suspiciously, she shrugged. “I get it. This is your deal, and you’re doing what you can do,” she conceded in a patient voice to stress her point. “However, if you need anybody—for decoys, backup, something, anything at all—just say the word,” she clarified. “I’m prepared to do anything to get those two little boys back.”

They nodded, yet stated, “We can handle it from here.”

She rolled her eyes at that and looked over at Alex. “Can Terkel track this guy if he sneaks away?” she whispered, leaning forward.

“Since we already know where he is, we can use Levi’s

satellite to confirm his movements," Alex explained in a quiet undertone.

Obviously the agents heard that. One of them asked, "But you haven't had any actual confirmed sightings of the twins, have you?"

"No," Alex admitted, "none that you'll listen to."

"Meaning what?" Delores asked, her tone hard.

"Meaning it's Riff and his word. Riff hasn't got any physical evidence. He just has ... that *different* kind of knowledge."

"*Right*," she muttered, "but everything we've heard from Riff so far means that Jack and John are *supposedly* there with the driver, and we should be moving on that with a sting operation."

"And yet we don't have any confirmation that our buyer's there," replied one of the other agents.

Taryn replied, "But you don't have any confirmation that he's *not* there. So far, Riff's in position, and we're not. So Riff's offering a lot better deal than no deal at all."

Delores turned to Taryn and asked her, "Do you really trust him?"

"Absolutely I trust him," Taryn declared. "I trust a lot of things that you guys can't see because I know that Riff's there, and I feel the energy flowing from him to the twins. I know people are at the end of this energy reading," she declared. "You haven't gotten to that point—and may never—so, from your perspective, this is all just intuition or abracadabra moments." Taryn snorted. "And I could talk until I'm blue in the face, but the truth wouldn't make any difference to you just because you can't see it, feel it, or touch it."

"You can't expect us to send anybody there on pure supposition," said one of the male FBI agents, staring at Taryn in surprise.

"Why the hell not? Do you have any better lead?"

"No."

"You've got Riff as a witness, who is right there, who has eyes on the truck that Jeff owns, and you're not even checking it out?" Taryn asked incredulously. The agent flushed, then glanced over at Delores, who frowned at Taryn.

"If we had something other than this woo-woo stuff," Delores stated, "it would be easier."

"Life isn't about *easier*," Taryn snapped. "Life is about living in the moment, and I can tell you that Riff isn't full of shit, and, if he says those two little boys are there, then they are there. Do you honestly think he would have driven all those hours on end making sure he didn't lose that truck if he wasn't sure the twins were inside? I fully expect you guys to at least send in a team. Something is there, and you are duty-bound to check it out."

"If our buyer is there, whether in the room or watching the room, we'll spook the guy," Delores noted, "and we can't take a chance of that happening."

"Well, you need to get your shit together a whole lot faster and get out there, so those two little boys don't go missing again or worse, succumb to their injuries," Taryn declared, her tone ominous. "There is no reason to bow out now. You already know the driver's location. You already heard the buyer's demands," she reminded the agents. "So set up whatever you need to go in there and to get those boys." And, with that, Taryn stormed into the bedroom, slamming the door behind her.

ALEX LOOKED OVER at the others and nodded. "I know you don't think our energy-working skills carry any weight, but I can tell you that Riff is very good at what he does. Plus, if you have any idea what *Terkel's* team used to do for the CIA," he shared, with emphasis on Terkel's name, "then you should realize that Riff works for Terkel, and the only way that would happen is if some of this *woo-woo stuff*, as you call it, is for real."

In a surprise move, one of the agents spoke up. "I don't see how we can avoid checking it out at least. If we had been given this lead by anybody else, we wouldn't have dismissed it," he pointed out. When Delores frowned at him, he just shrugged. "Time is ticking away, and they're right. We need to get those kids out of there. Plus, we really don't know the extent of their injuries."

"What do you propose we do?" Delores asked her fellow agent.

"I think somebody needs to go check it out. Sending in an unmarked car that the driver isn't expecting would be a good start." He frowned at the group. "I think we should probably still set up the sting, so that we're covering all our bases."

"Let me go check it out," Alex suggested. "I can get into the motel, back up Riff, and let you know." He decided to not share how Merk was on site already.

"Let us know what?" Delores asked. "As far as you're concerned, it's already a done deal. The buyer and the kids are supposedly there."

Alex nodded. "At least the driver is there, who could lead us to your infamous buyer. At this point in time, I could probably get those little boys out of there before your guys ever arrived for the sting op," he snapped. "I get that you're just sitting here, waiting for something, maybe for the real buyer to show. I don't see that happening. As your agent said, this guy's cagey. He can probably wait a week, parking his courier and the twins at a different motel each night, just to see if someone is following the driver. This buyer doesn't do things quickly, which doesn't bode well for the chances of survival for these little boys. The longer the twins are there, needing medical attention, the more likely they are to be abused and tormented, even by the driver or visitors who may come by, to the point that Jack and John will never recover," he declared, staring at Delores. "Therefore, so you won't be wasting any of your precious manpower, I can help back up Riff, and we can go in and get John and Jack, tying up the driver too—who would hopefully lead you to Gordon."

"How will you do that? Even if you can get all three, what about the ultimate buyer? You could scare him off, losing control of this op."

"Think about it this way," Alex replied, with a wry smile. "If we do lose control, and it all turns to shit, you get to blame it on us, save your own jobs, and live to do this all over again another day. And, if we do our jobs, and it goes well, you get credit because you were part of the organization behind it. Plus, you get your driver, who must at least have a money trail back to the buyer, and we save the kids. It's a win-win for you, any way you look at it."

Taryn's voice came from the doorway. "And if Alex is going, I'm going."

Cassie's voice added, "If she's going, I'm going. My brothers are hurting," she declared, staring at the agents.

"We have to get them and take them to the hospital."

"When you say, *hurting*, what do you mean, honey?" Delores asked, walking over to the little girl.

"They are crying," she whispered. "They are terrified, hurt, and crying. I'll go do something about it, even if you won't."

Alex looked over at Taryn and Cassie. "I'll go help Riff, and you two stay put right here," he suggested. "We can't take the chance of Cassie getting kidnapped again." When Taryn frowned at him, he nodded. "That's the deal."

"What the hell do you mean, *That's the deal?*" one of the FBI agents asked. "Let me remind you that this is our op."

"That's right," Taryn agreed, walking to the front door of their hotel suite. "The way I understand it, you FBI types are not to leave me alone with Cassie. So, if I leave with her, you must come along too, right? Even if we get there, and you refuse to help John and Jack, Cassie and I will help them."

"Whoa, whoa, whoa, whoa," Delores cried out, scrambling to her feet. "I do have the right to keep you here, and we'll restrain you if needed," she declared, instantly red in the face. "I don't want to go that route, but let me assure you that I can."

At that, one of the other agents piped up. "She's got a point though. They can go check it out and get some confirmation. Hopefully they can get something solid. Meanwhile, we set up a sting and come in a few hours behind them, as soon as we get *valid* confirmation."

"Why is it they won't believe Riff?" Taryn asked, turning to Alex.

He sighed. "Riff has his confirmation, but it's not tangible proof for the FBI."

Taryn nodded. "Sure, because, if he goes any closer, he'll give up his cover, and the last thing he wants is for the driver to take Jack and John on the run again."

"Exactly, which is why the Feds want to set up their sting, but they want proof first. A catch-22 for sure. So the motel is not very far away, just a couple hours. I'll go. I need to relieve Riff," he told Taryn. "I want you to stay here with Cassie. Regardless of what happens, I *will* come back for you, for both of you." When Cassie glared at him, he nodded. "I know. You don't want me leaving either, but we have to go pick up your brothers."

At that she stepped closer to Taryn and nodded. "Fine. I'll let them know you're coming." And, with that, she turned and walked into her bedroom.

Delores frowned from Alex to Taryn to the bedroom and asked, "What did she just say? What does that mean?"

"She's connected to her brothers telepathically," Taryn stated in a very cool tone. "She's been in communication with them off and on, but they haven't been very coherent or very conscious and can't speak properly because of their head injuries. That's why Cassie's been so worried. Now she'll tell them that Alex is on the way."

"Jesus Christ." Delores shook her head, as she glanced from Taryn to the men on her team and back again. "What the hell do we do with this woo-woo stuff?"

"At this point, I say we go with it," suggested one of the agents in exasperation. "They're right. We can always toss it off as them being difficult." He sent a smile toward Alex. "Let's take what we can and go with it."

"Okay then, fine," Delores muttered, raising her hands in mock surrender, while she turned and glared at Alex. "We'll put into play the sting op"—she shot a glance at her watch—"in six hours. You've got that long to get there and to get us confirmation that you guys are where we need you to be."

"I just need two and a half hours though, so move up that sting op." Alex grabbed his coat and took his coffee, snagging a couple breakfast sandwiches from the table. "I'll contact you in 150 minutes or less." Then he stopped to address Delores. "Better watch out for those two gals. They're priceless, and they're cagey."

And, with that, he was gone.

CHAPTER 17

Taryn sat down with a cup of coffee, as Cassie curled up beside her. Both of them had eaten and were now on Alex's laptop, wasting time on the internet, looking for anything that would make this go faster for them. But, so far, nothing was working.

Cassie once again looked over at her. "Did you hear from Alex?"

"No, not yet," she replied. "You and I both know that, as soon as he can tell us something, he will."

Cassie just nodded and didn't say anything.

"What about your brothers?" Taryn asked, repeating the same questions they had been trading back and forth time and time again.

"Nothing. John and Jack are out cold."

Taryn nodded.

The Feds kept looking at them sideways, almost as if they had timers on them going off every time Taryn and Cassie brought up anything that could be construed as woo-woo stuff. Each time the agents got an odd look on their faces.

Taryn couldn't imagine what it was like to live without at least some understanding of that innate level of intuition in all human beings, even in animals. She felt this to be true, even for humans who weren't energy workers. Regardless, these Feds seemed to have no problem sticking to their outdated notions as to what they believed and what they didn't.

At one point Cassie stated suddenly, "Uncle Jeff is waking up."

Taryn smiled down at her. "That's very good news," she replied. "And, in case you were wondering, your uncle is in the hospital, under guard, and he won't be getting out of jail for a very long time."

Cassie stared up at her, her eyes filled with an inner knowing. "He won't get out at all," Cassie noted calmly.

One of the Feds asked her, "Why do you say that?"

But Cassie didn't respond to him.

A little later Taryn whispered to Cassie, "Meaning, Uncle Jeff will die in prison?"

Cassie nodded. "He's a very bad man."

"That's very true," Taryn agreed, her voice soft. "I'm so sorry you had to live through that."

"He wasn't always a bad man," she whispered. "Only since my mommy died. Except that once."

"That's because your mom was such a beautiful angel, so maybe it was hard for your uncle Jeff to deal with the loss."

Cassie gave her a small smile and whispered, "I hope so."

"Jeff's life won't be very pleasant from now on, so that is his punishment for being so awful to you and your brothers." After that exchange, they didn't bring up the topic of Jeff again for a while.

It belatedly occurred to Taryn how these woo-woo discussions with Cassie could create a whole new problem she had to consider.

She needed to assume that any conversation she had out loud with Cassie could possibly go against them whenever a judge was involved in granting custody. Frowning, she sent Cassie a telepathic message, asking her to keep quiet about certain topics, just in case they decided that Taryn shouldn't go to England with Cassie. The little girl just shifted in her seat and stared, looking puzzled. Taryn gave Cassie a gentle smile, then, speaking telepathically, filled her in on the problem.

Remember that they don't understand this special stuff that we can do. So we need to choose carefully what conversations we have out loud and when to keep our discussions just between us.

Cassie looked around at the others, as if unsure why that would be.

Taryn explained further, *They can't hear us when we talk like this because they don't talk like you and your brothers do.*

My mom and I did too, she added telepathically.

That makes it even harder to lose her then, doesn't it?

She nodded, tears coming to her eyes. *I really miss her.*

I'm so sorry, sweetheart. Your world got flipped upside down when she died.

At Cassie's crying, one of the agents looked over at the child, but asked Taryn, "Does she understand what happened?"

Taryn gave him a flat response. "You tell me. She is a child. Her mom is dead. Her father abandoned them to her uncle Jeff, who is going to prison. Meanwhile, her uncle Bruce is recovering from torture at a Russian prison, and her brothers are missing. What do you think?"

He nodded and didn't say anything. Yet he cast Taryn a raised eyebrow.

She frowned back at him, wondering what he was thinking.

He finally asked, "How did her mother die anyway?"

"We're not sure. It's something to check into further. I was told it was a car accident."

He nodded. After a moment, he seemed to have considered it a bit and returned his attention to researching something.

Cassie shifted in Taryn's arms and asked, "Are there any movies? Is there any snack food or anything?"

"Do you mean, anything to take your mind off this?" Taryn asked. "We are getting there, although it doesn't seem like it. However, we do trust in Alex," she reminded the little girl.

"I know," Cassie replied, "and he's a good man." Then she looked up at Taryn and giggled. "He likes you."

"That's good to hear."

In the onslaught of the childhood giggles that followed, Cassie added, "I like him too. And he really likes you a lot, Taryn."

Taryn tapped the child on the nose, and Cassie gave a smile that was once again that of a happy, innocent child. "Good, because I really like him too," Taryn stated in a firm tone. "And that will be enough of that discussion, young lady."

Cassie burst into laughter. "Ooh, you really like him then, don't you?"

"Yeah, I really do," she admitted, with an eye roll. "I get it. We're back to being a child again, but could we potentially change the subject anyway?"

One of the Feds interjected, "Hey, it's the most fascinating subject we've heard in a while." He gave her a smirk. "It helps to keep away the boogeyman."

Taryn nodded. "Yes, you've got a good point there," she muttered, looking back at the little girl. Cassie was happy now that everything had shifted in her own brain. She was now searching for possible movies to watch online. With a fresh cup of tea, Taryn sat back and focused on sending as much healing energy as she could to Bruce and now to Jack and John, hoping that at least one of them could utilize whatever made its way to them.

She wasn't even aware how any of this worked, but she figured that the human body, as miraculous as it was, had to have a fail-safe and could accept whatever energy was coming its way and put it to good use. At least she hoped so. She couldn't stand the thought of doing nothing, so doing something would at least serve to make her feel not quite so useless.

Her phone rang ten minutes later, and everybody froze. She didn't recognize the number so answered it cautiously. "Hello?"

"Yeah, it's me," Alex confirmed. "I've got a burner phone."

"Okay," she said, looking around at the others. "Gosh, my phone ringing has never had so much attention."

He snorted. "Not the good kind either, I'm sure."

"Probably not," she agreed, with half a smile. "Are you there?"

"I am, and I've connected with Riff, who is taking twenty minutes to power up. Then we'll go take a look. Tell the Feds to get ready to move."

"Okay, I'll let them know."

And, with that, he disconnected.

"He's there. Riff is taking twenty for a power break, and then they'll do some reconnaissance. He'll send word when he has something to share. He wants you to get ready to move."

"*Great,*" Delores replied testily. "I guess Riff's not super-human after all."

"I think he pretty well is. Everybody needs a power nap every now and then. So I don't think fifteen or twenty minutes is asking very much, not when he's been driving for twenty-eight hours straight," she shared.

Delores shook her head. "You're the one who was dying to get the twins out of there *right now.*"

"And it's *finally* happening. Alex and Riff will rescue John and Jack very soon, so it's all good." Then Taryn waited for everybody to return their attention to their laptops.

As soon as Taryn relaxed and sensed Riff in her mind, along came Alex, not to mention Cassie. Taryn shared, *If the four of us work together, we could probably do something about this.*

Riff replied, *Yeah, we usually do it that way, but I'm used to having trained people, not family and friends.*

Well, you've got what you've got, Taryn declared. *Surely I would be better than nothing.*

He didn't say anything at first, then added in a clipped tone, *Surely you would. I suggest you keep this channel open, and we'll let you know more as we move in. It wouldn't hurt either if Cassie wanted to talk Jack and John through this process either.* And, with that, he seemed to leave.

Taryn felt a surge of energy and actually saw Cassie's energy weaving through hers, forming a trail to connect to the little boys.

Cassie shared with Taryn, *Jack and John are on the second floor, in the second bedroom, and are unconscious.*

Taryn called out to her guys, *Cassie's already in contact with the boys, in the second bedroom in a motel room on the second floor, but both boys are unconscious.*

That was a nice surprise to everyone.

We've got this, Riff replied. *Now butt out, don't distract us, so we can do our thing.* And, with that, he closed the door firmly and shut them both out.

She still felt the presence of Alex, who added, *We'll check back in a bit.*

She turned to Cassie. The little girl stared at her with both hope and fear in her eyes. "It'll be okay, honest."

Almost immediately the Fed nearest to her asked, "What the hell is going on? What are they doing, and how the hell are you even aware that they're doing anything?"

She turned and stared at him with her best incredulous expression, then stated in a flat tone, "As far as I know, you heard my phone ring as much as I did. I'm just reassuring Cassie that it'll all be okay." She shook her head. "God," she exclaimed, as she rolled her eyes, then sank back onto the couch. "When they call—which they will … and hopefully soon—you'll know at the same time as I will."

She then directed her energy to Cassie. *Wake me up if anything happens.* She closed her eyes, as if to fall asleep. Instead, she reached out with everything she had to soothe those two boys and their sister.

The question now was whether these agents would sit back and wait some more, or if the gals would have to save the twins.

RIFF AND ALEX were together in a nearby copse of trees, right beside the motel. Merk was up on the roof of a motel to the north of them, happy to have a bird's-eye view. Not wanting anyone to overhear them, they spoke telepathically, even with Merk, who still claimed to all that he had no energy-working skills.

Interesting partner you've got there, Riff noted, with a smirk. *Didn't know she had this level of abilities.*

I don't think she knew it either, Alex acknowledged, *and it seems to be growing, the more she's with Cassie.*

Yep, just like when you get energy workers together in Terk's castle, enhancing each other, but that little girl appears to already be quite strong and talented herself.

Apparently Cassie and her brothers communicated like this a lot.

That should make this easier, except for the fact that she's very aware her brothers are not awake. So she's pretty freaked out and worried about it.

I would be too, Alex replied. *Nobody could argue the love between siblings or family members who cared deeply about each other, but particularly with children who bonded together over the loss of their mother and the abandonment of their father, followed by an abusive uncle, beating them into compliance.*

As they moved closer to the motel, Riff shared, *Our driver's on the second floor too. Seems to be looking out the windows still. You know the room number. I'll go to the back, will enter through the bathroom window. You stay front and center.*

Yeah, I'm thinking about walking right up and knocking on the door.

What will you say to him?

I might let my fists do the talking.

Riff smirked. *Pretty sure that's not FBI protocol.*

Pretty sure I don't give a fuck either, Alex snapped.

As Riff disappeared around the back, Alex waited, keeping to himself and looking for the signal that Riff was in position. Meanwhile, his cell vibrated. He ignored it. But when more vibrations came in a row, he knew he had to at least take a quick look at his phone. *Guys, stand down for a moment. We got something. I'm forwarding two texts to you and to Taryn. Confirm with me when you finish reading them.*

Holey-moley, Merk replied.

Need to know, my ass, Riff stated with glee.

Can I tell Delores? Taryn asked. *You gotta let me do this, guys.*

Alex replied, *Let's put it to a vote. Yays or Nays.* And he heard three yays and added his own to it.

TARYN GOT A couple texts, the sounds like a ticking clock in their hotel room, which brought everyone's attention to her. She read them once more, smiling broadly.

Meanwhile, Delores was demanding to know what the hell was going on and complaining about the lack of communication again.

Taryn couldn't help but smirk as she faced Delores. "The original plan has now been expanded, due to some brand-new intel. First, Alex and Riff take down the driver. Second, Alex and Riff get Jack and John to the nearest hospital. Third, Alex and Riff get the driver to confess, especially any info about your elusive James Gordon. Fourth, the FBI talks to Levi." Taryn's smile just got bigger. "Levi's team has been doing a forensic deep dive into the black market, comparing notes with an international group of hackers, specifically following these illegal sales of children. They may have found some money trails leading to James Gordon. What with all his criminal activities, surely somebody can find a pattern here. No promises, but it's worth taking a good long look at, and Levi is willing to share this information with the FBI and other overseas governments. Fifth, the FBI speaks to Terk. Terk's team has worked up a profile for the man that Levi is tracking monetarily. Most likely James Gordon or someone of his ilk. Terk will share their findings as well. But the bottom line is, Terk thinks Gordon has *gifts*."

Delores frowned. "Do I want to know what that means?"

Taryn laughed out loud. "I think you already know what that means."

The two male agents shared a knowing look. "Gordon is psychic too?"

"Yep," Taryn declared loudly. "Which also means that the three of us you have sidelined all this time are now necessary to your op, with a compelling *need to know*."

Delores snapped at Taryn, "Let me see those texts." She frowned as she read them, probably twice. Then she went silent for a bit too long before she finally spoke again. "I'll make some phone calls." She walked out into the hallway, leaving Taryn smiling behind her.

IMMEDIATELY THEREAFTER, ALEX got the birdcall from Riff. So Alex walked up the steps, then quickly knocked on the door in question.

A surprisingly small man opened the door, frowning at him.

Alex smiled. "Hey, I heard a guy could purchase something special here." Immediately, he knew this guy had some energy skills. No wonder he was getting away from the authorities.

The other man stared at him nervously. "I don't know what the hell you're talking about."

Alex sent off a quick telepathic message to Riff and Terk. *This guy is playing the rube, but my bets are all in that he's the buyer, might even be James Gordon. He's paranoid and a control freak too, which matches the profile.* Alex rubbed his hands together, as he continued to play his part. "Not that I usually do this face-to-face, but I understand you're in a bit of trouble and maybe need to make a quick deal. In the interest of time, I'll just cut to the chase and say that I'm prepared to offer cash and take the twins."

The other man stared at him, backing up slightly. His gaze screamed bloody murder. "You get the hell out of my space and leave me alone. No kids are here."

Alex called out, "Hey, Jack and John, are you here?"

When no answer came, the other man snorted. "See? Told you no kids are here. Now get the hell away from me, freak." As he went to shut the door, Alex made sure his foot was in the center, just so it wouldn't close. "Get out," the perp muttered, "or I'll start yelling."

"Oh, now that would be great," Alex agreed. "Could you do that for me, please? I really want the cops to look at this room."

He cried out, "Leave me alone. Just get out of here. You don't know anything."

"I know too damn much about this." Alex snorted. "Too damn much about slugs like you infesting the world. And, no, I'm not the FBI agent you contacted to make a deal." He gave the guy a sneer. "I don't really give a shit about making deals. I'm just here to tell you that those boys are coming with me, whether you like it or not."

Gordon blinked several times, not sure what he was supposed to do. Then it looked as if he was about ready to cry.

Alex smiled at him again. "And you'll also tell me everything I need to know about everybody else in your lovely little circle of sickos."

"I'm just a middleman, a courier," he wailed.

Alex pulled his phone from his pocket, then put it on Record, totally ignoring the perv's lies. "Let's bring the Feds in to find out about *everything* you've got to say. I hear you're a pretty big fish too, so you must have *lots* to say."

"That's coercion," Gordon muttered. "That's against the law."

Alex smiled at him, knowing that, as soon as he wanted, Riff would make this man's life miserable. Meanwhile, Alex would do his best to make this pervert squirm right now. "Look forward to spending your life in a small cell, with bars and no window and where everybody else can watch you take a dump and where you never get a good night's sleep. Not unlike the way these children get treated, right?"

Gordon stared at Alex in horror. "What are you talking about?" he cried out. "Who are you? What are you doing here? Surely this is against the law."

"It doesn't matter who I am," Alex replied. "I came for those two little boys, and I'm not leaving without them." With that, he was about to poke Gordon in the chest, yet making no contact whatsoever with Gordon, caused him to step backward. The man looked around, as if seeking help, and, when he turned, Riff was right behind him.

The man's fear level was palpable at this point.

"Look at that, will ya?" Alex told Riff. "This guy seems to think that some coercion is going on here."

With a flip of his hand, Riff sent a probe to hit Gordon.

The man cried out, "My spine! Stop it! My spine!"

Alex shook his head. "We haven't touched you. See? … I've got it all on video, right here. Obviously, you've got some issues, maybe from drugs?" he asked. "So now that you're going to prison, we can get you some help, get you clean and sober."

Gordon started to cry and blubbered away. "You guys leave me alone. Just leave me alone."

"Why? Why should we leave you alone when two little boys are in that room, both of them hurting?"

"I didn't hurt them. I didn't touch them," he wailed, almost on the verge of hysteria. "That was their uncle."

"Yeah, don't worry. Uncle Jeff is already in custody," Alex confirmed, his tone hardening. "That's another sicko who doesn't deserve to see daylight."

Gordon went silent.

Alex decided to add some lies of his own. "And we have Jeff's brother too."

"You've got him?" he asked, his voice quivering.

"He's in custody with Jeff, and guess what?" Alex left it unsaid, looking at Riff.

Riff nodded. "You're next for prison." Riff was clearly enjoying this.

"No, no, no. I didn't do anything. I'm looking after the boys. They need help."

"Yeah, those boys need help all right, yet you didn't take them to a hospital, did you?"

"I can't. I'm not their uncle, but their uncle told me to get help for them. Only afterward did I realize how it would look."

"God," Alex muttered, looking over at Riff. "See how

he'll try and spin it?"

Riff tilted his head. "That's okay." Riff walked closer to the perp.

"You can't hit me. You can't. Then anything you get out of me, that's coercion," Gordon blubbered, "and anything I say can't be used against me."

Alex shook his head. "Amazing how much he seems to know about the law. Are you an attorney, Gordon?"

He was too busy sidestepping Riff to respond to Alex's question.

"Gordon, you are right, my man. I probably can't hit you," Riff admitted, sounding disinterested as he walked past the perp, then stood behind him. "I won't touch you at all." Then he sent another probe up and down the man's spine.

With a shriek, Gordon spun around. "What was that?"

Riff sighed. "Just the screams of a little psycho bitch, whining about your future, a future you already knew would come your way someday. It's called karma," Riff explained, with a laugh. "Looks as if the reality of all this crap you've been doing to kids is catching up to you."

"Not me. No way."

"What? You didn't know this is how you would end up?"

"Of course not. How would I? I'm just the middleman," Gordon repeated, staring around the room, avoiding turning to make eye contact with Riff. "Please, please, please, don't do that anymore. Whatever you're doing, please don't."

"Start talking," Riff stated. "If you talk, we'll consider the information, but other than that? Oh, hell no."

"What guarantees do I have that you won't turn me in to the Feds?"

"No guarantees whatsoever," Riff declared. "Absolutely

none. Yet I can tell you that I won't give you to the Feds, but my partner might. ... Plus, we can get you some real help, ... if you talk." Riff again twisted his wrist midair.

"They won't help me," Gordon shrieked, as if he were in too much pain. "Nobody can help me."

"Then you better sit down and start talking to us," Riff noted, "or you might just feel some more of ... What was it that is bothering you today?"

"Ghostly things, but I don't know what the hell it even is," Gordon muttered, looking around nervously. "You guys stay where you are."

"Sure," Alex replied, with a smile to Riff, who once again sent a probe to Gordon, who shrieked yet again.

"Okay, okay, okay. I'll talk." Then he opened his mouth, and the story that came from the dark recesses of this sick man's brain made both Riff and Alex sick to their stomachs. Thirty minutes later they had it all recorded, and Alex sent the recording to Delores, one of the FBI agents at the hotel, and then he phoned her.

"We have Gordon in custody," he told her, his tone filled with disgust, "and listen to the attached recording of his initial confession. I would suggest you have a barf bag nearby. If you're lucky, he might even still be alive by the time you get here."

"Don't you touch him, dammit. You'll screw up the case. Don't touch him," Delores warned.

"We haven't touched him at all, and he'll prove it, as well as our video."

Alex stood in the front room, one eye on Gordon and the other on Riff, who went to the second bedroom and checked out the little boys. He telepathically shared his findings with Alex, also asking Terk to call in an ambulance for the boys.

"And the twins?" Delores asked.

"Hurt, and they need a hospital, so that's where we're going. Do me a favor and bring the gals with you, when you pick up your pervert, will you?" And, with that, he disconnected, then looked over at Riff. "It's a sick world out there."

"It *is* a sick world," Riff confirmed calmly, "but today the good guys won a round. Just one round, not the war, but we gotta take the successes where we can. These little boys will get whatever help they need, and they'll live to see another day. ... That's the best we can hope for in this situation."

"We've got Uncle Bruce healing, and we've saved his niece and nephews," Alex noted, "and everybody will have a chance for a future they didn't have even ten minutes ago."

"Here's the ambulance," Riff said. "Let's get these little guys to the hospital. How about you follow the ambulance, while I keep our friend Gordon here entertained until the FBI comes to get him."

Alex nodded. "Will do. What about Merk? You want him to hang around?"

"*Nah*, I got this. Cut him loose."

And, with that, Alex sent a text to Merk, then directed the ambulance crew to Jack and John, and they were soon on their way to the nearest hospital.

CHAPTER 18

TARYN LOOKED UP from where she sat in the visitor's chair and sighed. Cassie was on the hospital bed beside her brothers, holding their hands, as Alex walked in again. Hopping to her feet, Taryn raced into his arms and held him close. "Thank you, thank you, thank you," she whispered into his ear.

He just smiled and nodded.

"Are you in trouble with the FBI?" she asked, pulling back enough to see his face.

"Always, but who cares? It was the right thing to do. And, since they got their man, Gordon, I think the Feds are just fine right now."

"It *was* the right thing to do. No doubt about that. I still don't get the hesitancy on the part of the Feds."

He smiled at her. "The FBI has its own internal rules and gets territorial. From the beginning, they more or less ordered us to stay out of it and to stay away, and I didn't want to get Levi or Terkel in trouble over this deal. We do try to work within their rules and those of the local authorities—somewhat. Yet, after too much waiting on the part of the FBI, even Terk and Levi were also of the opinion to just go with our instincts and get something done." He rolled his eyes at her. "That led Terk and his team to work up that spot-on profile, as Levi and his team coordinated with an international group of super-hackers to find some very interesting money trails. And it's all good."

"It's better than good," she agreed, with a sigh. "Two bad guys have been captured—well, three now that the missing father turned up, wanting his half of the sales proceeds. Can you believe that?"

Alex could very well believe it, and now the lie he told Gordon had turned into the truth. "Plus more bad guys to find and arrest, per Gordon's statement." Alex smiled. "But the best of all news is that we have these little boys here, finally getting some medical attention. The doctors say John and Jack will both be just fine, but they're keeping them for a bit. Both boys had a nasty crack on the side of their heads, definitely skull fractures," he muttered, looking at the twins, sedated but breathing just fine. "Both are pretty pale, but definitely some energy is moving in the air."

"You've got that right." Taryn laughed. "It's Cassie. She's connected with them," Taryn declared proudly, with a beaming smile.

"Has either one woken up at all?" Alex asked.

She nodded. "Yes, both surfaced a little bit, then went right back under, but it was enough for Cassie to let them know that they were okay, that they were in the hospital, and that good people were looking after them. Believe me when I say that John and Jack were relieved."

"Good." He stared over at the three united kids. "That has to be a pretty special bond among them."

"It is," she murmured. "Yet it's also one forged in pain, and I wouldn't wish that on anybody."

"No, of course not." He hugged her gently and asked, "You want to go for a coffee?"

She hesitated, then looked back at Cassie and Jack and

John. "I don't want to leave them," she murmured.

He nodded. "I get that you'll probably be like that for a while."

"I probably will. How can I not be, until I hand them safely over to Bruce?" she asked, with a smile.

Alex nodded. "Speaking of Bruce, have you heard anything from him at all?"

She nodded. "Not from Bruce himself," she clarified, "but I did hear from Terkel that Bruce is awake, and they've had a chance to really talk to him. He knows about his sister's death and that we've got the kids and will be bringing them his way. He doesn't know all the other horrid details though."

"Good, that's a bit much for anybody to assimilate all at once," he murmured.

"That is what I thought too," she agreed, "though I don't want to keep anything from him."

"You can tell him later," Alex suggested, "after he's had a chance to deal with what he's learned so far. Keep in mind that he's already got a lot to deal with from his own captivity."

She winced at that. "God, people suck," she muttered.

Alex burst out laughing. "Yeah, some people suck," he conceded, still smiling. "Yet other people are great." Then he squeezed her tightly to his chest.

She looked up at him, laughing, then threw her arms around his neck and just clung to him for a bit. "I don't know how to thank you," she murmured.

"You don't have to thank me," he whispered. "Helping kids? ... Well, it's special. It's what we do."

"I know. To even have the opportunity to do something like that? ... Well, it's why I told Terkel that I wanted to help."

Alex raised his eyebrows at her. "You did?"

She nodded. "And I meant it, though I don't know how or what I can do," she admitted. "It's not as if I really have any idea what I can do, but I sure want to do something."

"What did Terk say?"

"That we would talk about it when we get to his place," she replied absentmindedly.

"Well, that's good. And you're okay to go to England?"

"There's no *okay* about it," she declared. "I'm going because Bruce is over there, and because I've got the kids, of course. Now, *staying* over there, that's a whole different story. Yet Bruce will need some help for a while anyway, not just for him but for these children."

"He sure will," Alex agreed, with a nod. "I can't imagine waking up from what he's been through, only to find out he's suddenly got three kids to raise."

She laughed. "But he'll take it all in stride."

"Sounds like a nice guy," Alex noted. "I'm looking forward to meeting him."

"You'll love him," she stated. "He really is one of the good guys in the world."

He smiled at her. "In that case, I definitely want to meet him."

She didn't say anything for a moment but looked up at him. "When are we going anyway?"

"You tell me," he said, moving her away from the children. In a low tone, he asked, "Do you want to dive right into Terk's world, or would you like to have a weekend away with me first?"

"Well, that's definitely a yes to both," she said. "We will be hindered with paperwork before we can fly across the pond, right?"

He laughed. "We absolutely will be."

"And," she added softly, "the doctor said the boys will remain here at least a week or two, right?"

He gave her a smoldering smile. "Yes."

"So you and I and Cassie can take off a weekend here in the States, right?"

Alex smirked and tapped her on the nose. "You had me going. Yes, we three can have our weekend here in the US. After we are all in England, maybe you and I can have that special solo weekend?"

"You got it. Not immediately, but not too far off into the future either. I don't want to leave Bruce in the lurch."

"I understand," he murmured. Then he walked over to the hospital bed and looked down at Cassie. She opened her eyes, smiled at him, and reached up her arms, so he could give her a big hug. "Hey, little one," he whispered. "How are you doing?"

"Better now," she whispered. "Jack and John are waking up too."

At that, Alex turned to the twins.

Taryn checked Jack and John, their eyes opening, staring at her, puzzled. "Hey there," she murmured. "How are you doing?"

The boys blinked, then saw their sister, and immediately a connection of love and relief washed over the twins as their sister gave them a hug. Not too many dry eyes were in the room now, as they realized just how close and connected these three children were.

"It is pretty special," Alex murmured.

"Very," Taryn whispered at his side. "I still can't quite believe it."

"But, hey, it's all good. This is what was meant to happen."

She didn't say anything, her tears falling, and just nodded.

When the doctor finally came, he let them stay for a little bit longer, then explained that, since he would be running some tests, they should probably just take off for a while and come back a bit later to visit again.

Taryn looked over at Cassie, who was yawning, then asked Alex, "Do we have a hotel or anyplace to even go?"

"Yeah, I've got a hotel room already booked for us," Alex replied. "I suggest we all head over there and get some rest. Riff is over there sleeping right now."

"In that case, yes, let's go," Taryn agreed.

And, with the three of them in a rental vehicle that she didn't recognize but presumed was Alex's, they headed to the new hotel. As they walked inside the hotel lobby, Taryn held Cassie's hand. "This brings back memories. What about the FBI?"

"Oh, they'll be here to talk to you soon enough, don't worry."

She rolled her eyes at that. "Well, that's *great*," she muttered. "I was hoping they would be long gone."

He pushed the button on the elevator, and the door opened, and they all stepped inside. "No, there are still lots of questions. They are struggling right now, tying up loose ends and all that good stuff," he explained, "but it's not bad news. Not for us."

"If you say so," she muttered, with an eye roll. "It seems as if a lot of this is bad news, no matter which way you look at it."

He just smiled and waited for the elevator to open. He

brought them out into the hallway and led Taryn and Cassie into their hotel room. As soon as they got inside, Taryn noted it was a suite, with multiple bedrooms.

Cassie, having shaken off any remnants of her old reserved self, raced through the place and quickly claimed a bedroom of her own. Then she looked back at the others and announced simply, "I'm going to bed." And, without any argument from them, she headed to the bedroom, closed the door, then opened it again and shook her head. "I guess maybe I should leave it open."

"I think leaving it open is a good idea for now," Alex agreed, with a smile. "I would feel very cut off from you if you closed that door."

Cassie gave him a grateful smile for letting her off the hook, then headed back inside.

Taryn smiled at him. "Look at that. You already have a built-in radar for that sort of thing, which makes you totally father material."

He shook his head, frowning. "I don't think so. I don't have any experience. It's just called being human."

"Ah, but it's more than that. It's called being a *nice* human," she whispered.

He smiled. "It shouldn't be a hardship to be nice, particularly to children," he noted. "It's a sick world when that's the way it is."

"We already know it's a sick world," she pointed out, "but we won't dwell on it."

"I'm glad to hear you say that." He pointed to the nearby bedroom, its door closed. "Riff is asleep in this room, but there's still another bedroom, if you want to go rest."

She pondered it, then shook her head. "No thanks. Now, if we were alone, maybe, but like this? No."

He raised one eyebrow. "Why would being alone make a difference?"

Walking closer to him, she threw her arms around him and gave him a big kiss.

He stared at her in surprise, and then his face cracked into a big smile.

"I might follow up on that if we were alone," she muttered.

"You want me to chase people out of the bedrooms?" he teased. "I did say there was an empty one."

"Yeah, but they would know."

"Well, Cassie wouldn't care, and Riff already expects it."

She stared at him in shock. "Riff what?"

Alex chuckled. "Riff already knows what the deal is," he stated, with a knowing smile. "So, I just don't think it's a problem. Not for him."

She pondered that and then added, "I think it would still bother me to know that people would hear us." Then she shook her head. "On the other hand, I would really like to take a shower." She turned and looked back at him with a sexy grin. "Join me?"

"Hell yes," he said, then stopped. "Although that could be torture if it's really a shower you want."

"It would be torture," she agreed. "I really do want a shower, but, if we get lucky while we're at it, I won't complain," she clarified, with a waggle of her eyebrows.

And, with that, she ran to the third bedroom and into the attached bathroom. She turned on the water to give them a little bit more privacy. She wasn't lying. She really did want a shower, and a clean change of clothes, if such a thing was possible. If she got a chance to sleep a bit as well, she wouldn't argue.

Seconds later, she was nude and stepping under the water. When she turned around, Alex was climbing in behind her. She smiled as he picked up the bar of soap.

"If you want to do my hair that would be lovely," she whispered, "but other than that, I can manage."

"I've got the hair too," Alex stated easily, putting the soap down for the moment and picking up the little shampoo bottle. By the time Alex had her hair scrubbed and her scalp clean, Taryn turned around and did the same for him. She almost felt normal again. Of course, being in that hot shower with that incredibly sexy male body was a whole different story. She picked up the bar of soap and turned, smiling at him as she again waggled her eyebrows.

He rolled his eyes and chuckled, with a smile that just burned through her. "It sure won't be easy to stay quiet in here."

"Are you serious?" she asked. "You can't be quiet?"

"Are you sure you could?"

She didn't answer that question and just started at his chest with the bar of soap and worked her way down to his hips. Of course his manhood was already standing proud and firm in front of her. She smiled, as she slipped her hand around it and stroked up and down, the soap creating a smooth silky finish. He sucked in his breath, his hands on the shower walls over her head, closing his eyes as he enjoyed her ministrations.

She reached up and kissed him, her tongue loving his as they gently warred, their lips fused together in heated kisses, until she accidentally dropped the bar of soap.

He quickly retrieved it from the shower floor and chuckled, still in a crouched position. "My turn," he teased, looking up at her. Then he started at her ankles and slowly soaped his way up, stopping with a gentle caress at the V of her thighs, before sliding a finger between her legs, inserting one slowly inside.

She shuddered, her legs going wide, and she leaned against the back wall. "I never thought it would be so easy to lose one's self in a shower," she whispered. "But to feel as if I'll have my feet slide out from under me? … That is something else."

He straightened, lifted her up, and gently pinned her against the wall, all too conscious of the bruises and abrasions that covered her body. "I've got you," he murmured, kissing her deeply, flesh to flesh, chest against chest, his erection prodding her belly. "And, of course, from here, we're in the perfect position." He shifted ever-so-slightly, sitting right at the heart of her and then slipped inside just a bit.

She wiggled against him, as he dropped his head against her cheek, whispering, "God help me." She immediately increased her wiggling, her thighs tightening around his hips, his hands sliding down to grab her butt cheeks, as she whispered, "Do it. Just do it." But he held back, kissing her softly, over and over again. "Damn it, why aren't you doing it?" she panted.

He lifted his head and faced her. "Look at me."

When she opened her eyes to stare up at him, he lowered his head and kissed her softly. As his tongue slid inside, he slowly slipped into her body and rammed right to her center. She shuddered, impaled against the wall and completely overwhelmed at his possession of her. She wrapped her arms around his neck, shuddering, the ripples completely overtaking her body as they started to move, and she knew she was in for it.

She came apart in his arms almost immediately. By the time he exploded deep inside her, she was still pulsating from her own climax, only to have him do the same thing all over again. When they finally stopped moving, he turned off the shower, slid open the glass door, grabbed a towel, and wrapped her up in it, before carrying her to the bed. He laid her down gently, then returned to the bathroom and grabbed another towel, wrapping it around his waist.

When he rejoined her in the bedroom, she sat there, smiling up at him, looking bemused. He sat down beside her and whispered, "Are you okay?"

She nodded. "But I am feeling really tired now."

He nodded too. "Sleep," he whispered. Then he stretched out beside her, still wet, both still naked under their towels, as he pulled her into his arms and repeated, "Sleep."

She closed her eyes and slept.

CHAPTER 19

S EVERAL WEEKS LATER, with the kids laughing and giggling at her side, Taryn got off the plane and looked around at the tarmac. She expected to see Alex, or at least she hoped to. He'd told her that he would be there to pick them up. He'd gone back to England a little earlier to set up living accommodations for her and the kids. She was desperately hoping that she would see Bruce too. He'd gotten stronger, and, as soon as he'd woken up enough to realize what was going on, it had been a fight to keep him in bed. He'd been so adamant about healing as fast as he could.

She had hoped he might be here at the airport with Alex, but she would totally understand if he wasn't. As she disembarked, she was busy keeping the kids together, as they wanted to run and play, actions that she completely approved of, considering everything they'd been through. Jack and John were doing just fine now. Both boys had healed, but these head injuries would still be a concern for her every time she saw them.

Yet Jack and John were really doing well. They had been released from the hospital, after staying a couple weeks, while Alex got their visas and passports and other legal paperwork together. With that done and dusted, they had come over to England as soon as they could. Even then, it had taken longer than Taryn had wanted, but, hey, that was life, and now they were here.

As she walked along the tarmac, leaving the small plane they had ended their journey on, crossing to the nearby building, she heard a shout and looked over to see Bruce standing right there, tears in his eyes, as he looked at the four of them.

"Oh my God," he whispered.

She ran toward him, but the kids beat her to Bruce, racing up ahead and jumping into his arms. She didn't know how recovered he was, but they hit him with their combined full force, and Bruce didn't even appear to jerk from the impact. Tears streaming down his cheeks, he held them tight, as they all cried.

She was aware of her own tears, as she walked up and wrapped her arms around the four of them. Bruce opened his arms, then quickly snagged her into one big group hug and whispered, "Thank you, Taryn. Thank you. Oh my God, thank you so much."

When she finally extricated herself from his grasp, she looked around, and there was Alex. He gave her a slow, smoldering look that made her heart race, and she ran to him. He opened his arms, and she flung herself into them. "Finally," she whispered.

He nodded. "Yeah, you're not kidding. It seemed like forever."

"It has been," she murmured. "It's amazing, but Bruce looks almost the same."

"He's been to hell and back," Alex reminded her.

"So have they." Taryn pointed to the three children.

"Absolutely, and now they'll all get the chance to heal together," he added, with a gentle smile. He walked over to see the kids, and, when they noticed him, they all gave him big hugs.

With the joy of being reunited, all six of them laughed all the way to an awaiting SUV, and Taryn was so glad to be a part of it. The three adults sat in the front seat, with Taryn in the middle, while all the kiddos had the back seat to themselves.

"So, are you guys ready to start a whole new life?" Alex asked them, and such a bright smile filled his face that they all were soon grinning like fools.

"Definitely," Cassie said, grinning at him. "We'll go live in a *castle*."

Even Taryn had to laugh at that. "At some point in time that castle won't be big enough."

"Well, Terk's renovating an awful lot of outbuildings too," Alex shared, "so I don't think they'll run out of space anytime soon."

"And you're sure it's okay that I'll be there?" Taryn asked Alex.

"It's totally okay."

Even Bruce looked at her askance. "Of course you'll be there," he declared on a laugh. "Besides, no way I'm letting you out of my sight ever again, not when you did what you did for these kids."

Taryn shook her head. "I have it on good authority that a certain special someone may be around too."

He flushed, but a glint of anger now filled his gaze. "Maybe, but we still have some issues to resolve. We'll have to see how that works out."

"There will always be issues to resolve," Taryn shared comfortably. "The trick is to forget about them and focus on the happy things."

He looked at her in surprise, and then his big booming laugh filled the vehicle. Bruce smiled at Alex and added,

"She's always been my best friend."

"Glad to hear it," Taryn replied, "and I would certainly agree with that statement. I'm glad to see that you and Alex here are getting along too. I want my family to be close."

"Yeah, I hear that it's pretty serious between you two," Bruce noted, with a twinkle in his eyes, pointing a finger between Alex and Taryn, as she flushed a bit.

Alex nodded. "Taryn and the kids will love living here. The whole castle is just buzzing."

Bruce burst into a fit of laughter. "Are you kidding? There are babies everywhere," he shared. "I've never seen anything like it. It's an incredibly warm and loving environment, and, even better, it's perfect for people like us."

As they pulled up to the gates, Alex gripped Taryn's hand and said, "Welcome home."

She considered that phrase, remembering all the times that a home wasn't something she had ever really had, and then Bruce, almost as if he realized just how momentous this was, grabbed her other hand.

"This is how it should be," Bruce declared. "Our *home*. I can't even believe we'll be under the same roof again, the way it was always intended to be," he whispered. "I'm so damn grateful to have you back in my life."

With tears in her eyes, Taryn gave him a big hug and nodded. "It's been a pretty rough couple years," she muttered.

"Only because you're stubborn and had to work out things *by yourself*," Bruce noted.

She burst out laughing. "And *you* are perfect?"

"Of course I'm perfect," he replied, with a grin, and, with the tone he took, even Alex started to laugh.

"Seems we have a perfect new beginning," Alex announced, and, with that, he drove through the castle gates.

EPILOGUE

T ERKEL WALKED THROUGH the big patio doors out onto the deck of his own apartment, just seeking a few minutes of peace and quiet, something that was hard to come by in his household. He sat down in a comfy deck chair with a scotch and tilted his glass to the sky above.

"Not sure what you had in mind when you set this all in motion," he muttered to the world at random, "but good job." At a soft laugh behind him, he turned to see Celia. She wore a long soft gown and appeared to be floating, as she walked toward Terk. Her body was slim now, after only six weeks since the twins were born, mostly back to normal, but riper. The births of their twins, when it finally happened, had been an experience Terk would never forget. Celia had come through it like a trouper.

"What are you doing out here all alone?" she asked him.

"Well, it's the all-alone part I was looking forward to." When she stopped next to him to grab his outstretched hand, he added, "Except for you."

She chuckled. "Of course, but, hey, if you need alone time, that's totally okay, you know?"

"Nope. *Alone* is one thing, but *alone without you*? That's not what I meant at all."

"And yet it would still be okay."

"That's fine. … It can be okay but some other day."

She just smiled, and he opened his arms. Instead of sitting down beside him, she sat in his lap and curled up against him. "It's been a hell of a ride," she murmured.

"Are you kidding?" he asked, then burst into laughter. "That doesn't do it justice. I mean, a hell of a ride can entail all kinds of things," he clarified, "including the way you got pregnant."

"It sure as hell doesn't even begin to equate to the happy chaos that our world is now." She raised her head to see his face and smiled. "Any regrets?"

"None," he stated instantly, "no regrets, just a few little concerns. You know, some money issues, a little worry about the bills, all that stuff," he shared, "but definitely no regrets."

"Don't worry about the money issues either," she countered, with a chuckle. "We're making do."

"Yeah, *making do* won't cut it," he noted. "I am responsible for an awful lot of people now."

She traced his lips with her finger and whispered, "It's not just your responsibility. You're not alone in this," she said. "It's all of us together, and that makes a whole lot of difference."

He smiled, held her close, and whispered, "It sure as shit has been a ride. We've expanded way more than I even thought we could."

"And yet I don't think we're done, are we?"

"Oh, I don't know," he said, with a heartfelt sigh. "The world's such a mess. Sometimes it seems as if we might never be done."

"We may not," she acknowledged, "but you have created a special place, and … I hate to say, *a rescue*, but—"

"Oh, yeah, *rescue* fits," Terk agreed. "Jesus, we're creating a rescue for psychics." Then he burst into laughter again.

"Who knew?"

"Who knew what?" she asked.

"Who knew that so many psychics were in need, that so many psychics were out there? Who knew there were so many jobs out there that everybody desperately needed us psychics to do them?"

She smiled at him and added, "I think everybody but you." He rolled his eyes at that, and she giggled. "You're very special."

"*Right*," he muttered, but it was hard to argue with her. If ever somebody could turn his ugly day into something beautiful, it was Celia. "I presume the babies are fed and asleep?"

"They are," she replied, with a happy sigh. "Something else I never expected to happen, and, *boom*, there it is. *Motherhood*."

"Right. None of us expected that."

"And yet," she added, staring at him, "I can't help but feel that we're blessed."

He held her close and nodded. "Absolutely."

"What are we doing about Riff?" she asked.

"Yeah, I'm not sure what we're doing about Riff," he shared in a somber tone. "We still haven't had any news, and yet I feel as if we've been blocked time and time again. Then there is Angela, who just keeps coming back."

"Like a homing pigeon," Celia added.

"I don't know if either one of them are prepared to realize that the homing pigeon keeps returning because of Riff."

"I don't know that even she's ready to accept that yet," Celia agreed, "and the kids make her excuses all too real. Good excuses for her to keep showing up, you know?"

"Exactly," Terk noted, "though I was hoping maybe

some of that would slow down."

"It will soon," Celia pointed out. "Several more births will come, and then we shouldn't have any more pregnancies." She wiggled in his lap. "Unless you want one."

"God, no." He stared at her in shock, and now she burst out laughing. "You were joking, right?" he asked in horror. "Please say it."

"I was joking—or maybe I was just testing the waters."

"You mean, two isn't enough?"

She gave him a brilliant smile and shook her head. "*Hmm*, no. I don't think two is enough," she whispered, "but we don't need any more right away."

"Thank God for that," he declared, facing her. "We have lots more headaches to deal with before I want to go down that road."

"I don't disagree. I would like you to be a little bit more set up, a little bit less stressed, and a little bit more capable of taking some downtime with the babies."

"Babies?" he asked slowly.

"Yeah, babies," she repeated. "Another set of twins awaits us."

He sucked in his breath and winced, but almost instantly two tiny red-haired cherubs popped into his mind. "Good God, red-haired twins?"

Celia chuckled. "Red-haired *girls*," she clarified, almost too excited. "Yep, and I can't wait."

"Maybe," he said cautiously, "but we do have jobs to do."

"I thought you were out here, thinking about Jonas's latest MI6 op."

He sighed. "I came here to try *not* to think."

"What is it about and where?"

"Somebody in Iceland," he began. "I'm just not sure who to send yet."

"If it's somebody Jonas already knows, that would be an even bigger draw for him."

"Possibly, but I'm pressured on this because I'm pretty sure Jonas will be calling anytime now, looking for an answer."

"Well, if somebody's hurt and injured, there isn't much time to decide anyway."

"True, and he had somebody on the job, but apparently that fell through."

"When you say, *fell through* …"

"Yeah, they were killed," Terk stated, his tone grim, "which is why I've been holding off."

"And yet?"

"And yet nothing," he replied. "I'm not sure that we want to get into something like that. I don't want anybody here risking their lives anymore. Everybody's got families now, and somehow, it just seems different."

"Sure, but that also needs to be their decision," she noted calmly. "Everybody here has been affected by a case, one way or another."

"That's true," he conceded, "but at least it doesn't involve trafficking kids this time."

"What is this one about, though?"

"I think someone is marrying and then killing their spouse and then marrying and killing again," he said.

"So, why is MI6 concerned?"

"Because they think it's one of their diplomats, and nobody can touch him."

"Ah, so diplomatic immunity means he can travel the world, can keep committing all kinds of crimes, and nobody gives a crap?"

"Well, we give a crap, but it's hard to do anything about it when someone has diplomatic immunity all around the globe."

"So, Iceland, really?"

"Well, it's not as if he's an Islandic minister, if that's what you mean. He's from Iran, but he's currently in Iceland, and his fourth wife just died."

"But is Iran where the husband owes the wife a dowry after marriage, yet there is no rule about when to pay it? Oh, don't tell me that this was about not paying the dowry?"

"She did have a dowry due to her, and the problem is, he's now taken his wife's younger sister captive. The sister wasn't even raised anywhere close to his world, and, from what I am told, she's English. She reached out and asked for help to get away. That call went out two days ago, and nobody's heard from her since."

"Oh shit," Celia murmured, twisting in his arms to face him.

He nodded grimly, then picked up his drink and tossed it back. "So, we need somebody who can handle all kinds of BS. There is also a chance that the sister might have abilities. Apparently she kept her married sister entertained over her last months by reading tarot cards, thinking she could hide her gifts that way."

At that, Celia sucked in her breath. "That's dangerous," she muttered.

"Very dangerous, and nobody wants to acknowledge that she's gone missing. The diplomat has absolutely no ideas, of course, and says he's completely innocent. It's got nothing to do with him, *blah, blah, blah*, and he's heading home."

"So, we have two separate issues here. We have the sister

missing, and we have a diplomat who's killing off his wives." Then she frowned at Terk and asked, "Do you know that for sure?"

"No, not for sure I don't," he admitted. "However, with every marriage, he didn't have to pay a massive dowry debt, plus he gained an inheritance. So, my take would be an absolute flat-out yes on killing his wives. On an energy level, I can't read him," Terk added. "And whenever I can't read someone's aura or energy, I get very suspicious."

"Well, crap," Celia muttered. "I thought maybe things would calm down a little bit now."

"No, that won't happen. The real questions become, who do I send, and what abilities can we utilize in a situation like this to stack the deck in our favor?"

"I don't think there are any," she muttered. "Almost all of us know enough to hide our gifts from the world, so it's interesting that the sister was openly using tarot cards. That just makes her an easy victim for con men who want to use her gifts for their own selfish advantage."

Terk shook his head. "They had a Ouija board first, but it was removed from their possession."

"Well, I'm not against removing that as well," Celia agreed. "That can be dangerous too."

"Absolutely. We must actively protect ourselves."

She then asked, "What about Elena? She and her brother were involved in something similar," she reminded Terk. "They were part of one of the groups that I started up since we moved over here."

"Yeah, but I'm not sure that she's exactly what I would call *operative material*."

"I wasn't so much thinking of her as of her brother. He's ex-navy."

"His name?"

"Royce, I think."

"Royce," Terk repeated. "Seems as if I might know that name. Have you mentioned it to me before?"

"I think I did, but honestly, we've not had two seconds to even talk to each other," she muttered. "So who knows?"

"I feel as if I know that name."

"And you might. He had done a mission in Iceland and was stationed over there for quite a while, so he would know the area to some degree, and he might even know the players."

"I'm not sure that's a good thing though, is it?" he asked her.

"In this case it's hard to say, but it feels as if a connection is there."

Terk groaned.

"So, what's this sister's name? The one who's gone missing?" Celia asked suddenly.

He frowned at her and sighed. "Heather."

"Okay, Heather," she repeated slowly. "And we're helping because she's calling, or we're helping because Jonas is calling?"

"Jonas brought up the issue of the diplomat and the wives who he keeps murdering. I guess this diplomat has been on the MI6 watch list for quite a while, but they haven't done anything about him yet. However, now after the contact from the sister herself, it's more of a humanitarian mission. So at least we could dive in and see what we can do to help both cases."

"Right," Celia muttered. "So you need to contact Royce and Heather in whatever way you can. It definitely feels as if some connection is there."

Terk pondered that for a moment and then agreed. "I'm not exactly sure what that connection is at the moment, but yeah. It's there." He smiled, then reached for his phone and added, "Boy, did I ever luck out when I got you."

"You sure did," she declared, with a fat smile. "You need to remember that. You make your phone calls, and I'll go check on the girls." After giving him a big smacking kiss, she walked out, leaving him feeling as if he were the luckiest man alive.

This concludes Book 10 of Terk's Guardians: Alex.
Read about Royce: Terk's Guardians, Book 11

Terk's Guardians: Royce (Book #11)

In a world where diplomatic immunity can shield the darkest of sins, a sinister pattern emerges where wives mysteriously vanish without a trace. When MI6 finally connects the dots, even their hardened agents are disturbed by the implications. Terkel's team faces their most challenging mission yet—navigating international politics, while racing against time to prevent another tragic disappearance. The clock ticks by even faster when they discover the diplomat's latest target: the missing sister of dead wife number four.

Trapped in an opulent prison, Heather's heart aches, not just for her lost sister but for the freedom slipping through her fingers. Each passing day brings her closer to an unwanted fate—becoming wife number five to a man she suspects of unspeakable crimes. Her desperate plea for help echoes through secret channels, but the response brings only tighter security and darker shadows. The golden walls of her cage begin to close in, threatening to suffocate her last hopes of escape.

Enter Royce—dangerous, determined, and devastatingly

attractive. His calculated rescue plan seems perfect on paper, but the crackling tension between them threatens to complicate everything. As they navigate a deadly game of cat and mouse, their growing attraction becomes impossible to ignore. With both their lives hanging by a thread, Heather and Royce must trust not only each other's skills but also their hearts …

Find Book 11 here!
To find out more visit Dale Mayer's website.
https://geni.us/DMSRoyce

Author's Note

Thank you for reading Alex: Terk's Guardians, Book 10! If you enjoyed the book, please take a moment and leave a short review.

Dear reader,

I love to hear from readers, and you can contact me at my website: www.dalemayer.com or at my Facebook author page. To be informed of new releases and special offers, sign up for my newsletter or follow me on BookBub. And if you are interested in joining Dale Mayer's Reader Group, here is the Facebook sign up page.
http://geni.us/DaleMayerFBGroup

Cheers,
Dale Mayer

About the Author

Dale Mayer is a *USA Today* best-selling author, best known for her SEALs military romances, her Psychic Visions series, and her Lovely Lethal Garden cozy series. Her contemporary romances are raw and full of passion and emotion (Broken But … Mending, Hathaway House series). Her thrillers will keep you guessing (Kate Morgan, By Death series), and her romantic comedies will keep you giggling (*It's a Dog's Life*, a stand-alone novella; and the Broken Protocols series, starring Charming Marvin, the cat).

Dale honors the stories that come to her—and some of them are crazy, break all the rules and cross multiple genres!

To go with her fiction, she also writes nonfiction in many different fields, with books available on résumé writing, companion gardening, and the US mortgage system. All her books are available in print and ebook format.

Connect with Dale Mayer Online

Dale's Website – www.dalemayer.com
Twitter – @DaleMayer
Facebook Page – geni.us/DaleMayerFBFanPage
Facebook Group – geni.us/DaleMayerFBGroup
BookBub – geni.us/DaleMayerBookbub
Instagram – geni.us/DaleMayerInstagram
Goodreads – geni.us/DaleMayerGoodreads
Newsletter – geni.us/DaleNews